# Web of Malice

BOUND BY MISERY

Victoria M. Patton

Dark Force Press – www.darkforcepress.com

Dark Force Press
www.darkforcepress.com




Book Layout © 2015 BookDesignTemplates.com

Web of Malice/ Victoria M. Patton. -- 1st ed.
ISBN 13: 978-1-946934-12-3
ISBN 10:  1-946934-12-7

Library of Congress Control Number
2018941439


Editor:  Judith Boling

Dedication


Tony, thank you for your constant help and encouragement. Without you, I am sure this book would have taken much longer to complete. And thank you for putting up with my crazy.

# CONTENTS

# CHAPTER ONE

*Friday mid-day*

*Alicia exited her vehicle and caught her thick shoe heel on the uneven road surface, almost planting her face on the ground. She gasped as she grabbed her side view mirror for balance.*

*"Oh my God," she hissed out a breath. "I can't believe I have to come out to this Godforsaken place."*

*"What happened?" Stephanie's voice boomed through the speakerphone.*

*"I caught my boot heel on this stupid gravel road. I still don't know why he couldn't buy the Martin property."*

*"Because the Martin property cost a small fortune..."*

*Alicia cut her friend off in mid-sentence. "Well shit." She watched as the older model truck pulled down the drive. She waved at the handsome but creepy man behind the wheel. "Listen, Stephanie, my client is here...hang on..." Alicia looked up as he walked towards her. She held up her forefinger. "Mr. Bennett give me a sec to finish this call." She smiled returning to her friend on the phone. "Stephanie, I gotta go. Remember, I'm heading out to San Diego right after I leave here."*

*"Oh yeah, I forgot, but I thought the convention started this coming Monday."*

*"It does. It goes from Monday to Friday," she turned her back on Mr. Bennett, "but I may stay through next weekend. I may not. My return flight is scheduled for late Friday. I'll call you by Thursday and let you know my plans."*

*"What hotel are you at?" Stephanie asked.*

*"I'll have to call you from the airport. I had a mix-up, I'm not staying at the hotel where the convention is being held. I don't mind though. My new hotel is near the beach. I'll call you later with the details. My flight leaves at five pm."*

*"Okay, have a great time. Love you."*

*The line went dead as Alicia spun around and glanced up to find her client directly in front of her. "I'm sorry, I had to finish a call," she said taking a small step backward.*

"No worries at all. Sounds like you are going on a trip," David said.

"Yes, I am. I can't wait either. Going to San Diego for a realtor's convention. Getting out of Illinois for the winter is a great plan." Alicia glanced around. She stood in front of what amounted to a ramshackle hut. The wood had grayed and cracked from the harsh winters. She assessed the crumbling concrete stairs that would lead her to the decaying structure. They had shifted over time, and at the angle they rested, it was hard to tell if the house or the steps were crooked.

For all she knew the entire structure was sinking into the ground. Alicia glanced over at the new owner of the crappy shack. "Why did you buy this place? I have to know. I showed you so many other properties that were so much better than this."

David reined in his annoyance with the elf-like creature in front of him. Her shrill voice caused his skin to tingle like an itch that can't be scratched. "That may be true, but this one kind of spoke to me."

She frowned. "Well, I wouldn't want to be this close to Mallard Bay Campground anyway. That place gets crazy in the summertime."

"But I never have to worry about the campground being sold, and it's across the Fox River. I know I will never have an annoying neighbor." He followed Alicia as she led the way to the small front porch.

"You better have those stairs fixed. They look like they're about to fall apart at any given moment." Alicia reached for the tattered screen door, glancing back over her shoulder. She yelped taking a step away from him. "Umm, you don't want someone to sue you when they fall and break an ankle." She fumbled with the lock box on the door. "I don't even know why I kept this lock on here. Last time I came out here the lock on the back door broke." She sighed. "I don't know why you couldn't come to my office. I could have saved a trip." She forced an insincere smile his way.

David hovered watching over her shoulder as her trembling fingers fiddled with the lock. He rolled his eyes behind her back. She spent more time readjusting her oversize bag on her shoulder than she did unlocking the door. David took a long slow breath. He balled his hands into fists. Opening and closing them several times. "I do appreciate you entertaining me and meeting me here. I didn't want to go into town if I could help it."

Alicia stepped into the small living room. She crinkled her nose at the makeshift mantle Old Man Winston had put up. "You know, Mr. Bennett, the Martin property had a real fireplace. Not one made of plywood and a *potbellied stove."*

*David tilted his head. "I don't think you have the appreciation I do for the value this place has. The potential is limitless."*

*"Yes, but I know you have the money. After all, I had to run your credit. I know you're a frugal guy from the truck you drive, but I can tell you have good taste." She scrutinized his tailored shirt and expensive hiking boots. "I know you like the better things in life, so I still don't get why you didn't buy a better house."*

*David's eyes narrowed into slits. "It seems you pay attention."*

*"Don't let my pretty girl looks fool you. I'm smarter than most people like to give a natural blonde credit for."*

*David lifted a single eyebrow at her. He cringed at the sound of her cackling hyena laugh. He watched Alicia reach out and drag her finger across the surface of the potbellied stove, scrunching her nose at the black goop that stuck to her fingertip.*

*Alicia sniffed it and cringed as she vigorously tried to remove the substance by scraping her finger along the edge of the stove. "Oh my God, you are going to be cleaning for a month, to get this place livable." She wiped the remaining grease like substance on her black leggings. "Do you fish Mr. Bennett?"*

*David's eyebrows squished together. "No, I don't fish. Don't have the patience for it."*

*"Hmm, I thought as much. I didn't get the impression you were a fisherman. Although my friend Stephanie said that's why you bought the property."*

*David sneered at her. "No, I'm more of a bury the body kind of guy."*

*Alicia cleared her throat as she eyed the front door. "Ha-ha, that's funny."*

*"Hmm, I didn't mean it to be funny." He removed the six-inch blade from its sheathing and held it against his thigh as he took a step towards the mantle and Alicia. He raised the knife over his head, as he stepped closer.*

*Alicia's eyes widened; a bellowing scream escaped her lips. She took a step back and caught the heel of her shoe on the raised edge of the tile floor, sending her careening back into the stove. Her hand reached out to catch herself and slid in the black grease that coated its surface. She continued to fall back onto the dirty tile. She landed with a thud, as she watched David's knife stab the wooden mantle. Alicia exhaled sharply. "What the hell is wrong with you?" She panted as she tried to catch her breath. She looked up to find David's hand outstretched.*

*He leered at her as he grabbed her forearm and yanked her off the floor. Once Alicia was back on her feet, David pointed to the mantle. His knife firmly planted in the body of a giant Wolf spider. "I hate spiders."*

*Alicia gagged at the blood and guts that seeped from the gaping wound. She glanced around looking for something to wipe black icky goop from her hands. She found some old newspaper on the floor next to the stove. She watched Mr. Bennett out of the corner of her eye as he removed the knife and wiped it clean on his jeans. "That is so gross."*

*He smiled devilishly at her. "It's just a little blood."*

*She sidestepped him and walked to the lopsided table and chairs by the small kitchenette. "Well, umm, I have a few more papers I need you to sign and here are the keys." Alicia placed the paperwork and keys on the table. She turned towards him and held out the pen. "As soon as you sign the top two pages, I can get the hell out of here. And leave you and your critters alone." She nodded towards the mantle.*

*David still held the knife in his hand. The weighted blade had a serrated edge. It was the perfect instrument for gutting small animals. He smiled at the annoying woman before him. "Alicia, I'm sorry you had to drive all this way. And I'm sorry you're going to miss your flight."*

*Alicia's eyebrow wrinkled. She glanced at her watch. "Why would I miss my plane? I have about four hours to get to the airport and thank goodness, we are about ninety minutes from O'Hare."*

*David took a step closer. He held the knife next to his leg. "You see, Alicia, by your own words, you paid too much attention to who I am. I can't let you leave now. You may tell someone about me and this place," he squinted at her, "it seems you may have already done so."*

*Alicia took a step back. "Umm, no. No, I haven't really. I mean, I told the girls in the office, but that's standard information. I didn't tell them anything else. I mean, c'mon what's to tell?" She glanced at the knife in his hand and then back up to his piercing eyes. "Seriously, Mr. Bennett, I should be going." Her breath came in pants.*

*David reached out and grabbed her right shoulder. In a quick motion, he jabbed the knife into her flat stomach and yanked it upward. The sharpness of the blade, moved with ease as it ripped through flesh, muscle, and tissue, stopping when the edge hit the base of the sternum. "Sorry Alicia, but you're not going anywhere."*

*Alicia coughed as blood trickled out of her mouth. She placed her hands on the gaping wound trying to hold in her organs. Her intestines and stomach seeped through the opening and her fingers. A gurgling noise escaped just before she fell to the floor.*

*David watched as the last of her life vanished. He bent down and wiped the blade on her black leggings. "I don't want that much blood on my pants." He dumped the contents of Alicia's purse onto the rickety table. He grabbed her cell phone and left everything until he returned later. He checked his watch and estimated the drive to O'Hare, the time it would take to dump the phone, and then drive to his hotel. He figured it should put him back just in time for dinner.*

# CHAPTER TWO

Friday evening

Damien's stomach clenched. He exhaled the breath from his searing lungs. His heart raced, and he swallowed the bile that had inched its way up his throat. He now understood why Gage Price had told him to trust no one with this information. If he shared this with anyone, Damien would never be able to stop him. His eyes widened as he reread the note again. He had no idea how Glenn Rossdale had uncovered what he did before he was so brutally murdered.

*Damien,*

*I'm afraid if you're reading this, chances are I'm dead. I can only hope you found all my clues and have the Lockharts locked up. It also means Gage Price followed through and gave you the drive, and the one for the FBI too. He had said he would, but I wasn't so sure if self-preservation would win out.*

*That's not why I'm writing this now. While I was looking for the information that would lead to outing James Lockhart for rigging the election, I happened on some other information. I know you have already connected that train platform murder you and your partner covered five years ago, to James Lockhart, and that he hired a hitman to carry out all these murders. Price pulled those files and covered up the evidence, but he couldn't remove the name of the station victim. That information had already been entered from the medical examiner, so it could not be wiped.*

*Something about the victim's name, Kalvin Dale Draper, bothered me. I investigated it. Kalvin Dale Draper was an anagram for David Allen Parker. If that name doesn't mean that much to you, it should.*

*By all the records, David Allen Parker ceased to exist at ten years old. I don't know the name he currently uses, I'm sure he will continue to use variations of his real name. His mother changed their names after a tragic incident. She used the last name of Lindquist. David Arthur Lindquist. David's mother died a few years ago, and that was as far as I got. Best I can tell, she pulled that name out of a hat. I couldn't find any matching relatives in either parent's past.*

*I tracked David through high school and college. He left USC before graduation, then he disappeared. I established that David went off the grid the same time his father was executed.*

*Damien, David Allen Parker is George Henry Parker's son. George is the man who killed Dillon's family. Because of her testimony, George Parker received the death penalty. I believe David will come after Dillon.*

*You are going to have to stop him, Damien. If you don't, Dillon will never be safe.*

*Glen*


Damien reread the note. He held his head in his hands pulling on the ends of his hair. "*Merda, figlio di puttana!*" Coach slinked in and jumped onto the desk. Damien sighed. "Hey buddy, did I scare you?" The overweight cat nudged his hand until Damien scratched his head. "Okay, already." Damien rubbed the cat's soft fur. "How do I hunt down a ghost? Do you know, Coach?" The cat cocked his head to the side before head-butting Damien's chin. "You are no help."

Damien grabbed the bottle of whiskey he had left on his desk and poured a glass, he downed it then poured another. He leaned back in his chair and placed Coach on his lap. "Shit," he said as he picked up his phone. He punched in the speed dial number. "Hey Nicky, how's it going?"

"Damien, what's up *fratello*? How's Joe?"

"Fat and sassy. He went home yesterday after the news conference. He should be cleared to work by Monday. He may be on light duty until the middle of next week, but he is able to handle his weapon."

"Good, man, I'm glad to hear he is doing okay."

"Listen I need a favor." Damien fidgeted with a pen on his desk.

"Anything for you. What do you need?"

"Is Dillon still using the satellite phone you gave her during the last case with my stalker?"

"Yeah, she is. But we aren't tracking it. Why? You think she's cheating on you? She isn't Camilla, you know?"

"No, I'm not worried about her cheating. But with all this shit going on with the Lockhart case and her contentious relationship with Robert Lockhart, I want you to track her phone. Just to be safe." Damien cringed. The thickness in the back of his throat made it hard to swallow.

"You know, that's a good idea. She's been in the news a lot with this case, same as you and Joe. I'll have it up and going by this evening."

"Great. Can you set it up, so I get a copy of the log information? It will keep me from having to bother you when I want to check and make sure she doesn't have another boyfriend."

Nicky laughed heartily. "Yeah brother, no problem. I'll set it to copy you a running log. Where do you want me to send it?"

"Send it to my secure email." Damien pulled the jump drive from the computer and squeezed it in his hands. "Listen, don't say anything to Dad or anyone else. And don't say anything to Dillon. If she finds out I'm tracking her, she'll kill me. I want to keep her safe."

"No worries, Damien. I will set the log to stealth. Only you and I will get a copy of the log readings. You need anything else?"

"No. Thanks, Nicky. I love you."

"Love you, brother. Later."

Damien laid his phone on the desk. He stared at the jump drive in his hand. He closed his eyes as he tightened his fingers around it. He turned his chair towards the safe, the movement had Coach leaping off his lap in a huff. Damien placed the drive at the back, in a small compartment that wasn't readily seen. Before he locked the safe, he pulled out a folder and opened it. He had kept the original sketch from the previous case, and now he had a name.

The thickness of his throat constricted more. He inhaled, pushing the breath out through pursed lips. There was no turning back. Planning the murder of another person was something he had never done. But knowing a killer was coming after Dillon made the choice easy. Damien stared at the sketch. He was going to kill David Allen Parker, and send him to Hell with his father.

# CHAPTER THREE

Damien bolted up from his chair awakened by the garage alarm. He shook his head clearing the cobwebs. He dragged a hand down his face and glanced at his watch, ten p.m. The garage alarm shut off and he heard the living room door close. Stretching as he rose, he glanced at the safe.

As he exited the office, Dillon walked around the corner with Coach in her arms. Damien scowled at her as he leaned against the wall. "Really?" he asked. "That fat ass is the first thing you always hug when you walk in the door."

Dillon tried not to giggle, but the dejected look the man shot her was too much. "You're pathetic. Jealous of a furry cat." She kissed Coach's head and set him on the floor then moved towards the handsome Italian. She wrapped her arms around his lean muscled waist and craned her head to gaze into his eyes. Even though Dillon stood around five ten, Damien had about five inches on her. He looked down at her, and she saw the fatigue on his face. "Baby, you look exhausted."

Damien took her chin in his hand pulling her towards him. He laid his lips on hers. When she pulled away she released her hair from the ponytail, the vanilla citrus scent wafted around him. He inhaled hoping the smell would linger. "Yeah, I'm exhausted. I must have fallen asleep in my chair."

"Me too. How about we go up and snuggle in bed. I'm too tired to even stand in the shower."

He led her by the hand, to the master bedroom at the top of the stairs. They undressed and crawled under the covers. It didn't take long for Coach to make his way to his favorite spot. The cat walked across Damien's chest. He grunted as the cat put his massive weight on each paw. "Damn, Dillon. You've got to stop feeding him three meals at every sitting."

Dillon chuckled as the cat snuggled in between them. "He isn't fat. He's robust. And, he has big bones."

Damien snorted. "Big bones my ass. He's a tub of lard."

As if Coach knew he was being made fun of, he kicked Damien in the ribs.

"Man, he needs to be locked out." Damien scooted over an inch or so giving the cat more room.

"Don't you dare lock him out of this bedroom. I can't sleep without him." Dillon reached over and caressed Damien's chest as Coach snuggled closer to her.

"How did your day go?" Damien asked as he blinked his heavy-laden eyes.

Dillon yawned. "Oh man. We tried playing nice with the TV station to get the reporter to relinquish anything he had on the killer and the information he received from him. He held his ground. Until the Director of the FBI called the station. Come to find out the bastard didn't have anything to speak of, and he knew it all along, he wanted to look important and puff out his chest."

"You guys didn't get anything? You're not any closer to figuring out this guy's movements?"

"No, not really. The reporter had received the information minutes before the news conference."

"Do you guys have any leverage to make James Lockhart tell you who he hired? Seems like James would do anything to save his ass."

"We haven't gotten far enough into the investigation yet. AD Reynolds and Director Sherman are trying to keep any evidence from tipping off the Lockharts. Everything is on lockdown. Only a handful of us can even interview witnesses."

Dillon scooted a little closer to Damien before continuing. "SAC Marks is arranging to interview the crew from the plane in the next few days."

Damien waited for her to finish. He heard light snoring and knew he wouldn't get anything else tonight. He glanced over at the woman he loved more than life itself. No longer able to keep his eyes open, her beautiful face was the last thing he saw before he drifted off to sleep. As slumber overtook him, he vowed that if it cost him his own life, he would make sure she was safe.

# CHAPTER FOUR

*Saturday Morning*

*David pulled in front of his cabin. It really was a piece of shit property. But like he had explained to Alicia, the building wasn't important, he planned to burn it down anyway. He needed the seclusion for what he had in store for Dillon. He made his way up the stairs, pausing at the top. For a split second, they shifted underneath him.*

*The temperatures the night before had reached a record low. Upon entering the three-room shack, he shivered. Without the potbellied stove burning, the inside wasn't much warmer than the outside. He walked over to the near-frozen Alicia lying on the kitchenette floor. Her blood had congealed around her, making her look as if she floated on the glassy pool of crimson. Her intestines had seeped out of the wound, half in her body, half out. David grabbed Alicia by her wrists. When he pulled her the sticky blood peeled away from the floor. The noise sounded like cockroaches being crushed under someone's foot.*

*He dragged her towards the door, her entrails slithering alongside her. Focused on the path to the doorway, David didn't notice the mess trailing him. He felt a little resistance and looked up to see a one-foot length of her intestine had snagged on a protruding floorboard. He grumbled hanging his head. "Seriously, bitch."*

*David dropped her arms and walked over to the piece of intestine. He reached down and gave it a yank, the corded rope-like tissue tore, leaving a six-inch portion behind. He picked up her arms and continued through the front door. Again, he encountered resistance. This time her huge clunky heel was stuck on the raised edge of the door jam. His shoulders sagged. "For fucking sake. I swear Alicia if you weren't already dead, I'd kill you all over again." His jaw clenched as he pulled on her arms. He could feel the crunch of her shoulder joints as he yanked. Her heel gave way, ripping the thin piece of wood from the doorway.*

*Alicia's head hung at an odd angle. As David dragged her across the old withered porch, and down the small set of steps, her head banged precariously against the edges of the concrete. He dragged her to the back of her* car and popped the trunk using her keys. Stuffing the keys in his jeans pocket, he stared at the mess in front of him. The wound was rather large to begin with and split even more during the move to the car. He pinched the bridge of his nose, "I really should have thought about this."

Bending down he lifted Alicia up, her insides hanging on either side of her body. He stuffed her corpse into the trunk, her head hitting the edge of the vehicle with a heavy thump. David turned to go back to the cabin for Alicia's belongings. Almost to the stairs, he froze. He glanced over his shoulder. "Oh, just fuck me now." David jogged back to the car and slammed the trunk shut, just as a vehicle pulled up next to him.

"Hey there, fella."

David stepped next to the window of the old man's truck. "Hi, what can I do for you?"

"Ah, I'm Homer's neighbor from a few miles down the road." He reached his hand out through the window. "I'm Jimmy Eversol."

"I must be confused. Who is Homer?" David asked.

Jimmy laughed. "The man whose cabin you bought."

David smirked. "I guess my realtor always called him Old Man Winston. I ever knew his first name. I'm Allen Bennet, nice to meet you."

"Well Mr. Bennet, I wanted to come and see who bought the place." Jimmy looked down at the man's clothes. "By the looks of you and what's hanging from the back of the trunk, looks like you had to kill something."

David's heart raced, it nearly exploded in his chest as he glanced down at himself. Some of Alicia's bodily fluids covered a portion of his shirt. He turned to peek over his shoulder towards the trunk. A long piece of Alicia's intestines dangled from the edge. He turned back to Jimmy, a faint smile crested David's lip. "My cat got mauled last night. I scraped up what I could. I didn't notice I hadn't gotten all of him in the trunk."

Jimmy chuckled. "I have lost many a cat and dog to these wild animals out this way. But you might want to stuff it all in the trunk. A cop notices something dangling, and you're going to get pulled over. They're going to suspect you got a dead body in there. Anyway, Mr. Bennet, if you find you need anything, come on over and have a whiskey with me."

David stepped back nodding, "Thank you for the offer. If I need anything, I'll stop by."

"Hell, even if you don't, stop by anyway for a drink." Jimmy pulled away from the property.

*David wiped his hands on the sides of his jeans. "Well shit." He tried brushing off as much of the icky body ooze as best he could, but only managed to smear it. "Fuck, Alicia, I really hate you." He didn't have time to worry if his explanation satisfied Mr. Jimmy Eversol. David only hoped he didn't have to take care of him later.*

*He ran back into the cabin, grabbed Alicia's bag and all her shit. He threw that into the trunk with her. He drove her vehicle towards the back of his property. Trees surrounded the cabin with a dense thicket. Out past the trees, an open field led up to the Fox River. But the area right behind his cabin would offer a great hiding place to stash Alicia and her car.*

*Stopping at his truck, he grabbed a box with the items he would need later. Some surveillance equipment, a monitor, rope, and straps with hook and loop ties. He placed that stuff in the middle of the living room floor. He walked back outside, shivering slightly as a gust of ice-cold air blew through him. He grabbed the heavy metal chair from the bed of his truck. It resembled an old barber's chair, but a little smaller. It had the weight he needed to make sure his visitor wouldn't be able to escape her bindings.*

*Back in the cabin, David tried to clean most of the blood off the kitchen floor. He grabbed the bag of trash and headed out to his truck. Throwing the bag in the flatbed. He grabbed the two cans of gasoline and placed them at the back door of the cabin. Getting back in his truck, he smiled as he pulled away from the property. The next time he came back to the cabin, he would have the one person he had dreamt of since he was ten. His pulse sped up at the thought of making Dillon McGrath pay for what she had done to his family.*

# CHAPTER FIVE

Early Monday morning

Damien moved around the kitchen. Unable to sleep, he had risen earlier than Dillon. As he shuffled about fixing breakfast, he was trying to figure out how to convince Dr. Forsythe to help him without telling him too much when his phone rang. "Kaine."

"Hey, sweetie. I saw you on the news this weekend. How's Joe doing?"

The plate of bacon Damien had removed from the microwave slipped from his fingers. He managed to catch it before the bacon slid off and landed on the floor. The scratchy voice on the other end of the line curdled his blood. "Why the fuck are you calling me?"

"C'mon now. You know you miss me."

"Are you in need of medication? You must be fucking delusional if you think I miss you." Damien heard a noise behind him and turned to find Dillon glaring at him.

"Is that stupid bitch calling you?" Dillon asked.

He nodded.

"Is that your FBI girlfriend? Tell her if she threatens me again I'll have her up on charges." Camilla growled into the phone.

Damien smiled at Dillon. "She says hi." Dillon raised an eyebrow at him. He sighed, returning to his call. "Camilla, I told you last time we spoke, if you called me again, I would file a restraining order against you. Please don't make me." He hung up. He placed the bacon on a plate along with eggs, toast, and sausage.

Dillon eyed the massive plate of food. "Now who is trying to make who fat? What did witchypoo want?"

Damien frowned. "I didn't stay on long enough to find out."

Dillon stared at her food before looking up. "I'm trying hard to remember I'm a law enforcement officer, and murder, no matter how heinous the person may be, is not a viable action. But I have never wanted to shoot somebody like I do her."

"You know you don't have anything to worry about when it comes her and me right?"

She nodded as she swallowed. "I know. It doesn't make me want to kill her any less."

"Well, you don't worry about her. If she continues to call me, I will let Captain Mackey know. He knows about the last time."

Dillon finished her breakfast. She walked to the sink and rinsed her dishes after putting a few left-over morsels in Coach's bowl. "Damien, I have a bad feeling. Don't trust her."

Damien cocked an eyebrow at her.

She held up a hand. "Stop. I know what you're thinking. I'm not worried about you doing something. I'm worried about her doing something. She didn't call out of the blue because of her bleeding heart."

"No, she didn't. She called because we are back in the news and she wants a piece of the pie." Damien stepped to the sink and placed his dishes in it. He turned to take Dillon in his arms. As she snuggled against his chest, he kissed the top of her head. "I promise, I will be diligent where she is concerned."

Dillon inhaled. Damien's scent was both soothing and decadent. "Be extra cautious. She wants something."

He leaned back and lifted her chin. "I will be extra careful when it comes to Camilla."

# CHAPTER SIX

7:30 a.m. Monday morning


Damien parked in front of the Medical Examiner's office. He sat in his SUV for a few minutes, going over his plea in his head, and what information he would divulge to get the Doc on his side. He took a deep breath as he entered the empty lobby. Too early for a receptionist to man the front desk, he slid the magnetic strip of his ID card down the door lock. The light turned from red to green, and the bolt released. Damien pushed the oversized metal door open. He was assaulted by the heavy disinfectant smell. He groaned and winced knowing the scent would linger on him throughout the day.

The sound of his steps echoed off the concrete walls surrounding him as he made his way to Doctor Forsythe's office. Damien stopped midway down the hallway and cocked his head to the side. He swore he heard the whispers of the dead. He continued towards the Doc's office. A sly smile tugged at the corners of his mouth. Soaking up a bit of satisfaction that David Allen Parker would not have the luxury of visiting this place upon his death.

Damien entered Dr. Forsythe's outer office. "Hello? Anyone home?" He walked towards the closed door at the back of the cramped room. He knocked as he opened it. Dr. Forsythe sat engrossed in a file at his desk. "Hey Doc," Damien closed the door behind him. "You got a minute?"

Dr. Forsythe beamed a smile at his favorite lieutenant. "Well now, what do I owe the pleasure of an early morning visit?" Bernard Forsythe stared at Damien.

Damien took the seat in front of the doc's desk. "Have you done anything with the hair found on Glen Rossdale's body?"

Dr. Forsythe leaned back in his chair. "Not yet. I was going to put it in for testing. See, if by chance, we could get any information on who James Lockhart hired to kill all those innocent people. We are pretty sure it is the killer's." Dr. Forsythe leaned forward placing his elbows on the desk. "Why do you ask, Damien?"

Damien sighed as he stared at his hands. "Do you trust me, Bernard?"

"Yes. I do."

"I need you to do something for me. I need you to bury the hair. Just for a little while. I'm asking as a friend. Not a police lieutenant."

Dr. Forsythe's head tilted to the side. "Damien, why would you ask me to bury evidence in a major murder case? A murder case involving one of the most powerful political families in this country."

Damien dragged his hand through his hair. He placed his elbows on his knees and leaned into the Doctor's desk. "I can't tell you. Not without putting you in a compromising situation."

Bernard let out a robust laugh. "Don't you think asking me to bury the evidence puts me in a compromising situation?" he interlaced his hands, resting them on his desk. "You have to give me a better explanation, Damien. You want me to place not only my career but the integrity of this office in peril. I need to know why."

Damien squirmed in his seat. A million thoughts raced through his head. It always came down to trust, though. At the end of the day, it always came down to trust. Damien stared at the man before him. A marathon runner, he was thin but not sickly. His skin a little weathered from age and running in all kinds of temperatures. He had grown to care for this man as if he were family. "I have some information I have to verify before I can involve anyone. But it pertains to the safety of Dillon. If you run a DNA test on the hair, I can't protect her."

Bernard focused his laser-like stare on Damien. "I can put the test off for a week or two. There is a lot of other evidence I could look at first. I can bury this."

Damien flinched back. His eyes widened, and his jaw unclenched. Half stunned that the doctor had agreed so fast.

Dr. Forsythe nodded. "I see you were expecting me to grill you for the real reason you want me to hold the sample. The mere fact you are here asking me to do something I know goes against every grain in your body, tells me there must be a dire reason you are doing it. I trust you. I trust you wouldn't ask me to risk my career for something trivial."

Damien stood. He wanted to leave before Dr. Forsythe came to his senses. "Thank you, Bernard. I'll owe you." Damien turned and walked towards the door, only to be stopped by a hand on his shoulder.

"Listen to me. Something has you on a mission. I get the feeling you can't involve anyone. But you must remember you are surrounded by people you can trust. Don't ever forget that, Damien. Don't become so blinded you make a mistake you will regret later."

Damien nodded. "Thanks, Bernard."

Dr. Forsythe watched the burdened man leave his office. He feared his friend was going down a dangerous path of destruction.

# CHAPTER SEVEN

7:30 a.m. Monday morning across town

Rachel's feet pounded against the running trail. She needed to clear her head, and this trail was the best way she knew how. It had been a mile since she last passed someone. With the frigid temps and the flakelets that fell intermittently, she wasn't surprised she was one of the few diehards willing to get out and run.

Nearing the top of the hill, Rachel glanced at her watch. Fifteen more minutes, she would hit her mark. She frowned, a little behind the time she wanted. Training for a marathon had proven to be more work than she had bargained for.

Rachel heard the crack of branches. She glanced towards the noise but didn't see anything. The understory was too thick to see past the first few feet of the woods. Her pulse quickened. "Get a grip, Rach. No boogie man here." She panted a little harder.

Rachel picked up her pace. At the top of the hill, the trail opened to the Flat—the best part of this trail. It was an area surrounded by woods and ponds. On summer days this area was lined with people having picnics. A horse and rider could often be seen trotting these trails.

As Rachel's steps pounded against the smooth pavement, she thought about Tucker. She had met him at a business meeting a few months back. He was everything she thought she wanted in a man, yet something nagged her. It wasn't him. She couldn't pinpoint what it was that bothered her. Ever since she had become involved with him, something tapped at the back of her brain. As if it tried to warn her about something.

A shadow of movement caught her eye. Rachel turned her head, and her foot hit the edge of the trail. Her ankle twisted, sending her careening down onto the path. "OW!" She screamed. The swelling was immediate. "Oh crap," Rachel said as she grabbed her ankle. She glanced around. "I would have to fall on the one day all of Chicago decided not to run."

Rachel managed to push herself up off the ground. She put a little bit of weight on her foot. She sucked in air through her gritted teeth. "Son of a bitch, that hurts," Rachel hissed. She hobbled towards the end of her trail.

The distinct sound of crunching dead leaves and breaking branches came from the right of her. She picked up her pace as she peered over her shoulder, her heart pounded in her ears. Rachel saw the bend ahead that would lead to her car. She dragged her injured foot. The hair on the back of her neck stood on end.

"Hurry," Rachel said as she checked one last time over her shoulder. Nothing. She turned back just before she ran into him. The force knocked her on her ass. She screamed as she fell backward.

"Hey, are you okay?" The handsome man reached out a thinly gloved hand.

"Yeah, I think so," Rachel said as she reached for him. She smiled at him. "I'm sorry. I didn't mean to run into you."

"Don't worry about me. It looks like you have a nasty sprain. Can I help you back to your car?" he asked.

"No. I can see it from here." Rachel nodded towards the parking area. She regained her balance and hobbled to her vehicle. "Thank you for your help," she called out not looking back.

Rachel panted, trying to calm her nerves. She had never been spooked on this trail, but she could swear someone had been following her. She exhaled as she leaned against her vehicle. She closed her eyes as she slowed her breathing down. Her body trembled as she continued to breathe in through her nose and out through her mouth. "Way to go, Rach. That guy probably thinks you're a nut," she whispered.

Her hand shook as she pulled her keys from her pocket. She heard someone behind her. Her pulse sped back up. Rachel had a hard time catching her breath. She gripped her keys between her fingers ready to defend herself. She spun around and grabbed her chest. "Holy shit, it's you." She halfway laughed at the person standing before her. "You scared me half to death. What are you doing here anyway? I didn't know you liked to run here."

Rachel didn't see the blade before it slid across her throat. Her eyes widened at her assailant. She placed her hands on her neck, but the blood loss was coming at an alarming rate. Rachel felt woozy and off balance as she crumpled to the ground. She glanced at the person who just murdered her. Rachel's last thought as her life slipped away between her bloody fingers, was why?

# CHAPTER EIGHT

*730 a.m. Monday morning downtown Chicago*


*David pulled into a vacant parking spot, adjacent to the entrance of the parking garage. Exiting his vehicle, he strolled through the structure. He found cameras throughout the floor where the FBI personnel parked. He made mental notes on the specific type of cameras, their locations, and the direction they pointed. He had several signal jammers, and he was confident he would be able to jam their signal long enough to take his prey.*

*Back in his truck, David glanced around. The FBI office, located in the heart of the city, had access to shopping and restaurants. It was a busy area for tourists and locals who worked in the many high-rise buildings. He had decided that sitting outside her office was the best place to start learning her daily routine. He recognized her little red sportscar the moment it turned in front of him.*

*Within minutes, David watched as Agent McGrath walked out of the garage. Her lithe figure carried by long never-ending legs seemed to glide across the street. She had pulled her blonde hair back revealing her shapely neck. Dillon McGrath had grown into a beautiful woman. Several men that traveled the sidewalks turned to follow her with their gaze as she maneuvered past them on the way to a high-end coffee shop.*

*David watched as Dillon exited the shop with what looked like a few other agents. Their boxy blazers and slacks gave them away. Agent McGrath wore dark pants and boots. Her coat covered her shirt, but David guessed she wore a more stylish ensemble than her counterparts. She seemed observant of her surroundings. As the other agents joked and walked casually, McGrath continually scanned the area. Her head shifting from side to side as she made a note of her environment.*

*The moment Dillon and the FBI entourage were out of view, David headed towards the coffee shop. Upon entering he made his way to the side counter. It was packed with morning caffeine seekers, hoping to jolt their bodies from the weekend slumber. David noticed a young college-aged girl. He smiled at her as she stocked a shelving unit with the day's pastries.*

*"Hey there," he said. The young girl glanced at him. A slight pink hue*

*covered her cheeks.*

*"Hi. Can I help you with anything?" she continued to stock the shelves, but her gaze stayed on him.*

*"Well, I was hoping for a little information." He glanced around as he stepped closer to her. "I recognized someone, but I'm embarrassed to say I forgot the young lady's name. Can you help me?"*

*"Sure. I know most of the people who come in here. Although we have a lot of tourists, the regulars have been coming in here for years." She stopped stocking the shelf. "Who did you recognize?"*

*"Tall blonde, black pants, and riding boots. She came in with several of her colleagues." David leaned into the young woman. "I'm so embarrassed. I think she dated my little brother at one time, and I wanted to say hi. But it's been a long time since I saw her, I didn't dare to approach her."*

*The young girl's mouth pushed into a smile. Her eyes shined, locked on his. David waited as she tilted her head to the side. He watched as her brow wrinkled then relaxed.*

*"I bet you mean the FBI lady. Umm," she frowned then smiled brilliantly at him. "Dillon. Her name is Dillon. Not sure of her last name. We write the first name on the cup. Makes it easier to call out when the order is ready."*

*"Ah, that's her. I should have remembered. When does she come in here?"*

*"Well, every Monday morning for sure. Sometimes she gets a muffin to take back with her. She comes in on Thursday afternoons as well before she heads home at the end of her day."*

*David smiled. "I wanted to say hello to her. Maybe I will try and catch her this Thursday. Thank you for your help." He turned and headed back to his vehicle. David decided he would have the best shot Thursday afternoon. He needed that extra couple of days anyway. The event he had planned for Wednesday night at the farm was pivotal to carrying out the rest of his plans.*

# CHAPTER NINE

By eight thirty a.m. Monday morning, Damien arrived at the VCU. He entered the empty pen and glanced at the case board. Most of his detectives had two or more active cases they worked at any given time. It seemed this Monday morning most of them were out in the field. Damien had just entered his office when Joe bounded in.

"Where the fuck were you?"

"Well good morning to you too." Damien chuckled at his partner and best friend.

"Dude you forgot, didn't you?" Joe asked taking a handful of jelly beans as he sat in the chair in front of Damien's desk.

"Forgot what? I have no idea what you're talking about." Damien frowned at Joe. "Could you at least give me a hint?"

"We had a meeting with ADA Flowers today. She wanted to discuss the conversation we had with Gage before his murder. She will be assisting the Federal Government to make sure nothing falls through the cracks."

Damien sighed as he clasped his hands on his head. "Shit. I had to run an errand this morning and forgot. What did you tell her?"

Joe smiled. "I told her you had a sick cat."

Damien gaped at him. "You couldn't come up with anything better?"

"Dude, it's the first thing that popped into my head. You've never missed a meeting. I was ill prepared." He chuckled at Damien's scowl. "It's fine. The ADA said this was a prelim for her to get some background. I knew all the answers. Don't worry."

The knot in his stomach tightened. Damien had started out the weekend with a lie to his brother, and now he was lying to his best friend and partner. He had a feeling until he took care of David Allen Parker, the knot was there to stay.

Joe was just about to say something when the phone on Damien's desk rang.

"Kaine." He nodded to Joe. "Yeah, I got it. Detective Joe Hagan and I are on our way." Damien stood grabbing his jacket. "We got a homicide at the Palos Trail System."

Joe's head sagged. "Oh, man. It's going to be freezing up there. Who in their right mind would be running in the winter?"

Damien chuckled. "Grab your jacket, and we will find out."

Once in Damien's SUV, Joe settled in with his eyes closed. "Power napping big fella?" Damien asked.

Joe smirked without opening them. "Shit, only one of us needs to drive."

"Hey, I forgot to ask you, are you cleared?"

"Yeah. They had me run through a series of weapons test. Since I passed them all, there was no reason for me not to be put back on duty."

"I for one am glad to have you back. One day without you was one too many." Damien winked at his friend. He pulled into traffic. "You ever go running on the Trails?"

"Oh yeah, I love it. You remember the case from eight years ago? The one with the guy who killed those women at the jogging trails around the city?"

Damien nodded. "Yeah. I was still at the 12th precinct. I didn't get to work it at all, did you?"

"No, the state police had a task force working on it. Four or five girls were killed. Then it stopped. The killer vanished. Haven't heard anything from him since."

"I sure as hell hope that isn't what we're walking into." Damien squeezed the steering wheel.

Joe smiled. "You're preaching to the choir, boy-o."

Roughly forty minutes later, Damien pulled into the main parking area of the trail system. It was almost ten a.m. The sun was partially obscured by a massive gray cloud its glow cast an eerie shadow on the woods that lined the parking lot. The trail system here allowed runners, bikers, and horseback riders access to over forty miles of paved and unpaved trails. Damien had run these trails before. He always enjoyed the quiet serenity of them. However, no way in hell he'd ever let Dillon run up here by herself, and she had law enforcement training.

A CST van sat off to the left. They had rigged a few lights to allow the techs to collect evidence. Damien parked a few spaces over allowing the CSTs clearance to work.

Joe nudged Damien. "There's a cop over there. I bet that's the guy who called it in."

"Your power of observation is astonishing Detective Hagan." Damien laughed as Joe hit him on the back of the head as they approached the officer. "Hey Charlie," Damien said.

"Oh hey, Lieutenant Kaine. This is our witness."

Damien nodded. "What did you witness. Mr....."

"Tanner. Mike Tanner. I own a consulting company, Tanner Inc., here in the city."

"Mr. Tanner tell me what you know," Damien said as pulled his notepad from his pocket.

"I came here for an early morning run." He nodded towards the CST van. "The young lady bumped into me as I headed out onto the trail. She had been glancing back over her shoulder and didn't see me."

Damien's eyebrows pinched together. "Did you see anyone following her?"

"No, I didn't. The young woman had a nasty ankle sprain. I got the impression she had been spooked. After she had run into me, I offered to help her to her car, but she wanted to get away from me as fast as possible. When I came back from my run, about an hour later, her car was still here. I ventured over to it, thought maybe she would be inside. I noticed the blood on the ground, that's when I called the police. I didn't go looking for her."

Damien studied the man. "You're wearing gloves."

Mike Tanner snickered. "No wonder you're a detective." He pulled the gloves off his hands. "This time of year, I run with them. I don't like cold hands." He handed the gloves to the handsome man in front of him. "You are more than welcome to have them."

Damien held the gloves between his forefinger and thumb. "If you give your information to this officer, I don't see any need for you to hang around any longer. However, please remain in town for the next few days in case I have more questions."

Mike Tanner leaned into Damien. "You can call me anytime. If you would ever like to go out to dinner, I would love to take you."

Damien heard Joe cough behind him. He smiled at Mr. Tanner. "Thanks for the offer, but I prefer women."

Mr. Tanner moistened his lips as he winked at Damien. "You never know Detective, you may want to try something new."

Damien shrugged. "Thanks again for the information," he said as he headed towards the CSTs.

Joe glanced back over his shoulder at the guy. "You know Mr. Tanner is a handsome looking fellow. Seems to be successful. It's a shame you are already involved with Dillon."

"Fuck you, Hagan."

Damien and Joe came upon Roger Newberry, head CST for the Illinois State Police. "Hey Roger, why are you out here and not one of your lackeys? It must be bad if they're calling out the big guns."

Roger peered over his magnifying glasses. "Hey Kaine, Hagan. You remember those girls killed a few years back?"

They both nodded.

"Joe mentioned them on the way here," Damien said.

"Well, whenever a woman's body is found at one of these jogging trails, Division Central goes on high alert. Nobody wants this guy showing back up."

Damien held out the gloves. "These are from our witness. Check them for any contact with our dead girl. He did say he tried to help her up after a fall." He stared at the dead woman. He squatted down, to get a closer look. "Slit throat."

"You are so observant," Roger said as he placed the gloves in a paper sack. He scribbled a note on the sack as to where Damien had held the gloves. "Dr. Forsythe can give you better information. But from what I can see the killer didn't hesitate. One quick slash right across her throat. Not sure what kind of blade was used, but it was super sharp. Sliced right through muscle and tissue. I'm sure the ME will get a heck of a lot more information once she's on the table.

"Here's the deal, our victim's killer tried to make this look like our serial killer is back, but they didn't do their homework. Or they wanted to make it look like something it wasn't. Either way, this girl's killer did a poor job of it. See the previous killer stabbed the women once. Incapacitating them. He knew exactly where to stick the knife so that the victim wouldn't be able to scream out, but she wouldn't die immediately from the wound.

"He dragged them out of view, raped them, and killed them by slicing their throat, while he raped them a second time." Roger pointed to the dead woman. "This scene is a red herring."

Damien frowned as he moved around the girl. "I don't see any defensive wounds."

Joe chuckled. "Roger you're witnessing the great Lieutenant Kaine in action." Joe's Irish lilt a little heavier than usual.

"*Stai Zitto, idiota,*" Damien said with a smirk on his face. "Our helpful consultant over there said he didn't see anyone. However, he did say he got the impression our girl seemed spooked."

Roger lifted the covering he had placed over her genitals. "Whoever did this wanted to make sure the initial thought centered on a madman."

Both Damien and Joe cringed.

Damien knelt beside the body. The genital area looked as if someone hastily stabbed a sharp instrument into the victim's vagina. By the looks of damage to the surrounding tissue and the way the clothes had been shredded, it appeared the attack had a personal feel to it.

"Well fuck me," Joe said. "What was the killer trying to convey? Even the last killer didn't mutilate the women like this."

"No, that's why I believe the real intention is to lead you guys in another direction. I know I'm not the detective, but this scene screams staged to me."

Joe nodded at Damien. "Want my opinion?"

"I live for your opinion," Damien said.

Roger laughed at their exchange. "You two are in rare form today."

Joe grinned. "Damien fancies himself a comedian. Our girl here hobbled to her car after bumping into your new boyfriend. I believe someone spooked her on the trail and came up behind her here at her vehicle." Joe looked fixedly at Roger. "If the killer tried to stage this so the initial thought would be some crazy maniacal serial killer did this, I gotta wonder if it's someone close to the victim."

Roger pointed to her clothing. "Her jacket has an inside pocket with a zipper. She had her ID, Rachel Burrows."

Damien smacked Roger on the back of the head. "Why didn't you mention her name earlier?"

"You didn't ask," Roger said laughing. "I found it before you walked over here."

Roger stood up stretching his legs just as the ME's van parked.

Damien turned to see his favorite ME, Dr. Bernard Forsythe, coming towards him. He averted his gaze.  "Hey Doc," Damien said keeping his distance from the ME.

"Kaine, Hagan, Roger. I bet you three have this case almost solved.

Don't you?" Dr. Forsythe put on a pair of gloves.

Joe smiled. "Roger here has established it is not the work of the serial killer from a few years ago."

Roger snorted rolling his eyes. "I made the observation the scene was set to look like something it wasn't."

Dr. Forsythe examined the body. "It does seem as though this young lady suffered at the hands of a sick individual, but I would agree with Mr. Newberry. It isn't the work of our previous killer. This killer wanted us to think our girl here was raped and mutilated. Or to at least make this resemble a sexual predator of some sort. When you've seen as many sexual assaults as I have, you know when a scene has been staged to resemble one.

"After I perform a rape kit, I'll know for sure if she was indeed raped. I'll have more after the autopsy. However, these injuries to her genital area look post-mortem." He pointed to the cut flesh around the vaginal area. "This area is rich in blood flow. If she had been mutilated while alive, there would be more blood present." He ogled the two detectives. "Looks like you two now get to figure out who and why."

# CHAPTER TEN

Dillon walked back into her office after getting her Monday morning recharge from the coffee shop. Glancing at her watch, she sighed. The morning had just gotten started, and she already dreaded the day. Beginning her morning knowing Camilla was trying to sink her fangs back into Damien caused the acid in her stomach to churn.

She glared at the cup of coffee, knowing full well if she continued to drink it she would be chewing antacids for the next several hours. Sitting at her desk, she scrolled through the endless emails that seemed to propagate magically. She saved the ones needing extra attention and deleted the rest.

"SAC Marks and McGrath get your files on the Lockharts, and get into the conference room," AD Reynolds said as he walked past the two carrying his gargantuan cup of coffee and several file folders under his arm.

Both SAC Marks and Dillon followed their leader's instructions and entered the conference room to a melee of agents and support personnel talking about the prior week's events.

"Listen up. We have a lot to cover. SAC Marks, where are you with the interviews of the airplane personnel? Have you been able to track where they are?"

SAC Marks opened the file in front of him. "I have lined up a telecom conference for this morning at ten thirty. The entire crew that was on the flight with our suspect is together in Dallas. I'll put the sketch on the screen. See if they can ID him."

AD Reynolds scribbled on a pad of paper. "Okay. Make sure you get them to tell you anything and everything regarding the trip to Virginia. Can you also...." AD Reynolds trailed off as an excited young agent burst through the door.

"You got to see this," he said as he grabbed the remote for the TV that hung on the conference wall. "It just started."

All eyes turned towards the TV. Within minutes, the Lockharts, flanked by their attorneys stood at a podium that had been placed in front of the Lockhart's mansion.

*"Good morning. I am Jeffrey Patterson, legal representative for James Lockhart. Standing beside me is Stan Leland, legal representative for Robert Lockhart. We stand before you today to let you know the Lockharts are not guilty of the charges that have been levied against them. James Lockhart did not hire anyone to kill on his behalf. The mere thought he could do such a heinous act has made him sick and caused him to be under constant medical care."*

Dillon ogled AD Reynolds at the end of the table. "Are they serious right now?" she asked shaking her head.

AD Reynolds nodded in her direction. He placed a finger to his lips and turned his attention back to the screen.

*"The Lockharts have been besieged by false allegations and their family name has been forever associated with a vile and disgusting act. It has come to our attention that James Lockhart's longtime assistant, Tyler Bryce, plotted to cause trouble for the Senator, to continue an illicit affair with his wife. I know the good people of the State of Illinois can and will see past the lies certain government officials are spreading. All to keep James Lockhart out of the Governor's office. Thank you for your time."*

The conference room sat in stunned silence as AD Reynolds shut off the TV.

SAC Marks looked around the room. "Did he say the FBI was lying based on political motivations? You have got to be kidding me?"

AD Reynolds waved off the comment. "He is trying to sway any members of a potential jury. This conference was smoke and mirrors. The Lockhart's lawyers want potential jurors to have other scenarios. Just enough to create doubt in their minds."

He thumbed through some papers. "Okay, SAC Marks, get the conference set up. Make sure they can see the sketch. I bet with this statement, Tyler Bryce may be more willing to talk to us. I tend to think the reason he hasn't been forthcoming is due to some sort of promise. But now it must be clear to Bryce, he needs to protect himself."

AD Reynolds glanced over at two agents seated to his right. "Powers, you and Michaels find where Bryce is this morning and talk to him. Try his residence, don't call, just go there." He stood gathering his files. "Let's wrap this package up nice and tight, so the Lockharts don't have any chance in hell of getting out of this."

Everyone left the room, setting out on their respective tasks. Dillon grabbed a soda from the machine before returning to her desk. In the hour she sat in the conference, her inbound box now filled with fifty new emails. She was attempting to sort through the many requests for her to lecture at some venue when a message popped up on her screen. Marked priority from an unknown sender, she opened the email. It had two lines.

*James Lockhart is a liar.*

*Enjoy the audio file.*

Dillon opened the attached file. A phone conversation began to play through her speakers.

*"There are some extra loose ends I need you to take care of."*

*"What kind of extra loose ends?"*

*"A couple of people that may pose a threat to my plans."*

*"Well, if you had let me do my job five years ago, you wouldn't be in this mess now."*

*Now tell me who you want me to take care of."*

*"Two people, Officer Thadd Lynn and Brock Avery."*

*"Why Lynn now? He did his job, he doesn't know anything, and I thought Avery was taken care of when he received the money for his business?"*

*"Thadd may be able to figure out who gave the command to remove the file from the evidence locker. And as for Avery, I did take care of him, but I don't trust him to keep his mouth shut. Once the governorship is secure, I have a feeling he may come back to get a bigger piece of the pie."*

*"You should have let me take care of him when I silenced his overrated bodyguard. I would have one less mess to fix, and you wouldn't be out so much more money. By the way, my fee is double, and I want it in my account before I take care of your problems."*

*"Double? What the hell, you can't double it."*

*"Yes, I can. I don't think you can find someone else on such short notice, let alone get someone to touch the clusterfuck you've created."*

Dillon's body trembled, her pulse quickened as her mind raced. She paused the audio file and sprinted into her AD's office.

"You have to come listen to something." Dillon panted as she leaned through his office door.

"Excuse me?" he said. His head cocked to one side.

"I got the motherload in an email. You have to come listen to an audio file." She didn't wait for him to ask another question. She went to SAC Marks desk, "I need you to come to my desk." Again, she didn't wait for a response.

The two men came up behind her. She spun her chair around and looked up. "I received this email. I assume it's from our killer. Why he sent it to me and not you," she said nodding at AD Reynolds, "I don't know. But he did, and I think you are going to be glad." She spun around and pushed play. The conversation played through her speakers. By now a few other agents had stopped near her desk to see what had brought the AD out of his office.

When the recording finished, Dillon couldn't keep from giggling. Both AD Reynolds and SAC Marks had incredulous looks on their faces, complete with bulging eyes and wide-open mouths. "This, this is the smoking gun. Even Perry Mason would be proud," she said.

AD Reynolds stepped forward peering over Dillon's shoulder at her computer. He turned to SAC Marks. "Get the voice recording analyzed. It sounds as if the killer disguised his voice enough to keep us from matching it, but James' voice should be easy to match. The recording is pristine when it comes to quality."

SAC Marks looked at Dillon. "Get me the file. Call Trace, have them see if they can backtrace the email. I doubt this guy left us any bread crumbs, but it's worth a try. If we get lucky, he may have made a mistake."

She typed out a serious of commands. She turned to SAC Marks. "I sent it to you. I'll get ahold of Trace next."

AD Reynolds paced in front of her. "Why did he send it to you?"

Dillon shrugged. "Who knows. I often get shit sent to me. Maybe they think I'm sweet." She looked towards him and batted her eyelashes.

SAC Marks chuckled. "If only they knew the real you."

She swatted his arm and sneered at him. "Ha!"

"Don't engage this guy. If he sends you anything else, forward it to Trace and me. Go ahead and forward this email to me as well." AD Reynolds turned to go back to his office but stopped. "McGrath, what do you think about releasing this via a news conference? After James' voice is verified." He leaned against another agent's empty desk.

Dillon crossed her arms. "My first instinct is to say release it so everyone and their dog knows what a lying son of a bitch he is. However, I believe if you take the results of the audio comparison to each defendant, you can get them to plea. Once the stodgy bastard of a father, Roger Lockhart, hears his son on audio, he will reassess protecting him. But you will have to do it separately. Lay out everything against the son, offer the father a chance to die outside prison. I think this case can stay out of a courtroom."

AD Reynolds looked at SAC Marks. "Get the recording analyzed now. Get on the conference call with the airline crew—if we can get them to ID the sketch, I agree with McGrath, the Lockharts will fold."

# CHAPTER ELEVEN

Damien plugged in Rachel Burrows address. Her apartment was located on Division St. in the Xavier complex. "Let's head over to Rachel's apartment." Damien maneuvered through the mid-day traffic. "Roger said he would have a CST crew come over. I still want to go through it myself."

As Damien pulled up in front of the building, Joe whistled. "Man, we're in the wrong line of work."

"No shit," Damien said. "This place has all kinds of amenities."

Joe raised an eyebrow. "How would you know about the amenities of this place?"

"Before I purchased my condo, I considered moving in here. I liked the location, and I loved the view of the city, but the apartments can run a little small unless you spend a lot for one of the upper-level ones."

They were greeted by the doorman as they entered the building. "May I help you, gentlemen?"

Damien smiled at the man. "We're looking for Rachel Burrows' apartment."

"I'm sorry unless you're on the list, you'll have to be approved for entry."

Damien raised his badge. "This gives us approval. Do you know if she lives with anyone?" Damien asked.

The doorman lost his protective guard dog stance. "No, Miss Burrows lives alone. Her brother lives in this same though."

"We're going to need to get into her apartment. Can you let us in?" Damien asked.

The doorman straightened, his spine rigid. "I'm assuming you have a warrant?" He led them to the elevators and keyed in the code. "Has something happened to Miss Burrows?"

Joe showed his phone screen to the man. "We can email this to you, so you can print it. This is our warrant."

The doorman glanced at the screen. "That will suffice. If I need a copy, I can have you provide it to me later." The man led them down the hallway to Rachel's door. "Can you give me any information at all? I'm fond of Rachel. She always has a kind word to say to me. She never treats me like a doorman. She is polite and thoughtful."

Damien noticed the concern on the man's face. This part of the job bothered him the most. His shoulders drooped, he hesitated before he spoke. "I wish we could. However, this is an ongoing investigation. Would you get her brother's information for us? As well as any other contacts you may have for her."

He nodded. "Yes. I'll print all her information for you. I'll have everything I can gather ready for you when you leave here."

"Thank you. I appreciate your help. Before you leave, can you tell me anything else about Rachel? Is she dating one person, or did she see different people? Anything you know might help us." Damien asked.

The doorman sighed. "I try not to meddle in people's affairs. Rachel didn't do a lot of entertaining. She works with her brother. They own a graphic design studio. Very popular. She had a gentleman visitor every so often. I will pull all the information when I pull her visitor logs. How far back would you like me to go?"

Damien squinted at Joe, "Well?"

Joe shrugged. "I'd say go back at least two months. Maybe we will see a pattern."

Damien nodded. "That sounds good. I appreciate your help."

The doorman exited remaining stoic as he headed for the elevator. "You're welcome," he said over his shoulder.

Joe and Damien entered the apartment.

"Nice digs," Joe said. He walked into the living room. "Wow!" Through the wall of glass that led to an outside terrace, the skyline of Chicago filled the picturesque view. "I bet at night it is some sight to behold. I would never get tired of this view," Joe said.

Damien's phone pinged. "Roger said the team is on their way. In the meantime, let's see if we can find anything to give us some direction on a suspect."

Damien and Joe began a methodical search of Rachel's belongings.

From all accounts, this woman lived a very low-key lifestyle. Damien had the impression she didn't spend a lot of money on clothes, but what she had was of excellent quality. She didn't have expensive items lying about. All her decorative items seemed to be of a more sentimental rather than monetary value.

Damien stood in the center of the living room. "There's nothing here. I don't see anything pointing to a suspect. I haven't found a laptop. She must have one somewhere."

"You know, this would've been the woman of my dreams. She seems super low maintenance. Her place is comfortable, without any of those girly frills most women have to have."

Damien stared at Joe chuckling. "I thought Taylor was the woman of your dreams."

Joe laughed. "Well damn, you got that right. I meant if I hadn't ever met Taylor."

As they searched the last of the drawers, a young man busted through the door. They both spun around with their weapons in their hands.

"Rachel? Where the hell are you? I've been waiting at the office?" He stopped at the sight of the detectives. His eyes widened at the guns trained on him. "Who the hell are you, and why are you in here?"

Damien recognized the man from one of Rachel's photo. They holstered their weapons. He held out his badge. "I'm Lieutenant Kaine. This is Detective Joe Hagan. Who are you?"

The man's color paled. "Why are the police here? What's happened to Rachel?"

"Sir, can you answer my question?" Damien asked.

"Uh—yeah, I'm her brother, Jackson." He sat in the nearest chair. His hands trembled in his lap. "Now tell me why the hell you are here, and what the hell has happened to my sister."

Damien sat in front of the man. "Your sister was found dead out at the Palos Trail System. I'm sorry to have to tell you like this."

Jackson stared at the detective. He grabbed the sides of his head rocking back in his chair. "No. No. You've made a serious mistake."

Damien's lips pursed together. "No, sir. I'm sorry, there has been no mistake. We confirmed her identity from her ID."

Jackson's brow wrinkled. "What—what happened? Was it an accident? Did she fall on the trail or something?"

The corners of Damien's mouth turned down. "No, I'm afraid not. It seems she was attacked after she finished her run. Do you know what her plans were?"

Jackson couldn't speak. He opened his mouth to say something but closed it. All that came out was a muffled screech. He sat back in the chair his posture slumped. "I don't understand. She was attacked? By who?"

Damien reached out touching the man's leg. "Jackson, that's what we are trying to figure out. I need your help. Can you please tell me what your sister's plans were?"

Jackson heard the question, but he couldn't formulate an answer. His stomach hardened, and he had a tingling sensation in his chest. His thoughts scrambled to understand what the detective had asked him. "What? Oh, umm—what do you want to know?"

"Mr. Burrows, were you aware of Rachel's plans for this morning?" Damien asked.

Jackson focused on his hands. He picked at his nails. "Umm—she told me she was going for a run and she would meet me at the office later. We had an early morning appointment, but she never showed." The first tear spilled over and ran down his cheek.

"Jackson, did she have a serious boyfriend, or was she dating anyone?" Damien asked.

Jackson pinched the bridge of his nose, trying to stymy the flow of tears. His voice was hoarse and broken. "She's been dating this guy, Tucker McNeil. He owns an architectural firm here in the city. She wasn't sure if she wanted to stay in the relationship or not. Said there was something about him she didn't trust."

Damien glanced at Joe. "Did she elaborate?"

Jackson's knees bounced up and down. His hands shook. "No. She mentioned a few times something made her uneasy when she was around him at his office. Not when they were alone or like at his house or here. She never could pinpoint what it was." Jackson hung his head as the tears splattered on the floor.

"Mr. Burrows, can you prove where you were this morning? It will..."

Jackson stood and got in Damien's face. "How fucking dare you accuse me of doing this."

Damien restrained from taking the man down. "Mr. Burrows, I understand the distress you are in right now, but I need you to sit."

Joe had moved to flank Damien on his left side. "Jackson," Joe said his Irish lilt adding a calmness to his voice. "The quicker we can eliminate you, the quicker we can get on with finding who did this to Rachel."

Jackson sat and held his head in his hand. "I'm sorry. I'll do whatever you need. I want you going after the killer, not wasting your time on me." Jackson reached into his wallet and produced a business card. "There's a doorman on duty twenty-four hours at this building. The security is pretty tight after hours, you can verify my time in and out of the building with him." He handed the card to Damien.

"We can notify your parents for you." Damien took the card and placed his hand on the man's shoulder.

"It's just us. Our parents died a while ago." Jackson broke down in sobs.

"Jackson, I know you live in the building, I need you to stay in town for any questions I may need to be answered."

Still focused on his hands, Jackson didn't answer straight away. "I—I live in the apartment above. We were planning on connecting these apartments. Now, what am I supposed to do?" Jackson asked. Unable to catch his breath. He panted in between the sobs.

"Mr. Burrows, we'll need to get into your office and go through her computer. I can get a search warrant, but with your cooperation, we can move on this a lot quicker."

Jackson nodded towards the card in Damien's hand. "The doorman will let you in. I'll call him and tell him to expect you. Search whatever you need to." He glared at Damien. "Please find who did this to my sister."

Damien heard the CST's come in. "Mr. Burrows, I need you to go to your residence while the crime scene techs go over your sister's apartment. You'll have access in a day or two." Damien watched the broken man slink down the hallway, he heard the man's wailing as Jackson waited for the elevator.

Joe raised an eyebrow at Damien. "What do you think about him?" he asked nodding in the brother's direction.

Damien shrugged. "He stands to inherit a nice nest egg based on this apartment alone. He's at the top of our list. We'll do a run on him."

# CHAPTER TWELVE

Damien and Joe sat in Damien's SUV outside Rachel's office, eating their sandwiches from Kaufman's Deli.

"Thanks for stopping. Shit, I was hungry," Joe said munching on crispy salt and vinegar chips.

"When is your fat ass not hungry? You eat like you're still playing football for Syracuse." Damien smiled at the big Irishman next to him. "You know you aren't a spring chicken anymore."

Joe finished the last of his sandwich and took a drink of his diet soda. He stared at his partner letting out a long burp.

"Shit can you not burp in my face next time?"

Joe smiled. "You are obsessed with my ass. You can't help yourself, can you?"

"No, I can't help myself, Joe," Damien said.

Joe picked up the folder the security guard handed them on the way out of Rachel's building. "Let's see how many people came to see Rachel."

Damien took a bite of his sandwich. "You see anyone of interest in there?"

Joe frowned as he flipped through the pages. "Okay. When someone visits, they are logged in and logged out. Her boyfriend has come and gone a few dozen times. Nothing odd there. But over the last two months, when Tucker McNeil has been at Rachel's house, so has a one Sherry Breen."

"Who is Sherry Breen?"

Joe shrugged. "I have no idea. However, the odd thing is she came in, but the log shows she stayed less than two or three minutes."

Damien's brow furrowed. "Okay, means she just came in, checked on something, then left." He ogled Joe. "Does it say who she visited?"

Joe's lips pursed together. "No. All it shows was on a few of the nights when Tucker was a visitor so was this girl."

"I don't like coincidences. We need to find this Sherry Breen, maybe..." Damien held up his finger while he grabbed his phone from his pocket and answered the call via speakerphone. "Kaine"

"I want to see you."

Damien pinched the bridge of his nose. "Because of our past, I've given you some leeway. I'm not going to do it anymore."

"Damien, I told you it was a mistake. I'm ready to prove to you how much I love you. You don't have any time invested in her. Dump her."

"You're a fucking bitch." Damien hung up the phone. He fought the urge to throw it out the window. Inhaling deeply through his nose, the breath hissed out of his mouth. The knot in his stomach tightened a little more.

Joe closed the file. "Umm, I'm guessing that was Camilla."

Damien closed his eyes and sighed. "She's started calling me again. It's making Dillon and me off kilter."

"Damien, you are going to have to take steps to get her out of your life. You have let this go on far too long," Joe said.

"Yeah, I know." Damien began wrapping the last of his sandwich, his appetite gone, when his phone rang again. "Kaine"

"Hey, this is Detective Lawson out in California, returning your call."

"Hey, detective. Thanks for getting back to me. Unfortunately, I'm not at my desk, and I'm on a case now. Would you mind if I call you later? What time do you leave for the day?"

"I try to head out by seven p.m. You call me anytime, and I will get the message."

"I appreciate your help. I will call you this evening. Thanks again." Damien disconnected sneaking a sideways glance he let out a silent breath seeing that Joe was preoccupied with his phone. "You ready."

"Yeah. What detective you talking to? Something about this case?" Joe asked exiting the vehicle.

Damien walked towards the entrance of the building that housed Rachel Burrows' office. "Nah, something for my dad." Damien was thankful Joe couldn't see his face.

The doorman ran up to them noticing their badges on their belts. "You must be Lieutenant Kaine," he said extending his hand. "Rachel's brother phoned me. I am sick over the news. Whatever I can do to assist you, I will."

"Can you tell me what you know about Rachel and her brother?"

"They are super close. Have been ever since their parents died. Good people. Good at what they do. I've never heard of a dissatisfied customer."

Damien jotted in his notebook. "How about how they got along, any public fights?"

The doorman's focused narrowed in on Damien. "No. Absolutely not. I mean they had their typical brother-sister disputes. But nothing warranting a second look."

Damien glanced up. The doorman stood ready to defend. "How about Rachel, was she dating anyone?"

At the mention of the young lady's name, the doorman's expression softened. "She has been dating Tucker McNeil. I'd say for the last several months. I didn't pay a lot of attention to her love life, but I know she met him on a project almost a year ago. After the project ended, he still came around. I'm guessing six months or more."

"Has a young woman by the name of Sherry Breen ever come by here?" Damien asked.

The doorman led them down the hall to their office. "I don't recognize anyone named Breen. You don't have to sign in to get into the building." He opened Rachel's office door. "If I can assist you, let me know. I hope you find who did this. Rachel was one of those rare women who never thought of themselves. She always put the needs of others before herself."

Over the next hour, Damien and Joe combed through the Burrows' office. Stretching, Damien waved his hand as he spun around the room. "We aren't finding anything here. Which is unfortunate for her brother. As much as I think he was not involved with his sister's death, if we don't find anyone else, he stays on our list." Damien didn't want Jackson at the top of their list. Or on any list. He secretly hoped someone else would take the man's top spot.

"I'll notify Roger to send someone over to collect her laptop. They're going to have to comb through it to see if there is evidence anyway. I'm thinking the answers aren't going to lie here or on her computer." Checking his watch, Damien sighed. "It's still early. Call Tucker McNeil's office see where he is."

Joe dialed the number Google provided for the architect's office. He hung up and smiled, "He's at home today."

Damien used his phone to find his home address.

Joe closed the inner office door behind them as they exited into the main foyer of the suite. "Something about what the brother said has stuck with me. He mentioned Rachel had an uncomfortable feeling around Mr. McNeil when she was at his office. Stands to reason there may be someone there who made her uneasy. She may have keyed into something, but it never registered as threatening, so she didn't put two and two together."

Damien squinted. "You been watching late night TV again?"

"No, you *knacker*. For whatever reason, it has stuck with me. Something or someone made her uncomfortable enough for her to mention it to Jackson. Plus, since our initial reaction was that the crime scene was staged, we may have our first lead."

"Okay, let's see if the boyfriend can fill in the blanks for us. Maybe he has some insight into why Rachel was uncomfortable at his office."

# CHAPTER THIRTEEN

Tucker McNeil stepped to the side letting the detectives into his home. "I'm a little concerned why two of Chicago's finest are at my door. Last I checked I hadn't broken any laws." Tucker showed them into a dining room area. "Please have a seat. Can I get you two something to drink?"

They declined.

"Thank you for the offer," Joe said. He sat across from Mr. McNeil and an attractive young woman. "Sorry to bother you at home. We have to ask you some questions."

"No problem at all." Tucker McNeil pointed to the young lady at the table. "This is my assistant Sherry Breen. She brought some contracts over for me. I needed to have them for a meeting in the morning. We were going over those. What do you need my help with?"

Damien and Joe exchanged a glance. Damien scooted closer to the table. "Mr. McNeil, when did you last see Rachel Burrows?"

Tucker McNeil's eyes widened. "What's happened to Rachel? Has something happened to her? Is she in trouble?"

Damien noticed the assistant shifted in her seat. Her lips twitched. He glanced at Joe. His partner raised an eyebrow in his direction. Damien turned his attention back to the architect. "Mr. McNeil, Rachel was found dead at a local jogging area earlier this morning. Can you account for your whereabouts today?"

Tucker sat back in his chair. His eyes widened just before he turned away from the table and covered his face with his hands.

His assistant reached out to him. "Oh Tucker, I'm so sorry." She scowled at the detectives. "He was at a meeting this morning. Said he was coming home to work. I arrived before lunch to bring the items he would need for tomorrow."

Damien raised an eyebrow at the assistant but didn't acknowledge her response. "Mr. McNeil, I know this is shocking news. I am truly sorry we had to tell you this way. We need your input. Could you please tell me what time you left your office today?"

"Huh?" he wiped his eyes. "How can you think I had anything to do with this? I was in love with Rachel."

Joe noticed at the man's admission of love for Rachel his assistant stiffened in her chair. Her eyes squinted as she glowered at her boss. As if she sensed the stares, she made quick eye contact with Joe before softening her expression.

Damien's mouth flattened. "I understand your shock and concern for this line of questioning. As soon as we can rule you out of the equation, we can move on to someone else."

Mr. McNeil dragged his hand down his face. "I understand." He pushed the palms of his hands into his eyes. "I left my house around seven thirty a.m. I had an 8 a.m. meeting with a client, Jennifer Putnam. I can get you her information. After the meeting, I came home. You can check with the security of the building."

Damien nodded. "Thank you. Did you go to Rachel's house regularly?"

Tucker McNeil nodded his head. "Of course I did. We were dating. I went over there, she came over here. A few times we went to a hotel." His eyes filled with tears. "Our schedules kept us from going on a trip, so we would go to a fancy hotel and pretend we were far away from the city."

Damien gave Mr. McNeil a chance to collect himself. He turned towards Sherry Breen. "Miss Breen, what time did you show up here today?"

She frowned. "I'm sure it was around eleven thirty." She faced Tucker. "Isn't that about right, Tucker?"

He didn't answer for a minute. Tucker realized everyone was waiting for his reply. "Huh? Oh yeah, I guess it was. I returned home around ten thirty."

Joe turned his attention to the assistant. "Where were you before arriving here?"

She bristled. Sherry straightened her shoulders lifting her chin in the air. "I don't understand why my whereabouts are important. I didn't have anything to do with her murder."

Joe's eyebrows squinted together as he stared at the assistant. "We didn't say she was murdered."

Sherry's face reddened glistening from the sheen of sweat forming on her cheeks, chin, and forehead. "Well, I assumed she was. You are the police. Why else would you be here for a death if it wasn't a murder? Anyway, I was working out."

"Where do you work out?" Joe asked.

Her forehead wrinkled. "At Quad's Gym. It's near our office. I went there shortly after nine a.m.  I came here afterward." She rose from the table. "Unless you have other questions Tucker needs to rest. I'm sure you can understand this is horrible news."

Damien stood. "Thank you, Mr. McNeil, for taking the time to speak with us. We will need to come by and speak with you again. Do you plan on being at the office tomorrow?"

Tucker remained sitting. His head rested on the table. He didn't answer the detective.

"Mr. Tucker?" Damien asked.

He gazed upward. "I'm sorry, did you ask me something?"

Damien sympathized with the man. "Are you going to the office tomorrow?"

Sherry Breen laid a hand on her boss' shoulder. "We will be at the office." She turned towards him. "Tucker, we have a meeting with the Carlisle Foundation. They are expecting the final drawings on their proposal." She smiled tersely at the detectives. "As sad as this is, we can't put it off. Not everything can go on hold for the loss of life."

Damien tilted his head in her direction. "We will be by sometime tomorrow, maybe the day after." Before he headed for the door, he turned towards Sherry. "Miss Breen, can I please have your phone number?"

Sherry's forehead wrinkled. "Why do you need my phone number?"

"Miss Breen, we'll be checking everyone who may have had anything to do with Rachel Burrows. You don't have any reason you don't want to share your phone number with us, do you?"

She shrugged. "No. Of course not. I don't have anything to hide." She rattled off a number to him.

Damien nodded. "Thank you again." He turned to follow Joe out into the hallway then turned back to Sherry Breen. "Miss Breen, have you ever been to Rachel's apartment building?"

Sherry crossed her arms. "Why would I ever want to go to her house? I barely knew her."

Damien smiled at her. "I didn't ask if you knew her, I asked if you had ever been to her apartment building."

She huffed. "No. I have never been to Rachel's apartment."

"Thank you for your time," Damien said.

He and Joe stood in silence as they waited for the elevator.

Once inside and the doors securely closed, Joe smacked Damien on the arm. "What did you think about that?"

Damien giggled. "Our girl is in love with her boss. And I don't believe for one minute she is sad Rachel is out of the picture."

Joe rubbed his chin. "No shit. He has no clue either. Not one clue she would stop at nothing to keep him all to herself."

They exited into the frigid air. Damien shivered as the January winds blew right through him. "Shit it's cold." Climbing into the SUV Damien cranked the heater. "I think you're correct. The question now becomes, is she capable of committing a heinous murder to get the man she is in love with?"

Joe rubbed his brow. "Man, I don't know. I do think the assistant is what had Rachel's hackles up. Unfortunately, she didn't recognize it. Sherry lied about going to Rachel's apartment building. That's lie number one."

Joe pulled out his phone and typed out a text. Without glancing up, he spoke to Damien. "Hey, remember tomorrow I have court. It isn't until nine thirty, though. By the time I get to the VCU, I would have to leave to beat the traffic. I figured I could sleep late and go in from home."

Damien smiled. "You're texting Taylor, aren't you?"

"Of course. I'm telling her to tell work she will be late so she can sleep in with me. It won't be any fun to lay in an empty bed in the morning."

"You're a horny bastard," Damien said laughing.

Joe gave him a cheeky grin. "Well since I don't have to leave my house until eight forty-five, I will get a few extra hours with her." He eyed his partner. "You jealous again?"

"Yes, Joe. I'm jealous."

# CHAPTER FOURTEEN

Damien's shoulder's sagged as he walked into his office at the VCU. This new case added to the list of shit he had to do. When all he wanted to do was lock himself in his home office and find David Allen Parker.

He printed the photo of Rachel Burrows and placed it on his murder board. Damien stared at the picture of an attractive lady. From what little information he had, he figured she was a thoughtful and caring young woman.

He rested his head against his chair. He hated murder. The irony of that thought was not lost on him. It wasn't that he wanted to take the life of another person, Damien had to. David Allen Parker posed a severe threat to Dillon. And there was no way he would ever let anything happen to her.

Jolted by a noise in the pen Damien glanced at his watch, four fifteen. He had dozed for about twenty minutes. He walked out of his office to see DEA Special Agent Johnson with two other goons in his pen giving a few of his guys shit.

"You know Johnson, you need a johnson to do that, and we all know you ain't got one," Detective Alvarez said as her partner, Detective Hall, high fived her.

"Fuck you, Alvarez. We all know how you got into this unit. On your back," Agent Johnson said.

"That's enough Agent Johnson. What are you doing in my pen?" Damien asked as he stood next to his detectives.

"Is the big bad Lieutenant going to tell me I'm a bad boy for insulting his woman detective?" DEA Special Agent Johnson turned towards Damien. He stuck out his chest.

Damien leaned against Alvarez's desk and crossed his arms. "Johnson, Alvarez could whip your ass and put you in your place. Just like Agent McGrath did."

That comment garnered muffled laughs from a few other detectives who had gathered on the edge of the pen.

Damien saw the flame ignite in Johnson's eyes. The jab had hit the mark, dead on. "You need to leave this area."

"Fuck you, Kaine. You can't tell me where I can be." Johnson took a small step towards Damien. "You don't own this fucking building."

"Never said I owned it." Now Damien stood. "But I have the right to kick your ass out of my unit. Especially when you talk to one of my detectives the way you did."

Standing almost toe to toe, Damien towered over the DEA agent. But Damien knew it wasn't always about size. "I'm going to ask you nicely to leave this area."

"And if I don't, what is the great Damien Kaine going to do? You're all tough with a room of your fucking cronies backing you." Johnson smirked at the growing crowd of DC detectives.

"You're a dick, Johnson. I don't need anyone to back me up. Not where your fat little ass is concerned."

Just as Johnson was going to take a step towards Damien, a loud booming voice had all heads turning.

"You need to leave, Agent Johnson." Captain Mackey stood just inside the VCU pen. An entourage of DC officials flanked him. "If you don't have any business in this building, you need to leave. And I do have the authority to kick your ass out of here."

Agent Johnson took a few steps back. "I was just messing with these guys." He raised his hands in surrender. "No harm, no foul." He turned towards the stairwell. "I'm sure I'll be seeing you later, Kaine."

"Tell me when and where," Kaine responded. Damien glanced at the captain, who said nothing as he left.

Joe walked by. "Hey, Captain." Joe glanced at the detectives and scowled at Damien. "Shit, I go take one potty break and miss the good stuff."

Hall laughed at the red-head. "You missed Agent Johnson getting his ass handed to him."

Damien walked back to his office. "Shows over, everyone get back to work and quit slacking."

Joe followed on his heels. "What the heck, I go take a dump and all hell breaks loose. What did I miss?"

Damien dragged a hand through his hair pulling on the ends. "That fucking DEA Agent Johnson. I swear on all the holy saints I'm going to kick his ass one day."

"Did he say something about Dillon?"

"No, he insulted Alvarez."

Joe chuckled. "Alvarez could kick his ass."

"It's not about Alverez not being able to protect herself. It's about him coming into my house and disrespecting it and my detectives. And I don't like him," Damien said.

"Well, by all means, let's kick his ass."

# CHAPTER FIFTEEN

Damien entered his house about five thirty p.m. Coach sat at the ready. "Hey, buddy." Bending down he heaved the fat cat up. Coach nuzzled into his chin, purring. "Oh man, you're only this sweet to me when there is no one else here to feed you."

As if on cue, Coach leaned back meowed loudly and head-butted Damien. "Alright, I'll feed you." Placing the cat on the floor, Damien waited for a half step before heading towards the kitchen. Coach had a tendency to trip whoever led the way.

Damien made quick haste of the cat food then trotted into his office. Quickly pulling his phone from his pocket, he called the detective from California.

"Detective Lawson."

"Hey, this is Lieutenant Kaine, out here in Chicago."

"Hey Lieutenant, what can I do for you?"

"I'm working on a case, and I was hoping you might have some information that will help us." Damien glanced at his watch. He had about forty minutes before Dillon walked through the door.

"I will try. Tell me about it."

"I'm trying to find some information on a David Allen Lindquist. He was a student at USC about five years ago. I'm hoping you can pull anything on him. Maybe driver's license records anything at all. Also, maybe you could check his school records for me, see if you find any unusual activity associated with him? I'm hoping since you're the local police, the school may be willing to answer your questions."

"Yeah, I don't mind. It may take me until tomorrow. I have a few friends over there at the college who help me out."

"No problem. My father, Giovanni Kannetori, told me he thought you might be able to help me out." Damien winced berating himself for using his dad's name. He had pulled his dad's work history up on his computer, and he knew his father had done some work for this department and specifically with Detective Lawson.

"Heck man. I had no idea you were Kainetorri's son. Yeah, anything you need, buddy. Your father helped me out a bunch."

"I do have one other thing I'm hoping you can help me with. Do have any unsolved murder cases say from five to seven years ago, around the USC campus area? I'm looking for anything associated with USC including students, faculty, or anyone associated with the school."

"Give me until tomorrow at the latest. I'll call you when I get something."

"I owe you one, Detective Lawson. Anytime you need something, just let me know."

"Will do. Talk to you soon."

The line went dead. Damien took a deep breath. He leaned back in his chair as Coach meandered in and jumped up on his lap. With his eyes closed, he put his feet up on the desk and thought about how he could track down David Allen Parker. He had to figure he was somewhere outside the city. He also figured David wouldn't kill Dillon quickly. He would want to take his time with her, to have her to himself for a while.

Thinking back to what Rossdale said in his note, Damien thought if his father were being executed, he would want to go to the prison in hopes of seeing him. Damien sat up straight. He quickly turned on his computer. Glancing at the wall clock, his knee began to bounce. "C'mon—c'mon." He tapped on the desk with a pen. His computer came on, and Damien searched for the information he needed.

Typing in George Henry Parker, what Damien needed popped up on the screen. The Cummins Unit in Varner, Arkansas was where the state housed its death chamber. Damien booked marked the page for later. He started to look for numbers when his phone rang.

Engrossed in what he was looking at, he didn't check out the caller ID. "Kaine."

"I'm on my way over. I want to talk to you in person." Camilla huffed into the phone.

"I won't answer the door."

"Damien, I want to talk to you in person. If we don't do it at your house, I will come to your work."

"Camilla, if you show up here, I will call my Captain, and have you arrested for trespassing. If you come to the station, I will have you arrested for harassment." Damien was too engrossed in his computer and the phone conversation to notice the garage door had opened.

"I am coming over...."

"Do it, and I will call the police. I'm warning you." Damien heard Dillon's footsteps and hung up the phone. He closed the window on his computer as Dillon walked through the office door. He looked up and smiled as he moved to meet her. "Hey, your home." He grabbed the sacks from her hands and rushed into the kitchen.

"I heard you talking to someone. Were you on the phone?" Dillon studied him as he nervously placed the bags on the kitchen table.

Damien looked up, his gaze darting between her and the food as he fidgeted with the collar of his shirt. Shrugging he said, "I was following a lead on this case Joe and I got today." He turned abruptly to avoid her stare as he grabbed plates from the cabinet. His stomach soured. Today alone he had lied to just about everyone in his life.

Dillon squinted at him as she studied his movements. Usually confident in everything he did, Damien now looked as if he had never put dinner on the kitchen table before. She recognized the uneasiness in his jerky movement but decided it was best to leave it alone.

# CHAPTER SIXTEEN

As they sat at the table, spooning Chinese food onto their plates, Dillon needed a distraction from the unease that seemed to settle between them. "Did you hear any of the press conference James Lockhart and his father had at their house today?"

Damien's fork stopped halfway to his mouth. "Umm, no. I've been out all day investigating this murder we got."

"Oh, you want to tell me about it? When you're done, I'll tell you about my day."

Damien swallowed. "Okay. This girl was murdered at the Palos Trail System. Looks like someone tried to stage the kill to resemble those murders from about ten years ago. But they totally missed the mark, and the whole crime scene looked staged."

Dillon fed a few pieces of chicken to Coach, to the dismay of Damien.

He frowned as he continued. "We interviewed the boyfriend who happened to have his assistant with him. Joe and I both had the impression she did not like Rachel, and she is in love with her boss."

Dillon smirked. "I bet you have this wrapped up pretty quick. Seems like you have an idea who killed the young girl."

"Yeah. I'm pretty sure the assistant knows something. We have her in a lie right off the bat. She gave us an alibi. The next step is checking to see if it is a lie as well. If we can blow holes in it, we have something to go on. If not, the dead girl's brother stays at the top of our suspect list." Damien's head drooped just a bit.

Dillon ogled the man before her. Something was eating at him, but she wasn't sure what it was. "That bothers you, huh? I'm guessing you like the brother?"

Damien nodded. "I do. Oddly enough, I do like him. He's a nice kid. They lost their parents a few years ago. Now he is alone. I don't want him at the top of the suspect list. Right now, he is the main recipient of a large sum of money and property."

"I'm sure you will get the right guy or girl. You seem to always get your man." She smiled at his wrinkled eyebrows and frowny face. "C'mon, you've never arrested the wrong man. You're too thorough."

He shrugged. "Tell me about the press conference."

"Well, they held it in front of that castle they call home. Didn't seem like the place to win over the voters of Illinois, but what do I know. I'm sure the lawyers did it for a reason.

"We were having a meeting about the case when it came on the TV in the room. Do you know he blamed Tyler Bryce, the assistant? He also dared to say he was under constant medical care because of the stress."

"Seriously? What an ass. I sure hope his lawyers don't get him off."

She smiled at him. "You're not going to have to worry about either of Lockharts getting off."

Damien tilted his head to the side. "And you know this how?"

She smiled as she finished the last bite of her egg roll before continuing. "Alright. I get back to my desk and up pops this message. Only two lines and an audio file attached. The two lines: Lockhart is a liar and enjoy the audio file." Dillon giggled waving her hands in front of her face. "You will not believe what fell into our laps."

Damien stopped eating. He held his breath. "What?"

"The audio file is the killer talking with James, about the several kills he wanted this hired hitman to do. Including the evidence officer at the 17th, Brock Avery, and he talked about killing Avery's bodyguard five years ago."

Damien's heart pounded in his chest as his pulse beat wildly against his temples. "Who sent the file?" Damien rinsed his plate in the sink.

Dillon shrugged. "We assume it was the killer. He disguised his voice, but James' is plain as day. Trace is trying to find out where it came from. But they are not going to find anything. There is no way the killer hid his voice and didn't hide his location."

Damien inhaled slowly. "Was the email addressed to you or the email of the office in general?"

"No. Sent it to yours truly." She scraped some of her morsels into Coach's bowl. "I've been instructed not to engage the killer. If he sends me more, I'll forward them to the AD and Trace. Oh, as well as SAC Marks. He gets the audio files analyzed."

Damien nodded. "That's a good idea. Don't engage with him." Damien's phone rang. He glanced at the screen and sent it to voicemail. He looked up and flinched.

Dillon glared in his direction. "Did she call again?"

He sighed. "Yes."

"You know ignoring her calls won't make her go away?"

"Yes, I know." He set his plate in the dishwasher and the leftovers in the fridge. He turned to see Dillon had left the kitchen. He braced himself for impact as he walked into the office. "I turned around to speak to you, and you were gone."

He watched her as she spun around in her desk chair. A gift he had given her soon after she moved in with him. It was the exact same chair at the Springfield lab, where they worked their first case together. She stopped spinning abruptly when he stood in front of her.

"Why are you reluctant to turn her ass in and get a TRO against her?"

"A restraining order will go on her record. As an attorney, a TRO could mess up her job." Damien moved to his desk and plopped into the seat. The long day was fast wearing on him.

"Why the hell do you give a rat's ass about her? She's going out of her way to fuck with us."

"I dunno Dillon. As much as I want her to stop calling me, I don't want to ruin the girl's career."

She squinted at him. "Do you still have any feelings for her?"

Damien's eyes widened. "Why the hell would I have feelings for her or any other woman?"

"Why won't you stop this bitch from bugging you? You of all people have the power to make her go away."

Damien hung his head. He just didn't have it in him to argue tonight. He was about to say something when his phone rang. He looked up to see Dillon staring right at him. "Kaine"

"Hey, Lieutenant Kaine, this is Detective Lawson."

"Hey Detective, you got something for me already?" Damien asked.

"Yeah, I do. I'm still waiting for my friend at USC to call me back. But I researched around the time frame you asked about regarding unsolved cases."

"Great." Damien looked up to see Dillon ogling him. He winked at her continuing his conversation with caution. "Can you email me what you came up with?"

"Yeah, I can. I have two case files. They're still open, but I asked my Lieutenant if I could share them with you. He was excited to see if they had any connection to your case. These both fit your criteria. I'll keep looking for more, and as soon as I get any information from my friend at the University, I'll let you know."

"I appreciate it. Anything I can ever do for you, I will. Send the information to DKannetori@kannetorisecurities.com." Damien remained sitting while Dillon continued to spin in her chair.

"I got it. I'll talk to you later."

Damien placed his phone in his pocket. He was just about to say something when Dillon spoke.

"Who was that?"

"A detective out in California. I'm chasing a lead in another case I have."

She nodded and glanced at her watch. She was about to invite Damien to take a hot bath with her when the doorbell rang. She squinted at Damien. She could see the whites of his eyes when he bolted from his chair. "Are you expecting someone?"

Damien sighed. "Fuck no. I told her not to come over."

Dillon stood. She placed the palms of her hands on her desk. The doorbell rang three times in a row. "You have got to be fucking kidding me. That's her?" Dillon made her way to the door. She picked up her gun from the entry table and holstered it.

Damien tried to stop her. "Dillon put your weapon down. If you don't answer it, she will leave."

"The hell I will ignore it, and I will not put my weapon down. She's an intruder." Dillon flung the door open.

Camilla took a half step back. She straightened her spine and crossed her arms. "I want to talk to Damien."

"Well, I want to shoot you. Which do you think has a better chance of happening?" Dillon cocked an eyebrow at the annoying-as-hell woman.

"Are you threatening me?"

"The owner of this residence told you if you showed up, you would be trespassing. He gave you an explicit warning not to step onto his property. If he or I perceive a threat, we have every right to defend ourselves."

Before Camilla had a chance to irritate Dillon to the point of her following through with her threat, Damien intervened. "Camilla, I told you I didn't want to speak to you. Why are you here?" Camilla's round blue eyes narrowed in on him. He could feel the anger seep from every pore of Dillon's skin. Damien reached around Dillon's waist and pulled her into his side. "Camilla, I don't want you here. I'm asking you politely to leave my premises."

Dillon snuggled into the crux of Damien's arm. She leered at Camilla as she leaned into him. "Camilla, you have to know how pathetic you look. I mean, seriously, does he have to hold up a neon sign telling you to go the hell away? What self-respecting woman continues to bother a man who clearly has moved on? Oh, wait, you have no self-respect. You're a cheating whore who regrets the biggest mistake of her life."

Dillon wrapped both arms around Damien and looked up at him before returning to Camilla. "He isn't interested in you. And I'm not going anywhere." Dillon stepped back pulling Damien with her, giving her enough room to close the door. She reached for the door handle. Before she closed it, she took a small step towards Camilla. "Damien is a much nicer and patient person than I am. I live here. This is my home as much as it is his. If you ever bring your sorry ass back onto this property, I will have you arrested. I will use every connection I have to take your law license from you and fuck up your world. If you are lucky, that's all I'll do to you. Piss me off, and I will hide your body."

Dillon slammed the door. She turned to Damien. "I meant everything I said. I suggest you grow some balls and put her in her place before I do."

Damien cringed at the insult to his manhood. He watched Dillon's ass walk away from him. He followed her around the corner turning off lights as he watched her walk up the stairs. The more he watched that ass sway, the more he thought maybe she needed to be reminded of his love—and his manhood.

# CHAPTER SEVENTEEN

Monday evening

*David unloaded the security equipment from his truck. He didn't need an elaborate system. Just enough to keep him informed if anyone paid an unexpected visit to his cabin. Carrying the box with his newly acquired equipment up the rickety stairs, he stopped. He felt them shift. He glanced down waiting for them to give way under his weight.*

*He shook off the cold. He had lit the pot-bellied stove, and when he entered the small living room, he was greeted by the warmth of the small heating unit. The forecast called for temperatures to reach below freezing tonight, and he was glad he had loaded up on wood and kindling.*

*He placed the box on the table. Pulling his satellite computer from his bag, he connected to the internet via his portable hotspot. He waited for the slow connection to log on to the network. He didn't need much speed to check on one thing. Once connected he checked the mileage to Davenport, Iowa. David smiled at the screen. Less than two hours from here. "At least I won't have a long drive ahead of me."*

*David then pulled up the farm. Their visiting hours were Monday through Wednesday and Saturday. That worked perfectly for what he had planned. If he left Wednesday evening, he could get there, complete his task and then be back here with plenty of time to meet up with Dillon just before she left the garage at work.*

*He remembered the items in the box. He pulled out a small container. It held the latest technology when it came to jammers. He pulled one from a box. Reading its tech stats, he set it aside. He did the same with the remaining two. If he couldn't get to her after she bought her coffee, he would have a small window to take her in the garage. Closing his eyes, he reconstructed the garage at the FBI facility. He visualized moving through the floors.*

*Upon entering he would find a parking spot near her vehicle. When she showed up, he would jam the signals from the camera system. He figured he would have roughly ten minutes, maybe longer before anyone noticed the camera feed had gone out. Even if he shortened that time by five or so minutes that would still give him enough time to get Dillon into his vehicle.*

*David turned his attention back to his computer screen. The farm didn't have a huge staff, and they boasted about giving their employees Thursdays, Fridays, and Sundays off. David smiled. He looked into the box again and found the small camera he planned on using at the farm. He felt a little like a kid on Christmas morning. He couldn't wait to see the look on Dillon's face when she saw the movie he had planned for her. He chuckled to himself. He would be sure to pick up some popcorn.*

*He made a few notes about what he would need to do between now and then. He was just about to hook up the small security system when he heard a knock on his door. He turned, startled to find his visitor had entered the cabin.*

*"Hey brother," Jimmy Eversol said.*

*David stood walking towards his neighbor and apparently new best friend. "Hey there," he cocked his head to the side. "Umm...," he said.*

*The old man laughed. "Jimmy."*

*"Sorry." David extended his hand. "I suck at remembering names. What can I do for you?"*

*Jimmy reached out and shook the young man's hand. He glanced around the small cabin. He noticed the red stain on the floor. "You a hunter?"*

*David puckered his lips as he rubbed the back of his neck. "Uh, no. Why?"*

*Jimmy glanced in the direction of the stain. "Looks like you had to kill something." He smiled a wicked smile at him. "Or someone." He roared back in laughter at his own joke.*

*David nodded. "I remember the realtor telling me at one-point Old Man Winston had rented this place out to a few hunters one year."*

*Jimmy nodded in agreement. "Homer liked renting it out occasionally."*

*"Why are you here Jimmy? Is there something you need?" David wanted to hurry this conversation along. The old man was enjoyable enough, but he just didn't have time for chit-chat.*

*Jimmy raised a bottle of whiskey. "I was hoping you might be in the mood for a drink."*

*David eyed the amber liquid. He glanced at the table then back at the older man. "Sure, why not. Let me clear the table a bit. Have a seat." David began to put everything into the box. He closed the computer but made no effort to make the table a comfortable place to linger. Walking into the kitchenette, he grabbed two old mugs from the cabinet. Giving them a quick rinse, he walked back to the table.*

*He noticed Jimmy staring at the items in the box. He shifted the mugs to one hand and placed the other on the hilt of the knife at his waist. He watched as the old man looked at the items. David considered taking care of this problem right this moment, but he really had no reason to kill Jimmy. David held up his hand with the mugs in it. "This is all I got."*

*Jimmy turned and smiled. "Shit it's whiskey son, you don't need anything fancy. Hell, you don't even need glass." He took one from his host's hand. Poured a healthy amount into his cup then did the same to David's. Jimmy took a seat at the old lopsided table. "You got a wife?"*

*"No. Never been married. You?"*

*"My Milly died three years ago. Titty cancer. Damn, she fought that thing as best she could. I never had the desire to remarry."*

*Jimmy looked right at him, but David had the impression he didn't see him. He imagined he saw his Milly at that moment. "I can't imagine what dealing with cancer would be like."*

*Jimmy shrugged. "What you going to do? Life can sometimes suck." Jimmy motioned to the tech looking stuff on the table. "What do you do? Security?"*

*David took a sip of his whiskey. "You could call it that. I clean up the messes people leave behind. Help them out of a bind a bad decision got them into."*

*Jimmy drank the last of his whiskey. He looked at the empty glass and contemplated filling it again but thought better of it. It would only fill the void left by Milly for so long. Then the despair would return. He stood. "I didn't mean to barge in. I saw you were here and thought you would share a drink with me."*

*David rose. "I enjoyed the whiskey, Jimmy." He followed him to the door.*

*As the old man headed down the slanted steps, he turned back. "You know something, I got this feeling I'll be seeing you again." Jimmy waved as he drove down the long lane leading to the road.*

*Back inside the cabin, David resumed setting up the security system. He thought about the old man. He was a nice enough guy. Kind of reminded him of Allen, his grandfather. David had been really close to his paternal grandfather. After the trial though, it was as if his grandfather could no longer stand the sight of him. David looked so much like his father, and as he got older, David realized that his grandfather just couldn't stand to be reminded of what his own son had done.*

*David placed the last of the motion detectors along the perimeter of the porch. If someone came onto the porch, it would ping his phone. He set up the monitor in front of the chair that Dillon would soon sit in. A slow smile pulled at the corners of his mouth. Dillon would soon know what it felt like to have the last of her family taken from her.*

# CHAPTER EIGHTEEN



Damien stopped just inside the bedroom door. His gaze followed Dillon as she littered the floor with her clothes. Dressed in only a pair of purple panties, she glanced over her shoulder at him. A smirk tugged at the corners of her mouth, but she said nothing as she disappeared into the bathroom.

He chuckled shaking his head as he punched the six-digit code into the security panel next to the door. The system ran through a series of checks, then a green light blinked telling him the system was engaged.

Damien hummed as he stripped. He left his clothes in a pile at the foot of the bed. He entered the bathroom greeted by classic rock music that filtered through the sound system. The sweet smell of vanilla and citrus wafted around him. She stood with her back to the door of the shower. Her body surrounded by a swirl of steam.

He opened the door and stepped inside. Damien sucked in air through his gritted teeth as the 101-degree water pelted him.

"You are such a wuss," Dillon said without turning around.

He stepped up behind her. "I bet I can show you how wrong you are in your assumption." He reached around her. One hand grabbed a breast as he slid his other hand between her legs. Damien placed his lips on her shoulder and inched his way to her neck. Dillon rested the palms of her hands against the wall.

Damien's fingers teased and tormented her as they slid in and out of her with ease. Dillon moaned as she wrapped her arms around his neck and pressed her back against his chest. She lifted one foot and placed it on the long shelf opening herself up to him. Damien felt her body tremble against his. She turned her lips towards his, and he devoured her kiss. He pinched and rolled her nipple between his fingers. Another soft moan escaped Dillon's mouth just before she kissed him again.

He removed his fingers from her, and a small whimper escaped her. "Greedy little nymph, aren't you?"

He pushed her upper body down. Dillon's hands rested on the bench giving him better access to her. Damien bent over and bit her shoulder as he slid into her. "Dillon, you feel fantastic."

Damien moved in and out of her. With every thrust, Dillon pushed back against him. His hands grabbed her hips as he thrust harder and faster.

"Da-mi-en," she moaned. Drawing out each syllable of his name.

That was all that Damien needed. His orgasm exploded with force. He heard Dillon gasp as her orgasm overtook her. He leaned forward and pulled her body upright.

She placed her hand on the wall once more to steady herself. "Have I told you how much I love this shower?"

Damien snorted as he filled his palm with the vanilla shampoo she loved. He rubbed his palms together and massaged the silky cream into a lather on her hair.  "You may have mentioned it a time or two."

"It is by far the best bathroom I have ever had." She turned around and faced him. "I love you, Damien," Dillon said as she tilted her head under the water to rinse the shampoo.

Damien followed suit using the second showerhead. He stood and watched in awe at the fascinating creature before him. He'd never been with a woman so tough and yet vulnerable at the same time. She protected herself with her humor and a tough exterior.

She turned around and stared at him. He raised an eyebrow. "Why are you staring at me?"

"You're so pretty." She smiled at him.

"Pretty?" he asked rinsing off the shampoo. "I don't think I like being called pretty?"

She giggled. "No wonder Camilla wants you back. She has to be kicking herself every day for the mistake she made."

Damien shut off the water. He grabbed two towels off the heated towel bar and threw one to Dillon as he stepped out of the shower. He brushed his teeth at his sink. After a quick glance in the mirror, he decided he would shave tomorrow.

He leaned against the counter and watched Dillon go through her evening routine. She turned towards him and grinned. "What?" he asked.

"Oh, nothing."

"Uhhuh. What is it? I know something is up."

"I was thinking about having her arrested the next time she shows up here. I know she thinks I'm not serious."

She spun on him. "Damien, if she shows up again and you do not call the police on her, I will. I'm giving you fair notice."

Damien nodded at her. "Okay. Notice taken." He leaned into her and kissed her. "You have nothing to worry about, baby. I promise you." He hung his towel up and headed to the bed. He snuggled in and waited for her to join him.

Dillon dropped her towel next to the bed.

"Why can't you hang up your towel? You never hang your towel up."

She shrugged. "I like watching you blow a gasket." She winked at him as she snuggled up next to him under the covers. "Damien something feels off. It must be Camilla. She's stuck her nose back into your life, and I've been watching you over the last few days. You seem rattled."

Damien stared at the ceiling. He was a fool to think he could hide everything from her. At least Camilla gave him an excuse. "I promise you don't need to worry about Camilla. Yes, she has rattled me. But not because I have feelings for her, but rather because I don't want you to ever feel slighted. You are my life and what is important to me. I'm sorry I haven't taken care of her before. I should have, and I will. I promise you."

She snuggled against his chest, draping her arm across him. "I love you, Damien," she said just before she drifted off.

Damien heard her muffled breathing. "I love you too, Dillon. And I will do whatever it takes to protect you."

# CHAPTER NINETEEN

Tuesday Morning

Damien sat at his desk in the VCU with his office door shut. He figured he had about an hour before Joe showed up from his morning in court. He opened the file regarding the two cases from California. He'd had enough time to print the email from Detective Lawson before he left and that was it.

The first one was a professor murdered in the underground parking lot, inside the elevator. There were no cameras in use during that time in the garage area, there were no eyewitnesses, and no one remembered seeing anyone suspicious in the general vicinity just before the professor left his office.

As Damien scanned the notes, he saw that several students said they heard the professor arguing with someone earlier that day, but no one could recount the identity of the student. Only that the conversation had become very heated. Several eyewitnesses put the professor in a series of meetings the rest of the day. The professor held late office hours that night, and his teaching assistant had gone home before his last meeting was scheduled.

Damien was about to read the other case when his daily mail and message fairy showed up. Officer Baker walked through his door laden down with phone messages and interoffice mail. "Officer Baker, I'm beginning to think you hate me."

She gaped at him. "No, I don't." She placed all his mail on the corner of his desk. "I can't help the fact you get all this stuff."

He frowned at her. "Don't go for Lieutenant, Baker. It isn't worth the paperwork."

She smiled at him as she left his office. He was about to return to his case when several phone messages caught his eye. Rachel Burrows' brother had called over fifteen times. "Crap," he muttered. All this time spent on Dillon's past and he completely forgot about the case he had. "Crap, crap, crap."

He had the cold case files in front of him when Joe walked through his door. "Yo, Lieutenant, wassup?'

Damien shut the file covering it with his forearms. He raised an eyebrow at Joe. "Not much. Court was fun, huh?"

"Nah, had a great morning that's all." A big smile plastered Joe's face.

Damien raised a hand palm out. "I don't want to hear about your love life. I won't be able to look at Taylor the same way. Keep your sexcapades to yourself." Damien laughed at his partner.

"Your arse and parsley."

"What do I have wrong?" Damien chuckled at Joe's Irish slang.

"You wouldn't be able to look at me the same way." Joe winked at Damien. "You know you want me."

"Joe, you worry me sometimes."

Joe snickered at him. "What's in the file?"

Damien glanced down at the case file. He picked it up and put it in his desk drawer. "Paperwork, nothing important."

Joe grabbed a handful of jellybeans. "Yeah?" Joe asked. "I'm never going to be a lieutenant. Damn, you do way too much paperwork."

Damien cringed. The coil in his stomach tightened even more at another lie rolling off his tongue with ease. "Tell me about it."

"Where are we at on the Burrows case?" Joe dug through the jellybeans in his hand. Picking out his favorite colors first.

"Umm, well..."

"You haven't done shit on it, have you?" Joe asked gaping at his partner.

"I had a few things I had to do. But I have a few ideas."

Joe squinted at him. "Something is going on, and you aren't telling me."

Damien recoiled. "Whatever." He pulled the Burrows case from under the pile of mail on his desk.

"Okay, Sherlock. What are your ideas?"

"I want to call the phone company, and track Sherry Breen's phone number. Let's see if she was at the gym."

Joe wiggled his finger at Damien. "I'm not calling Suzie. You're the boss, you do it."

Damien roared back in laughter. "You avoid her all the time. You know that, right?"

"She scares me."

"She wants to marry you."

"That's what scares me. If I call her, she'll think it's an invitation, and she'll call me again. No. You do it. Plus, I got a lead to check out on our little assistant, too."

"Oh yeah? What's that?"

"I got a buddy at the gym where she's a member. I'm going to call him and see if he will give me any info."

Damien nodded. "Sounds good. Call Jennifer Putnam as well. Verify she had a meeting with Tucker yesterday morning. Let's make sure he was where he said he was."

Joe stood. "You got it."

# CHAPTER TWENTY



Dillon pulled into her spot in the garage. Ever since her car was vandalized, she made sure to park in perfect view of the cameras. A few coffees a week made sure the security guards paid a little extra attention to her vehicle. Dillon made her way through the busy lobby and entered the elevator. She closed her eyes wishing she was someplace else. The doors opened into the reception area of the FBI offices. "Hi, Margaret. How are you this morning?"

The long-time receptionist looked up beaming a big smile. Her hazel eyes were as big as saucers behind the enormous thick glasses she wore. Dillon had to stop herself from giggling. Today Margaret, who was in her fifties, had a big bright pink strip of hair in her usual gray locks.

"Good morning, Agent McGrath. How is that sexy man of yours?" Margaret leaned over the high counter. "You know, if you ever want to move on to someone else, I will gladly take him off your hands." Margaret winked at the agent.

"Margaret, there are some days I would gladly let you have him. Don't let his pretty boy looks fool you. He can be a royal pain in the ass." Dillon waved as she entered a long corridor through the large glass security door.

She glanced at the conference room as she headed to her desk. AD Reynolds, SAC Marks, and another Agent she didn't recognize were seated at the table. SAC Marks glanced up, his eyes locked on hers. The hair on her neck stood up. The intensity of his stare set off alarm bells in her head.

Dillon sat at her desk. She rubbed the back of her neck glancing in the direction of the conference room. Her insides quivered, and the speed of her pulse had her questioning that second cup of espresso. "Get a grip, Dillon. You haven't done anything. Let it go." She whispered the mantra over and over to herself.

She read through her email. Deleting all that she could. Several times she placed her hand on her knee, stopping it from bouncing up and down. Dillon busied herself on the computer. She couldn't stand it any longer, she had to see what was going on.

She left her desk and started down the hallway. Her phone beeped a message. Not paying attention to where she was going, she looked at her phone and smacked into him. "I'm sorry," she said glancing up. "Ah fuck. It's you." She tried to step around the fat pig, but he blocked the entire walkway.

"I don't warrant an apology? You think you are above everyone else and you can do whatever you want, don't you Agent?"

"Listen, Johnson, I was reading my texts. If your fat ass takes up the entire hallway, that's not my fault. And I did apologize." Dillon stepped to the side so she could squeeze by.

DEA Agent Johnson stepped in front of her. "Tsk tsk tsk. You got somewhere important to go? I guess you're the big wig huh? Always on the news, always the one everyone wants to speak with."

Several people had gathered in the open doorways of the offices. Dillon looked around at the faces of her colleagues. She turned back to Agent Johnson as he reached out to grab her ponytail. He got a few meaty fingers around it and was attempting to pull it when she punched him in the solar plexus. Unable to breathe, except in short, painful gasps, Johnson doubled over.

"I told you if you ever touched me again I would hurt you," Dillon said bending over and speaking in his ear. "Next time I will break a bone."

Agent Johnson recovered and stood haunch. "You're a fucking bitch. You know that?" He pulled his arm back aiming for the center of her face.

Dillon anticipated his move and sidestepped the punch. Johnson's fist landed on the edge of her eye. She grabbed the offending hand twisting it at an awkward angle. The pressure caused Johnson's knees to buckle, and the snap of his wrist bone caused him to cry out in pain.

AD Reynolds and SAC Marks, along with the third agent from the meeting stepped into the hallway. Two other agents moved on DEA Agent Johnson and secured him.

Dillon stepped to the side rubbing the bruised tissue by her eye socket. "You had no right to touch me." Her nostrils flared as she rounded on her boss. "This fucker blocked me, grabbed my hair, and when I protected myself, he tried to hit me." She pointed to her swollen eye, "I defended myself, and all these people witnessed it. I want to press assault charges."

Johnson fought against his restrainers. "That's not how it happened. I was messing around with her, in a playful manner, and she fucking freaked out." He shrugged off the men around him. "She has a problem. Not me."

One of the office personnel who witnessed the entire incident moved next to Dillon. "That's not true. He tried to pull her hair and put her off balance, then he tried to punch her in the face. Agent McGrath defended herself."

Others in the hallway nodded in agreement.

Agent Johnson stood defiantly. "The fuck I did."

AD Reynolds nodded to the agents next to Johnson. "Escort him to conference room three." He turned towards SAC Marks. "Call his supervisor, tell him he needs to get over here ASAP." He glared at the DEA Agent. "This is going to cost you, Johnson."

As the agents led Johnson down the hall, the crowd began to disperse. Dillon took the small ice pack that Agent Michaels held out to her.

The corners of Michaels' mouth inched upward. "Agent Johnson is going to need more than an ice pack. Looks like you broke his wrist." He winked at Dillon. "Sweet move by the way."

Dillon didn't return the smile.

# CHAPTER TWENTY-ONE

"Agent McGrath, step in here please." AD Reynolds motioned for her to enter the conference room. SAC Marks and the third agent followed in behind her.

"I didn't do a damn thing..." Dillon stopped mid-sentence when the AD raised his hand.

"I'm not worried about your scuffle. Although he is the reason you are here." He nodded towards a chair. "Have a seat Agent."

When everyone was seated at the table, AD Reynolds directed his attention to the third agent. "Dillon, this is Agent Parks. He is with Alcohol, Tobacco, and Firearms. He came in to tell us something he overheard at a bar, and it will shed some light on Agent Johnson's actions this morning. Agent educate Dillon about what you know."

"Hey, Agent McGrath. I was at Mulligan's last night. Most of us know about what happened last year with you and Agent Johnson after the press conference regarding the dismantling of the Metacruze Cartel." The agent glanced around the room. "A lot of us have had run-ins with Johnson. He usually fizzes out. But ever since you took him down a notch after the Cartel case, he has seethed." He shifted in his seat. "Anyway, last night at Mulligan's he was ranting about the confrontation at the VCU, between him and Damien, earlier that day."

Agent Parks stared at Agent McGrath. He found himself sucked in by her whiskey-colored eyes. The gold flecks picked up the light from the room and almost made you think her eyes had ignited. "He was in the middle a long rant about Damien when your picture came on the TV. He went batshit crazy. He called you the C word. Said someone needed to put you in your place and show you this is a man's job."

"Agent McGrath, do you know why he is hell-bent on ruining your life?" AD Reynolds asked.

"No. I don't. I know you guys warned me he hated Kaine for some of the work his dad has done with the DEA and FBI, which seemed to make him jealous. As for me, I had never met the man or had any dealings with him until I came here," Dillon said.

SAC Marks leaned forward with his arms on the table. "When you first got here, I remember him talking about you. Saying how he wanted to go out with you."

"Yeah. He asked me out. Not knowing I was already involved with Damien. I remember too, he didn't make a big deal when I told him I was seeing someone. He was still pretty nice. After he found out it was Kaine, he never said anything, but he was no longer friendly. I didn't think much of it."

"Well," said Agent Parks. "He's obsessed with you. When your picture came up on the TV, I knew something was going to happen. I had no idea it would be something like this."

"I'm not worried about him. I will press assault charges against him." Dillon looked around the table. The men didn't make eye contact with her. "I get the feeling I'm missing something?"

Agent Parks looked at Dillon. "Agent McGrath, you have bested him twice now. He has had some run-ins with other agents and law enforcement officers. When the VCU and Vice over at Division Central figured out how to take out the Cartel, he had another big black mark on his record. Now twice, a woman—you—has put him in his place. I heard you broke his wrist."

She shrugged. "I had told him if he touched me again, I would hurt him. I told him twice, I would defend myself. When he hit me, I did just that. I can't help it if I broke his wrist."

"He's going to come after you. I bet this will get him demoted, if not kicked out of the DEA altogether. This will make him a time bomb. You need to pay attention, McGrath. Keep your wits about you." Parks stood. "I'll give you any witness statement you guys need. I'll make an official statement regarding the incident at the bar. I know one other guy who will also make a statement. Those two things will go a long way to keep any blowback away from you. And trust me, he will try everything to get you in trouble for breaking his wrist."

The conference room door opened. A tall, thin but muscular man walked in. "AD Reynolds, mind telling me why my DEA agent is another room in what amounts to custody?"

A slight grin pulled at the corners of AD Reynolds mouth. "Jack, I was wondering when you were going to show up." He glanced at his watch. "It took you long enough."

AD Jack Gray held out his hand. "I wasn't about to rush over here for Agent Johnson." He glanced around the meeting room. "What did Agent Johnson do this time?" His eyes landed on Dillon. "Agent McGrath, have you been beating up my guy again?"

"Your guy has a serious problem with me. Or maybe every female who spurns his advances?"

AD Gray pulled out a chair and sat stoically for a moment. Then a wry smile crept across his face. "No. I think it's just you." He scanned the room then turned back to Dillon. "As he tells it. You took something he said and used it as an opportunity to show off your skills. You mind telling me what happened, from your point of view?"

Dillon leaned back in the chair as she faced him. "I was walking towards reception, he blocked my way, I bumped into him. Attempted to go around and he tried to get me off balance by pulling my hair, so I punched him. At which point I explained if he ever laid a hand on me again, I would break a bone. I guess he thought I was lying, and I imagine his ego was bruised. I'm a little more agile than he is, and when he tried to punch me, I saw it coming." She pointed to the now swollen and discolored eye, "he made contact with me, I defended myself."

"You broke his wrist."

"Not my problem. Was I supposed to get into a punching match with him? I've been trained to use minimal force to subdue an attacker and take control of a situation. That's all I did. When his fist made contact with my face, he was no longer an agent. He was an attacker, and he's an asshole."

"Agent," AD Reynolds said. "Stick to the facts of the incident."

"The fact he is an asshole is the reason there was an incident." Dillon looked at Agent Marks who hid his smile. "Listen, for whatever reason Agent Johnson hates me, he hates Damien as well. Those are two strong driving forces pushing him to put me in situations which make him feel superior. Unfortunately for him, it only puts a glaring spotlight on his stupidity."

"Agent." AD Reynolds dragged a hand down his face. "Jack, how do you want to proceed?"

AD Gray rocked in his chair before he answered. "You're right Agent McGrath. Johnson has a problem with you and Kaine. He has had some other issues as well. He used to be one of my best DEA agents. Not sure when the change happened or what facilitated it."

Jack Gray glanced around the table. "I hate to ruin anyone's career when he has some good to offer the organization—even someone like

Johnson." He turned towards Agent McGrath. "It's up to you and how far you want to push this. I'm assuming you have several people who can back your version of events, so it depends on what you want to do."

Dillon focused on AD Reynolds. She thought of Damien, and she almost understood his lack of pursuance of Camilla. Almost. AD Reynolds nodded at her. "I want to press this. I don't want to ruin him, but he has to understand his actions have consequences."

AD Gray stood. "I'm sorry this has happened, Agent. All I need from you is a statement." He turned towards AD Reynolds. "If you could get me a few statements from witnesses," he looked at Agent Parks who had remained standing, "I understand you to have some information needing to be reported. If you could give me a statement, I would appreciate it." AD Gray turned back to Dillon. "I am sorry my agent has done this." He headed towards the door. "Now I need to take Agent Johnson to the hospital and get his wrist cast."

They watched him leave.

AD Reynolds peered at Dillon. "Get your statement done." He turned towards SAC Marks, "I need you to get statements from everyone who witnessed the incident. And Agent Parks, if you could give me your statement regarding what you witnessed at the bar, I will turn all of them over to AD Gray."

Walking out of the conference room and back to her desk, Dillon took several deep breaths. The minute these incident reports were put in regarding her black eye and Johnson's broken wrist, coupled with the complaint and the witness statements, Dillon had enough experience to know that things would get worse before they ever got better.

# CHAPTER TWENTY-TWO

Damien pulled the Rachel Burrows case file. The ME's preliminary report at the crime scene said this murder was made to look like something it wasn't. Damien wanted to go through the proper channels, but with David Allen Parker out there, Damien also wanted to wrap up the Burrows case as quickly as possible. He knew Suzie would help get the information for him, saving him a lot of headache and paperwork.

Damien smiled as he pulled his cell phone out and dialed a number. "Hey gorgeous, how are you?"

"Well, if it isn't Damien Kaine. What have you been up to, sweet cheeks?" Suzie asked.

"Not too much," Damien said.

"Hmm, I heard you broke it off with that nasty woman. I have to say, I'm delighted you dumped her butt. At least I'm assuming you dumped her. No one in their right mind would dump you, Damien. How is Joe these days?"

Damien smiled. "Yes, Camilla and I are no longer dating. Joe's doing fine, Suzie. He says hi. He thought you might be able to help us with a case we have."

"I will if I can. What is it you need from me?"

"I have four phone numbers I need traced." Damien squeezed his eyes shut waiting for the refusal.

Suzie grumbled. "It will take me a little bit to pull the records. We have some upper management people hanging around. I will have to get it done while they aren't looking."

"Oh man, Suzie, I would be forever grateful for your help. It's regarding a nasty murder. I want to get this case closed as quickly as I can." Damien relayed Rachel's, Tucker's, Jackson's, and Sherry Breen's numbers. "Call me when you get the information, Suzie. I owe you a big favor."

"I'd be willing to let you off the hook if you have Joe call me later."

Damien chuckled. "I can do that. Thanks, Suzie."

"No problem. I'll talk to you later."

Damien felt a little bad leading Suzie on, but he would just about sell out his mother to end this case.

***

Joe pulled out his notes on the Rachel Burrow's murder. He located Jennifer Putnam's information they had gotten from Tucker McNeil. Joe leaned back in his chair as he waited for the phone to be answered.

"Hello, Jennifer Putman's office. How may I assist you?"

"Is Mrs. Putnam available?"

"I can check for you. May I tell her who is calling?"

"Yes, let her know Detective Joe Hagan from the Vicious Crimes Unit is on the phone." Joe heard an audible gasp.

"One moment please."

A mesmerizing tune played on the line. Joe closed his eyes rocking his chair to the music. He was thinking about his morning with Taylor, and he jumped when he heard the voice on the other end.

"This is Jennifer Putnam here. How may I help you, Detective Hagan?"

"Mrs. Putnam, I have some information I need you to verify for me. It's regarding a case I'm working on," Joe said.

"I'm not sure how I can assist you, but I will do my best. What do you need to know?" she asked.

"Yesterday morning you had an appointment with Tucker McNeil, can you tell me about the meeting?"

"I hope Tucker isn't in any trouble."

"No, Mrs. Putnam. Mr. McNeil isn't in any trouble. I need to clarify some information which has come into question. What time did he arrive and what time did he leave?"

Jennifer sighed. "Let's see. He got here just after eight a.m. Our meeting lasted close to an hour, after which he left. He could have left as late as nine fifteen."

"Was there anything in his demeanor which made you think something might be wrong?" Joe asked.

"No, I didn't notice any unusual behavior. Have I helped you with your case?"

"Yes, you have. I may need to ask you some other questions, may I call on you again?"

"Yes, Detective. Whatever you need from me."

The line went dead. Joe was about to call his buddy at the gym when

Damien came up to his desk. "Yo, I spoke with Jennifer Putnam. She confirmed Tucker's morning appointment."

Damien put on his jacket. "Let's get out of here for a bit. We will go see what the ME has come up with."

"Sweet. I love getting out of this place."

"You just got here."

"I still wouldn't mind leaving," Joe said.

"You don't do any work anyway."

"Hey now. I'm one of the hardest working detectives you got. Plus, you love me most."

Damien laughed. "Joe, I do love you."

# CHAPTER TWENTY-THREE

Tuesday mid-day

Damien drove along with the traffic. "I really don't like going to the ME's lab."

Joe turned to ogle his friend. "Why? You *sicín?*"

"No, I'm not chicken. But the dead, they wait in the corridor. You know that, right? My Nona used to say the dead don't always know where to go. They need help going to the other side. I think those that die violent deaths, I think they wait in that damn corridor."

Joe stared at his partner with a wide-open mouth. He giggled. "Your Nona had some crazy ideas. She used to talk about all those old Italian superstitions. Man, I miss her. But I still think you need meds."

Damien smiled at the memory of his grandmother. "She did have some crazy beliefs." He pulled into the parking lot of the lab. He led the way in and used his ID card instead of waiting for the receptionist to buzz them in. They took a few steps into the dimly lit corridor. Damien grabbed Joe's arm pulling him to a stop. "Listen," he placed his finger across his lips.

Joe cocked his head to the side. He raised an eyebrow. "I don't hear anything. Are you sure you're alright? I think you're losing it."

"If you just listen, you can hear the whispers. I'm telling you...this hallway is filled with the dead." Damien sniffed his shirt as they continued down the hall. "Crap, the smell of disinfectant and the dead are going to cling to our clothes."

"Now that, I agree with you. I hate the smell of this place."

They entered the autopsy room where Dr. Forsythe stood over a body. He had his music turned on. Dean Martin's voice crooned through hidden speakers. Dr. Forsythe glanced up smiling. "Lieutenant Kaine and Detective Hagan. How are my two favorite detectives?"

Damien laughed. "I bet you say that to all the detectives."

Joe frowned. "You mean we aren't his favorites?"

Damien smacked Joe on the chest. "You're a goof."

"Pfft. At least I don't think the dead are trying to talk to me." Joe smirked at his friend.

Damien gave Joe a crooked smile. He peered at the body on the table and wrinkled his nose at the sight. An older man with a bulging neck and eyes that looked as if they would pop out of his head at any moment. "What happened to this guy?"

"His wife poisoned him and watched him die. A slow and miserable death. She fed him raw Cassava."

Joe's brow wrinkled. "What the hell is Cassava?"

"It's a green leafy like substance. Once it hits the stomach acids, it produces Hydrogen Cyanide. It enters the bloodstream and sucks the oxygen out of the body, essentially asphyxiating the person. It is a languid and painful way to die." Dr. Forsythe took off his gloves. He reached behind him for a folder. "I bet you are here for Miss Burrows. First, she was in fantastic shape. Such a waste of a life."

Dr. Forsythe handed Damien the folder. "Rachel did have a severe sprain and few abrasions on her hands that I would attribute to her catching herself when she fell. Her killer sliced her throat from right to left. I didn't notice any hesitation marks. May indicate this wasn't the UNSUB's first kill."

Joe flinched. "Did Rachel die right away?"

"No, she did not. And she would have felt the knife as it entered and sliced across. She would have died within a few moments. However, she lived long enough to understand she was bleeding to death. I hate to imagine how horrific the last one or two minutes of her life was. From the amount of blood on her hands I'm guessing she tried to stop the flow." The doctor stuck his hands in his pockets. "The killer sliced so deep, a few more inches in and Rachel would have been decapitated."

"What about the sexual assault? Or the attempt to make it look like a sexual assault had occurred?" Damien asked.

Dr. Forsythe leaned against the counter. "Your killer used the knife on her genitals. Thanks to the Saints she was already dead. I believe the person wanted to deflect, lead the police to the conclusion it had a purely sexual nature to it." Dr. Forsythe pulled a pack of gum from his pocket. He offered the detectives a piece.

"Do you know if CSTs found anything?" Damien asked.

"As of a few hours ago, they didn't have anything they could attribute to a killer. A few fibers, nothing much until you have a suspect."

Damien tilted his head. "We may have a suspect if we can corner her."

Dr. Forsythe eyes widened. "A woman. Wow. That's unusual. However, at least I was right in my assumption."

"What assumption, Doc?" Joe asked.

"I'm not a head shrinker, but enough time at this job you develop an intuition of things and something has nagged me. I had the impression this killer hated Rachel. It seemed so personal. The damage done to her genitals was extensive. Your killer literally tried to flay her open from the pubic area up. If you're correct and it is a woman, my assumptions weren't too far off. Be careful. Any woman who would do this is a terrifying lady."

Damien gave the doctor a big grin. "Always, Dr. Forsythe."

***

Joe climbed into Damien's SUV. His stomach growled. "Damn, I'm starving. Let's grab a bite before we head back to the office. We can get it to go."

Damien missed hitting a car by mere inches as he pulled into traffic. "Where the hell do these people learn to fucking drive?" Damien flicked on the lights and siren. He caught the look from Joe. "What? I hope the lights scared the shit out of the crappy driver. Maybe they will pay attention the rest of their drive." He maneuvered through the Chicago traffic.

"Uh, it was your mistake. You're the one pulling out into traffic."

Damien scoffed at Joe. "You're crazy." He sighed as he headed towards his favorite eatery. "I'm pretty damn hungry too. Let's hit Kaufmann's."

Joe licked his lips. "Oh man, I love Kaufman's. They must put crack or something in their bread. Once you start eating it, you can't stop."

Damien laughed. "Is there any food you don't like?"

Joe's forehead wrinkled. "Cauliflower. I hate cauliflower."

Damien remained quiet.

Joe kept glancing at his partner. "Is there anything wrong, Damien? You seem like something's up?"

Damien didn't turn from the window. "No, nothing much." He sighed as he followed the traffic.

Joe frowned. "Damien, I have known you for some time. I'm pretty apt at figuring out there is something going on with you. You seem pre-occupied."

Damien didn't say anything. He kept his face front. He was afraid if Joe saw his face, he would see right through his lie.

"Okay. I get it must be something you don't want to talk about. I hope you know you can trust me with anything."

Damien nodded but kept his eyes on the traffic. He finally turned towards Joe. "Yeah, I know. I'll tell you when I can. Okay?"

Joe reached over and squeezed Damien's shoulder. "Sure buddy. No problem."

# CHAPTER TWENTY-FOUR

Joe sat at his desk. He pulled his phone from his pocket at the sound of a text message. Looking at the screen, Taylor had sent a very detailed set of instructions as to what she wanted to do to him that night. "Oh, you're such a wicked woman," he whispered to himself. Quickly gathering his faculties and adjusting his jeans, he called his friend at Quad's gym. "Hey Jeff, it's Hagan. What's up buddy?"

"Not much, haven't seen you in the last few months, crime keeping you busy?"

The echoes of weights clanking against the racks in the background filled Joe's ear. "You know it."

"Hey Joe, you have to come in and see this new virtual reality running system we got. I can set it up to look like you're back in your hometown of Dublin."

Joe smiled at the memory of his Irish home. "No shit, I'll have to come in and try it."

"I'm sure you didn't call to talk about gym equipment. What can I do for you?"

"Listen, Jeff, I need a favor. Can you tell me if someone came in for a workout yesterday morning? I can get a warrant to keep your ass from getting in trouble, but if I can get the information now, it would save me some time."

He heard Jeff speak to someone, then the rustling of papers.

"No need for a warrant buddy. Who do you need me to look up?"

"Her name is Sherry Breen. She claims to have been at the gym yesterday between the hours of say six-thirty to seven-thirty a.m."

"Well, I'm looking at her membership. The last time I show her coming into the gym was three days ago. As a matter of fact, we have a new video system. When you use your card in the scanner for entry, a camera snaps a photo. It cross-checks the membership to make sure you haven't given your card to anyone to use. Here's the secret, so don't let this out, we haven't told our clients about the photo ID scanner. We have had a lot of problems with non-members using the gym. It's a way for us to stop the policy breakers. You know, Kaine's dad put the system in."

"I know it's a foolproof system, then. This is great information. Would you be comfortable emailing her gym usage for the last week?"

"Yeah, no problem, man. Hey, you need to come in," Jeff said.

"I will," Joe said. "Thanks, buddy." Joe pocketed his phone and headed across the pen. He walked into Damien's office. "Well, our Girl Friday may have some explaining to do."

Damien looked up through heavy lids. "Oh, yeah? What did you find out?"

"She wasn't at the gym. She hasn't been to the gym in over three days. Makes me wonder why she lied twice, and what else she has lied to us about."

Damien looked at his watch. "I want to go to Tucker McNeil's residence. I want to establish his whereabouts. I also hope to get any information on how often our Girl Friday is at his house."

"Let me grab my jacket, and I'm ready to go."

"You want me to bring you back here or take you home and pick you up in the morning?"

Joe's eyebrows squished together. "Hmm. Is this a test question?" Joe put on his jacket as he followed Damien to the stairwell. "Yeah, drop me off. By the time we get to his residence with this wonderful Chicago traffic, we'll be lucky if we get home by mid-day tomorrow."

# CHAPTER TWENTY-FIVE

Damien parked in front of Tucker McNeil's residence. They entered the building to a front desk area manned by three people. He and Joe walked towards the counter. They both held out their badges. An older lady looked down her nose at them as they approached. Damien considered the tight woven bun on the top of her head. He noticed the corners of her eyes were pulled slightly upward and attributed it to her current hairstyle. He held in the small giggle that threatened to escape. "Is someone from security available to speak with us?"

"Can you tell me the nature of your business?" the old spinster asked.

Damien peered over at Joe. "No. I can tell you it is a police matter. That's it. Now could you call someone from security to come and speak with us?"

She huffed out a breath, grabbing the phone from its cradle. "Hang on a moment." She punched in a number, "Ralph, I have two police detectives here. They want to speak to someone in security. I will." She glared at Damien. "Someone will be right out." She turned back to her computer.

Joe raised an eyebrow looking over Damien's shoulder at the woman. "Man, she must have realized she is as ugly as a blind cobbler's thumb, and it has put her arse in a foul mood."

Damien sniggered. "Where the hell do you come up with half the shit you say?" He nodded towards the older woman. "And why do people have to be so damn rude?"

"They hate their life. So, their sole purpose is to make everyone else's miserable."

An overweight man in an ill-fitting suit walked towards them. Damien raised his eyebrow at Joe. "Oh boy, here we go," he said out of the side of his mouth.

The man scrutinized the two detectives before him. "You two are needing to speak with the security of this building?"

Damien shook the man's clammy hand. He and Joe both held out their ID's. "Yes, sir. I'm Lieutenant Kaine, and this is Detective Hagan. We are investigating the death of a young woman early Monday morning. We need to confirm one of your resident's statements. Tucker

McNeil said he left the building before seven thirty Monday morning. Can you confirm that for us?"

"I didn't hear about any death."

Joe tilted his head to the side. "Mr.?"

The man shuffled his feet. "Harper. Jack Harper."

Joe gave the man a wry grin. "Mr. Harper, can you please check your entry log and tell us when Mr. McNeil left Monday morning."

The man sighed. "Come on in my office. I can pull it up there." He led them to a small room just off the lobby. "Okay, what time frame are we looking at?"

Damien leaned across the desk. "Should be somewhere between seven and seven thirty a.m."

"McNeil, huh." The man typed on his keyboard. "Alright, the keypad log shows he exited the building at six-fifty." The man focused on Damien. "I'm assuming you want the video as well?"

Damien's eyebrows pinched together. "We weren't aware there was video."

Mr. Harper typed on the computer. "Every time someone leaves or enters before or after hours when they use their key card, or they buzz someone's residence, we have a camera set up to take a series of photos and bursts of video." He continued typing. "During regular hours we have other cameras which pick up all entrants into the building. Anyone who doesn't reside in the building must check in at the desk. "Here, this is the video of Mr. McNeil's departure."

They leaned into the screen. The man still wore what he had on when they interviewed him Monday afternoon. "Can you pull up a time frame from say ten thirty until say four p.m. for me?"

His lips puckered before they turned down into a frown. "Alright, sure I can."

"I'm trying to ascertain when Mr. McNeil may have had a visitor. Sherry Breen. She stated she came here before the lunch hour on Monday."

Jack huffed. "Yeah, let's see." He keyed in a few commands. "At eleven eighteen someone came through the doorway." He turned towards the detective. "Is this who you're looking for?"

Damien looked at Joe. On the screen, before them, Sherry Breen walked into the building and stood in front of the security desk. "Do you show her coming in or leaving any other time, maybe earlier the Monday morning in question?"

"Hang on." Jack Harper sighed as he ran a search. "Okay, how about I pull up, say for the last month, all the times she has come here, would that help too?"

Within a few moments, the computer generated a list of all the times Sherry Breen came to her boss' apartment. "Could you print it for me? As well as the photos of her entering the building Monday morning?" Damien asked.

"If it gets you two out of my office, I sure will," he said.

"Can you email me all the video you have of her as well?" Laying a business card on his desk, Damien patted the man on the shoulder. "We appreciate this. You may have helped us in our case."

The man's forehead wrinkled. "I helped you?"

Damien nodded. "Yes, sir. You have saved us a lot of unnecessary legwork." Damien took the papers the man held out to him. "Thanks again for this," Damien said as they left the claustrophobic room.

Once in the vehicle, Damien turned to Joe. "Are you thinking what I'm thinking?"

Joe read through the pages. "If you think our little Miss Breen is as mad as a box of frogs when it comes to her boss, then yes."

Damien almost ran off the road laughing. "Jesus you have to stop."

"Stop what?" Joe said as he thumbed through the file. "Umm, if you had an assistant, say Baker, how often would she come to your house? After hours?"

"Maybe once in a blue moon. I guess. Why?"

"Miss Breen comes over here whenever she can. This chick might as well move in. Shit." Joe looked out the window. "We caught her in the lie about the gym and about going to Rachel's apartment building. Now if Suzie gets us any information on her cell phone activity, all of this may help us back her into a corner."

Damien pulled up in front of Joe's house. His phone rang. He smiled at the screen display. He gave Joe a lopsided grin as he held his finger to his lips. "Hey Suzie, what do you have for me?" As Suzie's voice streamed out through the Bluetooth, Joe's head hung to his chest, and his shoulders sagged.

"Hey Kaine, look those names and numbers you gave me I ran them. You want me to send them to you?" Suzie asked.

"Yeah, send them to my email."

"Text me your private email. Since I'm giving you a gift without a warrant, they can't go anywhere near the Division Central system. If this information pans out, put in for a warrant, and I'll send them through the proper channels. Until then, I don't want it known it came from me." She sighed. "You tell Joe to call me. He still owes me a drink."

Joe cringed in the passenger seat.

Damien had to swallow his laughter. "I sure will Suzie. He'll call you in the next day or two. I promise. Thanks again." Damien disconnected the call as he broke out into laughter.

Joe's nostrils flared as he squinted at Damien. "Why the hell didn't you tell her I was dating someone?"

"I wanted her to give me the information, and I knew she would give it to me without a warrant." Damien doubled over in laughter at his partner's expression.

"Oh, fuck me. Now I have to tell Taylor about her, so Taylor knows I'm not trying to hook up with someone. No warrant for you means a crappy night for me."

"I'm sure you'll live."

"You don't understand. Last time I hung out with her, she called me almost every damn day. I didn't even have sex with her. I have to make sure Taylor realizes this is all your doing."

Damien continued giggling as he pulled up his email on his phone. "Fine, I'll make it up to you." He studied the phone records showing the location of each of the cell phones he asked Suzie to check out. "Well, my, my, my."

"What did she give us?"

"The brother Jackson and McNeil were where they said they were, and so was Rachel. I had her check Miss Breen's phone. She was nowhere near the gym. Care to guess where she was?"

Joe tapped his chin. "Hmm, I'm thinking somewhere near the Palos Trail System."

Damien nodded slowly. "Oh yeah. Our Miss Breen's phone pinged off the towers near I-55 and I-294, at the same time she said she was at the gym."

"Well hot damn! How do you want to play this?"

Damien sighed tilting his head to the side. "You got Tucker McNeil's office number in the file?" Damien held out his phone.

Joe scanned through his notes to find McNeil's number. He punched it in then handed the phone back to Damien. The receptionist's voice came through the speakers. "Architect Inc. how may I help you?"

"This is Lieutenant Damien Kaine, I need to speak with Tucker McNeil please."

"Just one moment Lieutenant."

A few moments later Tucker McNeil came on the line. "Yes, Lieutenant Kaine, do you have any information regarding Rachel?"

"We do. Can we come to your office tomorrow?" Damien asked.

"Whatever you need from me. Just tell me when and I will be here," Tucker said.

"Great we will be there around nine a.m. Please make sure Miss Breen is there as well."

"We will both be here. See you tomorrow, Detective."

Damien disconnected the call. "Well, looks like you get to sleep in two days in a row." Damien smiled at his partner.

"You know what, it's easier to have Taylor drop me off at your place, McNeil's office is closer to you than to me. How about if I have her drop me off at eight-fifteen? Ish?"

"That'll work. I'll see you later, buddy." He watched his partner run up the stairs to his second-floor apartment. Damien pulled away from the curb cringing at the tightness in his chest. His thoughts filled with self-loathing concerning all the lies he told. They flowed smoothly now. The burden of the secret that Glenn Rossdale had given him was becoming a weight around his neck.

# CHAPTER TWENTY-SIX

Damien pulled into his garage. Bombarded by two equally opposing emotions. The elation that Dillon was home early, and dread that Dillon was home early. Damien glanced at his phone, double checking his messages. "C'mon Detective Lawson call with my information." He stood in front of his door, staring at his messages. He pulled up his email one last time before he entered.

Coach was nowhere to be found. Damien had a pretty good idea where he was, and he was right. Sitting on the counter while Dillon stood over a pot of what smelled like leftover spaghetti, he watched as she fed the cat cut up pieces of pasta. "You know, you are going to make him the fattest cat in Chicago?"

Dillon turned around with a smile. "He is pleasantly plump, not fat and I wish you would quit calling him names."

Damien stood with his mouth gaping open. "What happened to you?" he moved towards her. Placing his hands on both sides of her neck and face, he twisted her head so that the light gave him a better view of her bruised and swollen eye. "What happened Dillon?"

Dillon kissed him sweetly on the lips. "It's nothing. Had a run-in with one of the other Agents. A slight misunderstanding you could say." She turned back to the pasta.

"Excuse me? A slight run-in with an agent? Which agent, and what kind of run-in gives you a swollen black eye?"

She avoided his eye contact as she pulled some freshly grated parmesan cheese from the refrigerator as well as a bowl of salad.

"Dillon. Please tell me the truth. What happened today?"

Dillon spun around. "Okay. I had a run in with Agent Johnson. He tried to block my way, and in the process, we had a minor kerfuffle. Nothing more."

Damien sat at the table as he watched her methodically place the meal in front of him. He tamped down the irritation. "You have a fucking black eye. How can you call a black eye minor?"

Dillon raised an eyebrow at him. "It's nothing to get upset about. Can we put it aside for tonight? I have had to deal with the Lockharts, and I have had enough of work. The last thing I want to do is talk about an asshole. It's bad enough I have to deal with him in my workplace. I don't want to bring him home with me too."

"Fine." Damien stabbed at his spaghetti. The nausea was overwhelming. He took a deep breath and drank some water. He twisted his head from side to side. The burn of stomach acid began to recede. "What's going on with the Lockharts?"

"The recording we received, is paying off in droves. They are trying to negotiate a deal allowing them to see daylight outside a prison cell before they die."

"Sounds like the case is all but wrapped up."

"It is. And I can't wait to bury the damn file." She sipped her wine before continuing. "How is the case you got, what yesterday, right?" she sat back and sighed. "My days are starting to run together."

Damien swallowed the bite he had chewed for the last few minutes. "Yes, we should have it wrapped up by tomorrow. Joe will be coming here in the morning, and we will go to the boyfriend's office. If it goes as planned, it should be wrapped up in the next day or so."

Dillon began to clear the plates. When she turned around Damien was checking his phone. "Expecting a message?"

He looked at her then placed his phone back in his pocket. "The detective from California. I'm hoping he will give me a little bit more information to help with another case."

"Hmm, what other case?" Dillon asked as she put the last of the dishes in the dishwasher. When Damien didn't answer, she turned back to the table. He sat with his phone in his hand oblivious that she had said anything. "Hello?"

Damien's head snapped up. "Hey, yeah," he said pocketing his phone. "You need help?" he rose from the table and moved to finish the last of the cleanup.

"No. I don't need any help. I asked you a question."

"I'm sorry. I didn't hear you, what is it you want to know?"

Dillon stopped what she was doing. "Damien, are you texting Camilla?"

Damien's mouth fell open, he stared at her. "Why the hell are you asking me that? No, I am not texting Camilla, or talking to her. I am not having secret meetings with her, nor do I fucking want to." He stepped back from her. "I don't understand when the hell you started thinking I was cheating on you. But I am damn tired of you thinking I have something going on with Camilla."

Dillon watched Damien storm out of the kitchen. She heard him go into the home gym and turn on some music. Instead of following him, afraid she would push him away more, she opted to go to the office and work. She needed to finish up her statement on the incident with Agent Johnson. She glanced over her shoulder at the closed door to the gym and sat at her desk. Maybe she projected onto Damien her own secrets. If he ever found out the whole story about Agent Johnson, she would have a lot of explaining to do.

# CHAPTER TWENTY-SEVEN

Wednesday Morning

Dillon left the condominium on the ruse of an early morning meeting and went into the office. The previous night had been filled with tension and an underlying feeling that Damien was hiding something. She really didn't think he was seeing or even wanted to see Camilla, but if it wasn't her, she had no idea what it was.

As she worked on her statement regarding the Johnson incident, making sure what she had added last night at home made sense, another email came through. This one had a file attached. It was a series of payments that were made to an offshore account. The number had been blocked, but the name of the bank was still visible. Dillon read through the file. "Holy shit." She thought her eyes were going to pop out of her head. All the payments originated from accounts that James Lockhart owned or had access to.

She hurriedly finished her statement then printed it. She also printed the attachment and carried both into the AD's office. She knocked on the door. "Hey, I got another email concerning James." She laid the print out of all the payments on his desk. "I forwarded the email to you as well."

AD Reynolds read the paper. A smile filled his face when he looked up. "Well now, I can't wait to see what James does with this information. I know the voice file had James and his father scrambling to get as light a sentence as possible." He held the paper up. "This will put the nail in their coffins."

She nodded. "I thought so too." She handed him her incident report. "Here is my statement."

"Great, I'll get this over to AD Gray." He leaned back in his chair. "You still want to go through with this?"

She squinted at him. Her brow furrowed. "Do you think I shouldn't?" She folded her arms across her chest.

"No. Not at all. I'm just making sure. When I turn all this in, you'll find yourself the subject of several inquiries." He pointed at her eye.

"Does it hurt?"

She reached up and touched her sore eye. "It looks worse than it is."

"What did Damien say?"

She leaned against the doorframe. "He wasn't too happy."

The AD cocked his head to the side. "You didn't tell him everything did you?"

"I may have neglected to tell him all the details."

"Dillon, that's going to get you into trouble."

She waved him off. "I will tell him everything. He has been preoccupied with another case." She turned to leave when the AD called out to her.

"Don't wait too long to tell him. Trust me on this Dillon."

She continued to her desk and was just about to sit down when her desk phone rang. "McGrath here."

"Agent McGrath? You have a visitor up here. She says she won't go away until you come up here."

The hair on Dillon's arms stood up. She didn't have to be told who it was. "I'll be right up." She stood and did something she never does while on duty. She removed her weapon and placed it in her drawer.

Walking into the reception area, Dillon's eyes landed on the slender bitch. Her pulse sped up as the fight or flight response kicked in. Leaning heavily towards the fight side. "Camilla why the hell are you here?" Dillon peeked over her shoulder and was grateful Margaret was involved in a phone call.

Camilla spun around placing her hands on her hips. "I want you to move out of his house."

"Well, I want to shoot you, neither of which is going to happen. Unfortunately." Dillon noted Camilla's maladroit attempt to be intimidating.

"I want Damien back, and I will do whatever it takes to get him."

Dillon stepped towards her. She noticed Camilla leaned away from her but stood her ground. "You can do whatever you want. If you think you can win him back, go for it. However, all it does is make you look pathetic."

"He doesn't have any time invested in you. I'll show him he is making a mistake." Camilla crossed her arms.

"Camilla you are a whore. You slept with so many men during the time you were with Damien, even if I weren't in the picture, he wouldn't have anything to do with your ass."

Dillon heard the ding of the elevator. A delivery man wearing sunglasses stepped out carrying a giant bouquet of flowers. Slightly distracted by the beautiful arrangement Dillon didn't hear Camilla at all.

"Hey, blondie?"

Dillon turned to see Camilla waving a hand at her. "Are you having a seizure?" Dillon asked.

"I'm warning you. You either leave Damien or I will make your life miserable." Camilla turned on her heels and followed the delivery man into the elevator.  She stared at Dillon who stood at the counter of the receptionist desk. As the door closed, the man beside her said something. "Excuse me?" Camilla said in response.

"I said I get the feeling you don't like her. She's a pretty girl." He smiled at her.

Camilla's eyes narrowed in on the delivery man. "She may be pretty, but she is stupid if she thinks I'm going to give up that easy."

"Give up what?" the man asked her.

"She has moved in with my old boyfriend, and I have decided I want him back." Camilla fluffed her hair and straightened her shirt. "I don't care if he thinks he is in love with her or not."

The man nodded. "I bet it would be nice if you could get her out of the way altogether wouldn't it?"

The elevator opened, Camilla and the delivery man stepped out into the lobby. She turned towards the man. "You don't even know the half of it."

The man led the way out of the building and held the door for her. Camilla watched as he walked to an older model truck. She wondered why he didn't have a delivery truck. As the man climbed in, he turned back to her. At the same moment, her cell phone rang. She started to turn away when the delivery man spoke to her.

"You never know Camilla, you might get what you want."

"Huh?" she asked as she held the phone to her ear. But the man just drove away.

# CHAPTER TWENTY-EIGHT

Damien sat in his home office. Dillon had just left. He tried to eat breakfast, but the heated coil in his belly kept his appetite at bay. Damien nursed his open can of diet soda and pulled the files from his desk drawer on the two cases from California. He rolled his shoulders twisting his head from side to side. He couldn't help shaking the feeling something was looming, just waiting to strike.

He scanned the first case again, refreshing his memory. The second case involved another student. This young man was killed in the basement of his apartment building. He was murdered while working out in the gym that filled the entire basement floor. Joshua had his throat crushed under a weighted barbell.

The report stated that Joshua had an argument with a young man over a disputed grade just two days earlier. Damien read through the report. There was no mention of the young man's name. However, it did state that Joshua had mentioned to his instructor that he worried the student in question may try to take the grade dispute to arbitration.

Damien frowned. The local police never could track down the name of the other student, and no one who worked with Joshua could give the police any information as to who the student was.

These two cases had no connection between them. Neither victim ran in the same circle or worked in the same part of the University. But Damien was positive they both had everything to do with David Allen Parker. However, he wouldn't be able to do much more without help from Detective Lawson. "Well, fuck me." He pulled out his phone and called the detective. Damien realized the time difference in California, the same moment the detective's voicemail answered. "Hey Detective Lawson, it's Damien Kaine. When you get a chance to speak with your friend at USC, would you get me a list of David Lindquist's classes throughout his entire enrollment? Also, could you get me all his relevant school data, like loans, housing, or anything else about his time at USC? Thank you."

Damien pulled on the ends of his hair. His constant stomach ache and nausea were beginning to take a toll on him. Coach sauntered in and jumped up on the desk. Purring, he head-butted Damien's hand until he got what he wanted. "Alright, Coach. Man, you are relentless." Damien scooped up the hefty fur ball and placed him on his lap. Coach snuggled in as Damien drug a hand from the top of his head down his back. At one-point Coach positioned himself so Damien could scratch his belly.

Just before eight-thirty, Damien heard the garage door open. Looking at his watch, he was surprised it was already eight thirty. A few moments later Joe entered the condo.

"Yo, you decent? Or is Dillon naked?"

"In the office." Damien frowned at Joe. "You don't need to see my woman naked. You have a woman."

"That may be true, but I wouldn't look away if Dillon walked out with a towel around her head and nothing else."

"You're a pig." Damien chuckled and placed Coach on the desk. He stretched and then jumped down. Sulking over to Joe, Damien watched as his partner picked up the cat and snuggled him against his chest. "You ready? Or you want to stay here and love on Coach?"

"Hey, I can't help it if your cat loves me."

"He loves everyone."

"He didn't love Camilla." Joe saw the cringe on Damien's face. "I must have hit a sore spot. I told you to cut her out. You should've taken steps to get her out of your life long ago."

"Yeah yeah, I heard you." Damien dragged a hand through his hair. "She's calling almost every day. Dillon thinks I'm interested in her."

Joe hit Damien on the shoulder. "Get out? Why would Dillon think that?

"Who knows." Damien swallowed the bile inching its way up his throat as the knot twisted a little tighter. "Let's go."

"Take care of it. Talk to the Captain, do something," Joe said.

They headed out to Damien's SUV.  "Shit it's cold," Damien said as he started the vehicle.

"Why don't you use the damn remote start? Now I have to sit here and freeze until your heater kicks in."

"I forget most of the time," Damien said as he pulled into traffic.

Joe opened the file and began to thumb through it.

Damien called for police back up to meet them at Architect Inc. He gave instructions for the officers to remain in their car until he showed up on the scene.

Joe looked up with a raised eyebrow at his partner. "You expect our

Girl Friday to cause a scene?"

Damien shook his head. "No. To be honest, if we can't trap her or back her into a statement which gives us probable cause, we won't even be able to arrest her."

"We have her in three lies. That's huge, should get us some warrants. All three lies place her around Rachel," Joe said.

"Lies won't get us much, but they show she was obsessed with Rachel."

"You think we can get her to give it up?" Joe asked.

Damien maneuvered around a garbage truck. "If we hit her with her lies I think we can get her to cave. At least that's what I hope."

Joe closed the file. "If we ask her direct questions about her whereabouts, and everything she says we contradict, we can get her off-kilter. Plus, when Tucker finds out she is lying, he will help push her over the edge. Unknowingly of course." Joe grinned.

They pulled onto Architect Inc.'s street. Damien spotted the patrol car and pulled up behind it. The two officers exited their vehicle meeting them at the curb. Damien reached out to shake their hands. "Okay, so this is what we have. We are going to go in and interview a suspect in a murder investigation. I don't think she will try to run, and I'm pretty sure she doesn't even know we are on to her.

"When we go in, I would appreciate it if you would stay outside, don't let anyone else come into the office and do not let anyone leave. If we can get our suspect to admit to the crimes or we can trip her up, you two will escort her to DC. Any questions?"

Both officers said no as they followed Damien and Joe into the office foyer.

Damien saw Sherry Breen as she stood at the reception desk. Her attitude seemed jovial given her boss had just lost someone he was in love with. She spoke with animated gestures to the person behind the desk. Sherry turned towards the sound of the door opening. Damien noticed her happy go lucky demeanor vanished.

Sherry grimaced as she folded her arms across her chest. "Detectives. I assume you are here for Mr. McNeil?"

Damien and Joe stood a few feet from her. "Yes. However, we need to speak with both of you."

She hissed out a long breath. "We answered your questions the other day. Can't you give Tucker a little breathing room? It doesn't matter, I don't believe he is even available. I believe it would be best if you come back another day. Setting up an appointment would ensure his availability." She turned her back to them.

"We already called Mr. McNeil, he scheduled this meeting. He is expecting us," Damien said.

Sherry Breen turned around. Her mouth fell open. Her eyes narrowed, and she balled her hands into fists at her side. "Wh-when? I was unaware you had called." She pursed her lips together and leered at the receptionist who cowered behind the desk.

"Yesterday. I'm surprised he didn't tell you. I was under the impression you took care of most things around this office," Damien said.

Joe stepped up to the counter. He smiled his sexiest smile and winked at the young lady. "Would you call back to Mr. McNeil and let him know we are here?"

The young girl blushed as she avoided eye contact with Joe. "I sure can."

While she called back announcing their arrival, Damien glanced around the office. "How long have you worked here Miss Breen?"

Sherry blinked rapidly. Her hands made flighty movements as she fidgeted with the buttons on her sweater. "I've been here for about three years. Came to work for Tucker, I mean Mr. McNeil, right out of college."

Damien turned towards the approaching footsteps. Mr. McNeil came into the waiting area, and he noticed Tucker's haggard look, puffy eyes, and dark circles.

"Detectives, please come back to my office. I'm anxious to know what information you've come up with. I spoke with Jackson this morning. He has been gracious enough to let me help plan the funeral."

Damien noticed the icy stare Sherry Breen gave her boss. He motioned for her to follow them down the hall. "You'll need to come with us. We need to get an official statement from you as well."

Once in the office, Damien and Joe remained standing. "Mr. McNeil, by chance were you expecting to see Miss Burrows the day she died?"

"Umm—no we had plans for the next night. When I spoke with Rachel on Sunday, she told me she had wanted to go for a run Monday morning. She and her brother have been working on their current project, and she needed to clear her head. Running seemed to help her refocus."

Damien's brow wrinkled. "Did anyone else know of her plans to run?"

Tucker shrugged. "I'm not sure. I didn't tell anyone. I'm not sure if she did. Other than her brother." He tilted his head. "Sherry was with me at my house on Sunday when I spoke to her, other than her I don't know if anyone else knew or not."

Damien turned towards Sherry Breen. "Were you aware Rachel was going running Monday morning?"

She looked at Tucker, then the detective. "Yes. I mean I may have overheard their conversation." Sherry wrung her hands.

Joe shifted his stance. "Miss Breen, did you like Rachel?"

Sherry tilted her head back slightly as her brow furrowed and her lips turned downward. "She was pleasant enough. I didn't hang out with her. But yes, I would say I liked her."

"Miss Breen, you told me the other evening you had never been to Rachel's residence. But we have logs showing you visited Rachel Burrow's apartment building," Damien said.

Sherry gasped. "I have never been to her apartment. I'm not even sure where she lived." She glanced at Tucker. "I don't know what they are talking about."

"The security desk at the Burrow's residence keeps a log of anyone who comes into the building. On several occasions, it shows you came into the building and left within a few minutes." Damien eyed her, waiting for her response.

"Well, I don't know why it would show that. I have never been to Rachel's apartment," Sherry Breen sat with her hands folded in her lap.

Damien noticed her breathing increased and a light sheen of sweat formed on her forehead. "Mr. McNeil we were able to confirm your departure from your building the time you said." He faced Sherry. "Tell me again, where you were Monday morning. Before you ended up at Mr. McNeil's house?"

Sherry huffed. "I already told you. I went to work out since I didn't have to come into the office at my normal time. I went to Quad's Gym. From there I went straight to Tucker's house."

"Miss Breen, about how long did you work out before you left for Mr.

McNeil's residence?"

Sherry bit her bottom lip shifting her gaze between Joe and Damien. "My exercise routine lasted for at least forty-five minutes, it could've been longer."

"Are you aware Quad's Gym uses a card scanner?" Damien asked.

"Yes," she said.

"Are you aware they have a new system there. It takes a photo of you as you enter the building?"

She shook her head, saying nothing.

"Miss Breen, they have no record of you entering the gym Monday morning. Can you explain why?"

Sherry fidgeted with her sweater and her watch. "Well, their scanner sometimes doesn't register your card."

Damien gave her a mocking smile. "No. I spoke with an employee. He said their scanner was working fine. He checked the video log, and there's no record of you entering the gym. The last time you were there was two or three days ago. He pulled your workout usage. Can you explain where you were?"

Tucker focused on his assistant. "Sherry, if you weren't there, where were you?"

"Tucker, there's been some kind of mistake here. I'm sure the gym is incorrect," Sherry said.

Damien leaned in. "Miss Breen, we were able to verify Tucker and Jackson's whereabouts by checking their phone location. If you were at Quad's at the time you claim, how did your phone ping off the towers at the junction of I-55 and I-294, near the Palos Trail entrance?"

She stood glaring at Damien. "You can't pin this on me. I know where I was Monday morning when Rachel was murdered." Sherry started for the door.

Joe blocked her exit. "We aren't finished here."

Damien stepped towards Sherry while Joe maneuvered himself closer to her. "If you were at the gym when you said you were, how did your phone end up near the trails?"

Sherry stepped back, rolling her eyes. She crossed her arms. "The phone company is incorrect. They make mistakes all the time."

Mr. McNeil came around his desk. "Did you have something to do with this? Why would they say these things if there was no truth to them? Tell me, were you there Sherry? What are you hiding?" His voice quivered as he spoke.

Sherry flinched waving her arms around. "They've made a mistake. Tucker. You can't believe what they're saying."

Damien looked at her. "You lied in your original statement, allowing us to obtain a search warrant. At this moment we have a CST crew heading to your house. They'll find the clothes you wore Monday morning, and I'm sure they'll find Rachel's blood on them." Damien glanced at Joe. "No one realizes how hard it is to get blood out of clothes or off shoes, you know Joe?"

"Yup, that's right. The criminal always seems to forget about the little things. I bet you didn't wash the blood off your shoes as well as you think you did, Sherry." Joe said.

Sherry Breen began to shake. Her bottom lip trembled. She stammered as she tried to speak. "There has been a horrible mistake made."

"Miss Breen there has been no mistake. You were envious of Rachel and her relationship with Mr. McNeil. When you overheard Tucker's conversation with her, you took the opportunity and went there. From eyewitness accounts," Damien watched her eyes widen as she swallowed. "You didn't know there was a witness, did you? He bumped into Rachel before you killed her. He was there before and after you left."

Joe moved a little closer to Sherry. "You tried to take her on the trail. When you couldn't get close enough to her there, you ambushed Rachel at her vehicle. You cut her throat, nearly slicing her damn head off. You staged the scene to look like she was raped and murdered." Joe held out his handcuffs and stepped up behind her. "You're in love with your boss. The thought of him being with Rachel infuriated you."

Sherry's gaze shifted between the two detectives. "No. No. You're wrong." Her shoulders sagged as she stared at Tucker. She tried to reach out to him, but Joe grabbed her hands and placed her in handcuffs. She struggled to pull away.

"We aren't wrong Miss Breen. You killed Rachel because she had something you wanted—Mr. McNeil," Damien said.

Sherry resigned herself to what was about to happen. She held her head up and stared at Tucker. "I did this for you. She would've destroyed you. She didn't love you as I do."

Tucker stood his hands clenched into fists. His body trembled. "I can't believe this. You killed Rachel. I don't understand." He glanced at the two men then turned and faced Sherry. "Why? Why would you kill her? She never did anything to you."

Sherry's jaw dropped. She gazed dumbfounded at him. "Ever since you started dating her, you haven't had time for me. You were always busy with her. I used to bring files over to your house, and we would eat Chinese food or pasta, and we would hang out. You started to see her, and you didn't have time for me."

Tucker ran his hand through his hair. His breath became rapid and labored. "Those were business meetings. I never had you come to my house for anything else. I never spent time with you outside this office except in a working capacity. You're delusional, you're—you're a psycho."

"No! I did it for you. Everything I do is for you. I've always loved you. I take care of everything for you. She did nothing! It was me, I did everything. I love you—me—not her!" Tears streamed down her face. "Please Tucker, tell me you love me. You know you love me."

He growled as he charged towards Sherry. Damien grabbed him before he reached her.

"You're a monster. A sick, ugly monster." Tucker yelled at her. "I could never love someone like you. I hope you rot in hell." He screamed at her.

Sherry struggled against the restraints. "Tucker, I know you love me. You'll realize your true feelings for me. When I get out of jail, we can be together. We can have the—the life she was trying to take from me. Please Tucker, please tell me you love me?"

Tucker turned his back to her.

The officers had entered at the sound of the screaming. Both officers now flanked Sherry Breen as she tried to get close to Tucker McNeil. They escorted her from the office and led her down the hallway. She screamed that they had it wrong. She babbled it was self-defense that Rachel became enraged.

Joe and Damien followed the two police officers from Tucker McNeil's office. Damien glanced over his shoulder as he left. In the middle of the room, Tucker McNeil fell to his knees and cried.

# CHAPTER TWENTY-NINE

Damien watched as the officers loaded Miss Breen into the back of the patrol car. He had given them instructions to book her on murder charges. He started the SUV and was about to pull away from the curb when his phone rang.

Not paying attention to the caller ID, he answered it using the vehicle Bluetooth. "Kaine."

"Well, you never sent me flowers, and now you're sending them to Dillon?"

Damien struggled to follow the ramblings of the mad as a hatter bitch on the phone. "What in the hell are you talking about Camilla?"

"Today I paid a visit to your girlfriend."

"Wait, back the truck up. You went to Dillon's office? Why, Camilla? Why in the hell would you go to her place of work? What is wrong with you?"

"I may have made a mistake, but I'm not going to give up on us. If you would give us a chance, I could show you how much you still love me."

"Camilla, answer my damn question. Why did you go to Dillon's workplace?"

"I went there to tell her I wanted her to move out of your place..."

"Are you fucking crazy? You might be fucking mad."

"No, Damien. I'm not crazy. I decided I want you back."

Damien could hear the smugness in her voice.

"Since when did you become a flowers kind of guy anyway?"

Damien rubbed the sides of his temples. "Camilla, what the fuck are you talking about? What flowers?"

"When I was there, Dillon had a huge bouquet delivered to her. At least I assume they were for her. Just before the elevator door closed, I saw her pick them up."

Damien looked at Joe who sat with his mouth open. Fuck. This isn't what he needed to happen right now. "Camilla, I need you to tell me everything you can about the delivery guy."

Camilla sighed into the phone. "This guy delivered the flowers. In the elevator he asked me if I wished she was out of the picture. Of course, I said yes. He said I may get what I want one day. When I tried to ask him what he meant he pulled away."

Damien's heart raced. "Can you tell me anything about the man?"

"Nothing stands out. Average height. The one odd thing was he got into an old truck. Not a delivery truck. I mean c'mon, Damien. If you're going to send flowers, you should use Meagan's Floral. You know it's the best florist in the city...."

"Camilla, I have to go. I'm going to tell you right now...are you listening?"

"Yeah Damien, I'm listening."

"I want nothing more to do with you. I don't want you back in my life. I don't want to spend time with you. I don't want to talk on the phone. Do you understand?" Damien reached for his phone in the cradle. "Camilla I am done with you." He disconnected the call.

Joe sat and stared at him. "What's going on Damien?"

"You heard her. She's trying to get me back."

"No. That conversation had nothing to do with Camilla. You were more interested in the delivery guy than the fact that Dillon got a bouquet of flowers from some unknown admirer."

Damien pulled out into traffic. He didn't respond.

"Damien, something has been up for several days now. You have missed meetings, been absent-minded. You aren't handling the VCU or the cases like I've seen you do in the past. Tell me what the hell is going on with you."

Damien's jaw clenched. He couldn't keep it from Joe any longer. "You know when we met with Gage Price?"

Joe's eyes narrowed in on his partner. "Yes?"

"He gave me a jump drive. A special one from Glenn Rossdale."

"And?"

"When you went to the bathroom, at the end of our interview, that's when Gage gave it to me." He filled Joe in on what Gage had told him and what was on the drive. When Damien finished telling him everything Joe sat quietly. After about five minutes, Damien turned to find his partner staring at him. "What?"

Joe huffed. "I can't believe you didn't share any of this with me. All this time you have been hiding it. Why?"

"I didn't want to involve you in my plans. If you know them, you can be held as an accessory."

"What the fuck? An accessory to what?"

"Joe, I'm not bringing David Allen Parker in for questioning or arresting him. I plan on killing him."

"Are you fucking crazy? How the hell do you think you can get away with killing him?"

"Because no one will find his body." Damien turned towards Joe. "Trust me on that."

Joe leaned his head against the seat. "I should beat the shit out of you. Of all the people you should and could tell—me—you didn't. And you wouldn't have if I wasn't sitting here." Joe ogled Damien. "I'm gathering by your reaction you think the delivery man is David?"

"Yeah, I do. He's been sending her files which have nailed the Lockharts. He is purposely doing all this to fuck with her." Damien glanced over at Joe. "She doesn't know any of this, and you better not tell her a damn thing."

Joe gaped at him. "Okay, wait. You haven't told her any of this. Who this guy is?"

"No. And I'm not going to."

"Damien, you've got to tell her. She needs to know her past is coming back to haunt her. She deserves to know."

"No. She doesn't."

Joe reached out and grabbed Damien's arm as he opened his door to get out of the vehicle. "I'll back you and help you. Whatever you need me to do. But at some point, you are going to need to tell her everything."

Damien nodded. Bile rose burning his throat. He swallowed several times. "You know there is no coming back from this. I'm not arresting him."

"I know what I'm getting into. Whatever it takes."

# CHAPTER THIRTY

Wednesday mid-day

Damien and Joe entered the VCU. Three of his detectives sat at their desks.

Jenkins looked up and nodded at Damien. "Hey, Lieutenant. I figured you would be beating the shit out of Johnson right about now. Of course, Dillon seems capable of protecting herself."

"Shit, Jenks. Dillon could be your bodyguard." Alvarez said.

Damien cocked his head to the side. "Uh, okay. I must have missed something. I know they had a minor scuffle yesterday, is that what you're referring to?"

The detectives glanced at each other then back at Damien.

Joe took his seat at his desk. "You guys look like you know something he doesn't. What gives?"

Jenkins leaned back in his chair. "Yesterday they had more than a minor scuffle. Evidently, Johnson tried to fuck with Dillon, and she broke his wrist. The word on the street is he was the instigator, and she is pressing charges against his ass."

Alverez chimed in. "Yeah, this is one in a long list of incidents, but Dillon is the first to press the issue. Johnson may get demoted, or he may get booted out."

"His ass needs to be booted out," Joe said.

Damien remained expressionless. He could hear his pulse beating in his temples. His heart beating twice as fast as usual. He halfway nodded. "Oh, yeah. She mentioned it. I wasn't putting it together. Johnson does have some issues."

"Hey, whatever happens, you two need to keep your eye on him. He is going to be pissed. She has kicked his ass twice now, and she is going to fuck his career." Jenkins popped some gum into his mouth. "I don't think he'll go away easy."

"I hear ya. You guys good on your cases?" Damien asked wanting to change the subject.

They all nodded and gave quick updates. He waved them off as he headed to his office. He closed the door and sat at his desk. The irony of him being pissed at Dillon for hiding shit from him hit him over the head like an anvil. "Talk about a double standard," he whispered to himself. For the first time in his life, he felt like he had absolutely no control.

A knock at the door brought him out of his funk. "It's open."

Joe bounded in with a file. "Hey here's the file on Sherry Breen. She's in holding now, I just got off the phone with the ADA. She's getting ready to file murder charges against her."

"If anyone deserves to be put away its Sherry Breen. Along with James and Robert Lockhart," Damien said. "I have to say I hope they lock all of them in the bowels of the jail."

"I'll be glad when those fuckers get off the damn TV. I'm tired of having to keep answering questions. Did you hear James' wife filed for divorce? Looks like she is going to be a wealthy woman."

"As much as I hate cheaters, I do love the fact she will at least get everything, and he will rot in jail."

Damien was about to say something else when his cell phone rang. He looked at the number and motioned for Joe to shut the door. "Hey Detective Lawson, what you got for me?" Damien put his phone on speaker and laid it on his desk.

"Hey, Lieutenant Kaine. I heard back from my buddy at the college. He pulled all of David's files. I owe him a big favor."

"I can help you with a favor. You tell me what I can do, and I will."

"I'll remember that. As for all the information I got, it's quite a bit. I'll send it to your email. However, after going through some of this and looking back at those two unsolved cases, we might have a connection, David Lindquist."

Damien's eyes widened. "Hey, I will owe you big time if you can do something for me."

"Okay. What is it?"

"Listen, there is a big chance this guy could go underground. If he hears a whiff of this investigation, he may poof. Do your investigation but leave his name out."

There was silence on the phone. "It's kind of hard to investigate a cold case and keep a name out of it. We do have to interview people from the past, you know?"

Damien dragged a hand through his hair.

Joe saw the concern ebb across Damien's face. "Hey Detective Lawson, this is Joe, I'm Damien's partner. I get you see a connection, but we are talking about several murders we could solve in both our states. Your cases have been cold for five years, just like a few of ours. Could you give us say a week before you go poking around in Lindquist's past? We'll share everything with you from our case. Access to every piece of evidence. It will help tie your cases to him."

Silence on the phone. "Oh hell, I can put this on the bottom of the pile. Shit, I got four other cases staring back at me. I can push this off for a few. But it will cost you, Kaine," Detective Lawson said.

"Just ask," Damien responded. "You got something in mind?"

"I do. I bought my dream home. I'm going to die there as much as it cost me. I want one of your dad's security systems at cost. Deal?"

Damien smiled at Joe. "Listen, I'll give you the system, and install it for you if you bury your cold case till I tell you when. Deal?"

"Uhm, I'm sorry, what cold cases?" The line went dead.

"Well, once again being a Kainetorri has some perks," Joe said as he took a handful of jellybeans.

"Shit, that's gonna cost me a fortune." Damien hung his head in his hands. "But it's worth it." He glanced at his watch. "I got a quick meeting at two. Shouldn't take thirty minutes. Afterward, you want to go to my house and look at these files. See if we can track this fucker?"

Joe stood stretching. "Man, I'll do just about anything if it means I get to leave early."

"Anything Joe?"

Joe smiled as he walked out of his office. "As long as I don't have to kiss you, yeah pretty much anything."

# CHAPTER THIRTY-ONE

*Wednesday afternoon*

*David pulled into the little diner in Davenport, Iowa. Thanks to the Chicago traffic, the trip took longer than expected, just under three hours. The farm's website said they closed at five pm on Wednesdays. He glanced at his watch, he had two hours to fill before he could head to Dillon's childhood home.*

*He settled into a booth at the back of the diner. He pulled out his phone and double checked how far he was from his destination. Less than thirty minutes. David smiled at the waitress when she brought his drink. "I'm not in a hurry. You can take your time putting in my order."*

*The young brunette put her hand on her chest and sighed. "Thank you. We got slammed, my replacement is late, and the kitchen is in the middle of a shift change."*

*"Put it in when things settle down." He added sugar to his tea and looked at the news on his phone. He read the Lockharts were waving their trial for a plea deal. The evidence was just too damning. David thought that was the smartest thing old James had done. If a jury ever heard all the details, they would make an example out of the Lockharts. He relished the thought of the arrogant fuck spending his life in a damp, dark cell.*

*David pulled up the Google earth view of the farm. Making a note of the entrances in and out. A long drive set the main house apart from the rest of the farm. There was a big barn on the premises that the website said was used to let the visitors have a hands-on experience.*

*David's stare hardened at the picture of the property. His shoulders hunched as he leaned into his phone. While he and his mother moved around more times than he could count, Dillon got to grow up in what amounted to a sanctuary. He shut his phone screen off and laid it face down when the waitress brought another drink and some freshly baked rolls. He spread butter on one roll and thought of his plans for later that evening. A slow grin pushed the corners of his mouth upward. Dillon had no idea how much her life was about to change.*

# CHAPTER THIRTY-TWO

Damien and Joe walked into the condo. Coach sat at the ready, scowl and all. Damien peered at the cat, which he swore raised one cat brow at him, as Coach drooled over the sandwiches they carried. "Hey fatty, you hungry?"

At the mere mention of the word hungry, Coach spun in a circle, racing them to the kitchen. Damien grabbed two sodas from the fridge and tossed them to Joe. He filled Coach's bowl with his favorite stinky food. Both stood listening to Coach growl as he ate.

"What is Coach's problem?" Joe asked as he led the way to the office.

"How the hell should I know. Maybe it's a way to gain his masculinity back. Shit, someone cut off his balls by the time I got him. And between Dillon, Taylor, and Mrs. C. dressing him up, the poor cat has to prove his manhood somehow."

"Where is Mrs. C.? I haven't seen her the last couple of days."

Damien opened his soda. Joe pulled a chair over to his desk. A few commands later and the monitor display filled the big screen that hung on the wall. "She's traveling. She and a friend took their dogs and went on a road trip."

"You are tracking her right?"

"Oh, hell yeah. I switched out her phone a long time ago for one of my dad's tracking phones. It's programmed with a panic mode. If she feels unsafe at any time, all she has to do is hit a series of numbers, and it notifies Nicky at the compound, and me. A trace is started immediately." Damien pulled his phone. "Here. Look at this." He pulled up a series of pictures and handed his phone to Joe.

Joe barely swallowed his bite of sandwich. "For shit's sake, what is she doing to her poor dog?" Joe scrolled through several photos of Mrs. C.'s little dog dressed as a cop, a fireman, a princess, and a hotdog. "She has a severe problem." Joe handed him his phone back laughing. "But damn if I don't love that old woman."

"You and me both." Damien pulled up the emails from Detective Lawson. "Okay. Let's see what my new best friend in Cali has sent me." Opening the files, he read the information. "Alright. I've read over both cold case files. Let's set those aside for now. I know he used David Arthur Lindquist through high school. His mother was smart to keep his first name. It would be hard for a ten-year-old to remember a new first name."

"I know if my father was sentenced for the murder of a family I wouldn't want anyone to know," Joe said.

"It looks like she tried to erase anything associated with his father." Damien scrolled through the college documents. "See, look here. At some point, he changed his name. Dropped Arthur for Allen at the beginning of his sophomore year."

Damien searched online for the records for David's mother's death. "Look. She died the summer before his sophomore year. That's when he went back to his middle name too. Must have some significance to him."

"Maybe it's his father's middle name or a grandfather." Joe reached for his chips. He looked at his feet to see Coach staring at him. "Hey there buddy." Joe placed a chip on the floor and watched as the cat munched on it.

Damien ran another search. "Yes. It was his paternal grandfather's name. Looks like he died when David turned eighteen. According to what I can find, it doesn't look like the grandfather had much communication with David and his mother after the murders. He gave one interview before his son was scheduled to be executed." Damien read through the interview. "Wow. In this interview, he said he didn't have any family left. His wife died right after the trial, and he no longer was on speaking terms with his grandson or his former daughter-in-law."

Damien looked up at Joe. "That had to mess with a kid. Being blamed for his father's actions. His own grandfather wouldn't speak to him. That tells me a lot about why his mother changed everything but the boy's first name. "

"She wanted to put as much distance between her and her ex-husband." Joe stared at the information on the big screen. "It looks like they moved around a lot before settling in California. She got a good job and started to make something of her life."

"Okay. His mom dies, he changes his middle name back, why?"

Joe shrugged. "You do weird things when someone dies. Maybe he wanted to capture those memories from when he was a kid. Something to hold onto."

Damien's mouth hung open.

Joe frowned at him. "What?"

"Have you been watching those doctor shows again?"

Joe chuckled. "No, you ass. But it does make sense." Joe snapped his fingers. "Wait...when did his father get executed?"

Damien did another search. "Ahh. Later the same school year the execution was put on the docket. The corrections facility in Arkansas schedules their executions one to two years out. Looks like George's was scheduled for the following year. David would have been in his senior year of college. And I know from Ross he left school before graduating."

"We need to get the list of people who attended the execution." Joe glanced at his watch. "We will have to get it tomorrow. When is Dillon expected home?"

Damien shrugged. "Any minute. What about Taylor?"

Joe nodded. "She should be showing up too. She wants to get miso soup, wontons, and eggrolls. I will get something more filling than soup." He patted his stomach.

Voices filtered down the hall from the living room. "Shit," Damien whispered. "I didn't hear the garage open. Did you?" He had just enough time to darken the screen and nothing else.

"No. Dillon must have parked in front," Joe said as he stood.

They heard laughter from the other room.

"Well, I guess they're both home," Joe said as he followed Damien out the office door.

"Damn it, Coach. If you would give me five seconds to set this down, I will pick you up." Dillon maneuvered a giant bouquet of exotic flowers.

Damien and Joe looked at each other.

Taylor smiled at Joe as she made her way to him. "Hey, baby. You never buy me flowers." She winked at him as she stood on her tippy toes to kiss him.

"And I never will. Flowers are a waste of money." He returned her playful kiss. "I would rather buy a new sex toy. Something we both can enjoy."

"Joe!" she said as she swatted him across the chest.

Damien goggled the flowers. "Who sent you those?"

Dillon turned on him. "I thought they were from you." She watched as Joe pulled the card from the holder. "If you didn't send them, who did?"

Joe noticed Damien's body go rigid. His hands were balled into fists, and Joe was sure steam wafted from his ears. "Umm, Dillon. Think about it for a minute. If it isn't Damien, who has been sending you gifts, so to speak?"

Dillon's brow wrinkled. She gazed at everyone in the room. "Oh, crap. The hired hitman from the Lockhart case. Well shit."

Joe read the card out loud. "I have been thinking about you. I hope you like the flowers. All my love." Joe slipped the card into his back pocket.

"Did you see the delivery guy?" Damien asked through gritted teeth.

Dillon squinted at him. "No. I didn't."

"Why the hell not? You know it was the killer, right?"

"Why would I pay attention to a delivery man? I didn't know he was the Lockhart's hired hitman." Dillon rubbed her temples. She let her arms drop against her body before rounding on Damien. "Wait for a second, how the hell do you know it was a man that delivered the flowers? And why the hell do you think the delivery man was the killer, our hitman? Are you psychic now?" she gave him a fake smile.

Taylor peeked at Joe who nodded at her. "Hey guys, we are going to head out," Taylor said as she reached for Joe's hand.

Damien's head nodded in Joe's direction as he and Taylor walked out of the condo. Staring at the floor, his breath came out in short, clipped pants.

"Who told you I received flowers, Damien? And how do you know for sure the delivery man and the killer are one and the same?" Dillon crossed her arms.

"We'll get to that."

"The fuck we will. Camilla, the bitch, called you, didn't she?" Dillon began to pace the living room. "You have got to do something about her."

"I'm not worried about her. She called me to try to talk me into dumping you and letting her back into my life." Damien pursed his lips together. "In case you didn't hear me before, I don't want a relationship with her. I'll talk to Captain Mackey tomorrow about the best way to handle her. I want her to leave me alone as much as you do."

# CHAPTER THIRTY-THREE

Dillon walked into the kitchen and grabbed a beer. She chucked the cap into the trash and began to guzzle it. She stopped, taking a breath. She glared at Damien as he leaned against the door frame.

"Don't give me the evil eye. I haven't done anything," he said.

Dillon cocked her head to the side. "Camilla thought it was a great idea to come to my place of work, the FBI nonetheless, to tell me she wants you back. She said you don't have feelings for me and I should move out now." She took a long pull on her beer. "I wanted to beat the shit out of her right there."

"She said it in hopes of putting a rift between us. She's hoping you will believe her, you and I will fight, and break up. Which will never happen. Just saying." He raised an eyebrow at her.

"I'm not worried about her breaking us up. I'm more curious as to why you think the delivery man is the killer. I mean, the killer could have paid for the flowers to be delivered." She tapped her foot, the clicking sound of her boot echoed off the tile floor.

Damien dragged his hand down his face. "When Camilla told me about the flowers, I asked her a bunch of questions. She said the delivery man got into an older truck. Not a delivery truck."

"What the hell does a delivery truck have to do with anything? Florists contract out all the time to individuals. Hell, he could've been an employee of the florist and delivered the flowers in his own truck."

"No! It wasn't just one of the employees."

"You can't be sure. C'mon, the Lockharts' hired hitman has no interest in me. He wants to fuck with James Lockhart ensuring his ass is protected. I'm the vehicle to do it."

Dillon walked past him, heading towards the office. Damien grabbed a beer from the refrigerator, he stared at the many things to eat but had no desire for food. He carried the beer and stepped into the office. The bottle slipped from his hand. He caught it before it hit the floor.

Dillon stood and gaped at the monitor. On the screen, she read the interview with George Parker's father. "Why are you reading this?" she pointed to the screen.

Damien set his beer on Dillon's desk and wiped his hands on his jeans. "I came across it when I was researching another case." He leaned against the desk. "Is there anything you wanted to tell me about the incident at your work yesterday?"

She cocked her head to the side. "What incident?"

"C'mon Dillon? You're always telling me I keep shit from you, and here you're not telling me the whole truth. I had to find out about what happened with Agent Johnson from my detectives."

"What's to tell?"

"Are you fucking kidding me? You never mentioned you broke his wrist or you were pressing charges against him. Why?"

She sighed. "I didn't want to make a big deal out of it."

"It is a big deal. This asshole put his hands on you. It wasn't an accident he gave you a beautiful black eye. He fucking punched you."

"And I didn't tell you everything because I knew you would react this way."

"Uh, what way is that? Because I care some asshole punched my girlfriend? FBI or not, a guy lays his hands on another man's woman, that man has a right to be pissed. Not only that, but you didn't tell me about you breaking his wrist and pressing charges against him."

"I didn't tell you because I didn't want it to turn into this." Dillon looked at him. "Listen, this will work out. But I have to show Johnson he can't put me in these situations and get away with it." Dillon wanted to use the large monitor on the wall. She went to close the browser on Damien's computer and stood immobilized by what showed on the screen. She looked up at Damien. "Why are you looking at the prison where George Parker was executed? First, it's the grandfather's interview, now the prison itself. Why Damien?"

Damien placed his hands on his hips. He was looking down at his feet, but the weight of Dillon's stare burned through him. He opened his mouth to speak but closed it. "I received some information which leads me to believe the hitman James Lockhart hired is a former associate of George Parker." The words hung in the air. His hair on his arms stood on end, the static electricity filled the space between him and Dillon.

Dillon's mouth hung open. "Wha...I don't...you need to explain."

Damien's head hung. He looked up to find Dillon's whiskey-colored eyes, glowing back at him. "The day we met with Gage Price, at his wife's café, he gave me two jump drives. One I turned in, to the captain and to the FBI. The second one I did not."

Dillon's fists clenched next to her thighs. "All this time you had other evidence in the Lockhart case?"

"No, Dillon. It didn't have anything to do with the Lockhart case."

"You said Gage Price gave you a drive. How could it not have anything to do with the Lockharts?" She flung her hands in the air. "I can't believe you. Again, you have taken a case and withheld evidence. Evidence which may have gotten this case shut earlier." She began to pace the area in front of Damien's desk. "I can't fucking believe you. You have no right to withhold evidence as it suits your fancy. You..."

"Dillon!" Damien said, but she kept talking. "Dillon! It had nothing to do with the Lockharts."

"Bullshit, what else could it have to do with?"

"You. It involves you."

Dillon stopped pacing. "What? What do you mean, me?"

Damien leaned his head back and sighed. "Glenn Rosedale uncovered something when he was researching the Lockharts. He gave it to Price to give to me."

"Wait, the drive was from Rossdale? I don't understand this."

"He came across some information which relates directly to you."

"Okay. Why didn't you turn it in? This might have helped us, in this case."

"Because, if the FBI acted on this information, David would go underground. And you would be looking over your shoulder the rest of your life. I'm not about to let that happen."

Dillon rubbed her temple. "I'm not following you. Who is David?"

Damien moved to stand next to Dillon. "David is an associate to George Parker, and he is coming after you."

She stared at him. Her brow furrowed.

Damien reached out and placed his hands on her arms. "David Arthur Lindquist has a vendetta against you. Glen uncovered this guy had some kind of connection or relationship with George Henry Parker."

Dillon felt as if a hammer had just smacked her on the head.

"Dillon, Glen Rossdale thinks David will come after you. He gave me the file to warn me. There is no way I'm going to let this fucker go underground and remain out there waiting to pounce on you."

"What are you planning on doing Damien? If you aren't going to turn in the information and let the FBI hunt for him, what are you going to do?"

"I'm going to protect you the only way I know how."

"Damien you can't go after him. If this guy is the hitman James Lockhart hired, he has abilities and resources."

Damien turned from her and moved back to the desk. He picked up his beer. Taking a long sip, he thought about just how far he was willing to go. "Do you get this guy wants you dead?"

"Yes, I get it. But I still can't stand by while you plan something to catch this guy and arrest him. Just so you can take the credit for it..."

Damien slammed his beer on the desk. "You think I'm going after him for the arrest? To make myself look good?"

"No, that's not what I meant."

"What did you mean Dillon? You want to explain it? Cause that's what it sounds like to me."

"That's not what I meant. But I'm not going to let you run an off the books investigation. I don't care if this asshole wants to blame me for George's execution or not. My boss needs to know what's going on."

"You can't tell anyone about this, Dillon. You can't."

"I'm an officer of the law. How can I not? You are an officer of the law. How can you even consider trying to go after this guy and arrest him?"

Damien tossed his bottle into the trash. "I never said I was going to arrest him."

Dillon's eyes widened. Her hands trembled at her side. "What is it you plan on doing Damien?"

"I'm not arresting him."

"You can't be planning to kill him. Are you fucking crazy?"

"No, Dillon. I'm not crazy. But I'm not going to let this fucker follow your every movement the rest of your life, waiting to take his shot at killing you."

"I can't be a part of this, Damien. I can't." Dillon walked towards the door.

He reached out and took her hand. "Dillon, I can't let anything happen to you. I will not let this guy get to you and hurt you." He pulled her close to him. He felt her tremble as she wrapped her arms around his waist. "I love you so much, Dillon. I will stop at nothing to protect you."

# CHAPTER THIRTY-FOUR

*Wednesday 6 p.m.*

*David pulled through the open gates on the farm. The main house was located down a small lane on the right, set off from the work area. He could see workers off in the distance finishing up the day's chores. He took note of his surroundings as he drove to the front of the house. The driveway had a half circle in the front and a spur that pulled around back. David followed the spur and pulled his truck up a little, hiding it from the view of anyone passing by.*

*He grabbed his small hand-held video recorder from his bag and exited the truck. This one was similar to the nanny cams on the market. It had a wide-angle lens and would pick up an entire room in its view. He wanted to make sure Dillon saw everything. He came to the edge of the house and peeked around the corner making sure no one was in the vicinity. David stepped onto the porch and glanced around one last time as he knocked on the door.*

*A rather sizeable sounding dog barked from behind the door. David reached back and patted the sheath that held his six-inch blade. He slid the sheath a little to the right making the handle more accessible.*

*"Hush up Gunner. Go on now—get."*

*David stepped back as the front door opened.*

*"Hey there. What can I do for you?" Jonas McGrath asked. He studied the young man before him. Something seemed familiar, but he couldn't place him.*

*"Hi, I'm David Lindquist. I know I've never met you, but I went to college with your granddaughter, Dillon. I was driving by and thought I would see if she lived here."*

*Jonas unlocked the screen door and pushed it open. "Well, hello, David. C'mon in. Dillon doesn't live here, but we are always excited to meet her friends."*

*David entered the spacious living room. He could see the dining area and the kitchen from the open doorway. It was an open concept with huge wooden beams that lined the vaulted ceiling.*

*Gunner, a giant creamy brown bullmastiff, took a protective stance next to his owner. The dog rumbled out a long low growl.*

*"Gunner. Stop." Jonas grabbed the dog by the collar just as his wife walked in. "Kitty, will you take Gunner and put him in his room." Kitty walked towards him. He looked at his visitor, "this is my wife Catherine, and I'm Jonas."*

*Kitty smiled as she walked towards the men. "Nice to meet you. I'm not sure how long the door will hold, Jojo." She grabbed Gunner's leather collar and led him to a back room. Too small for a bedroom or even an office but worked great as a dog room. "Gunner, you got your bed and your toys back here. You entertain yourself for a bit." Kitty rubbed the big dog's head. "We'll be back for you when our guest leaves." As Kitty pushed the door close, she was surprised to hear the dog howl and bang against it.*

*She walked back into the living room to find her husband and the visitor sitting at the table. "You guys start on the food. I'll fill the glasses with tea."*

*"Tell us how you know Dillon." Jonas held out the basket of bread towards the man. "David, right?"*

*"Yes, sir. I went to school with her. Spent many a night studying for our psychology tests together. I was passing through and remembered she had mentioned you guys and your farm and thought I would see if by chance she was here. I guess I should have called." David looked over his shoulder towards the hallway. He heard the dog howling and scratching at the door. David kept expecting to see the giant creature barreling towards him. "Does Gunner always act this way?"*

*"No. He's usually a quiet, lazy dog. Not much of a watchdog," Jonas said glancing over at his wife. "He isn't always happy to go into the back room. I hope he doesn't bust the damn door again, Kitten."*

*"I hope not either." She looked at their visitor. "Sometimes we have to put him back there. And when he decides he doesn't want to be in there, not much will stop him."*

*David again looked over his shoulder. "Well, I won't keep you too long."*

*"Tell us what you do now." Jonas sipped on his tea. Gunner's howling was getting increasingly loud, and a tingling sensation began to fill Jonas' chest.*

*David stood and removed a small box from his sweatshirt pocket. He walked over towards the bar area that separated the kitchen from the dining room and placed the small box on the bar. Angling it so that it picked up the entire area from the dining room to the living room.*

*"What are you doing?" Jonas asked attempting to stand from his chair.*

*David stepped behind Kitty. "No, no, no. I wouldn't do that if I were you." One hand rested on Kitty's shoulder. David reached under his sweatshirt and pulled the blade from its sheath. Placing it at the base of her throat he grinned at Jonas as the old man sat back down. "That's better. Now, I bet you're wondering what's going on, huh?" a small giggle came out. "I haven't been honest with you. I know this is no way to begin a friendship, but if I told you who I was, chances are you wouldn't have let me in."*

*"Who the hell are you? Why are you doing this?" Jonas watched as his Kitty stared back at him with tear-filled eyes. "It's going to be okay, Kitten."*

*David smirked. "Uh, no. It's not going to be okay, Kitten. So cute, too. Your little pet names for each other."*

*"What do you want? Take whatever you want and go." Jonas' heart broke as the tears now spilled down his wife's cheeks. He lifted his gaze and met the madman that held their fate in his hands. "Take what you want. Leave her alone."*

*"It's only fair I tell you who I am. I'm kind of surprised you don't recognize me. I know I resemble my father. My grandfather made that known to me." David leaned down and put his mouth next to Kitty's ear. "He couldn't get past my resemblance to the biggest disappointment of his life."*

*Jonas' mind raced. All he could see was the whites of Kitty's eyes. He couldn't understand what this man wanted from them. "I don't know what you think we have. Why you're telling us about your family?"*

*David guffawed at the old man. "You don't recognize me, do you? All those days in the courtroom, and you don't recognize me." David's hand that held the blade trembled.*

*"What, what do you..."*

*A small chirp like sound came from Kitty's throat. Her eyes pleaded with Jonas. Her heart raced. "Why are you here? We didn't do anything but support our granddaughter." Kitty winced in pain as the man's hand gripped her shoulder in a vice like pinch.*

*Jonas saw the flash of the courtroom. "George. Your George's son."*

*"Ahh, no Alzheimer's here. You win a prize. Although. I'm a little disappointed you didn't recognize me sooner."*

*"Again, why are you here? We had no involvement with your father or the case. He killed my son, his wife, and my grandsons."*

*"Technically that is true. But had it not been for Dillon, they never would*

*have figured out it was my father. I wouldn't have spent the next several years traveling around with my heartbroken mother until she finally pulled herself back into fucking reality."*

*"But it wasn't our fault! Or Dillon's. It's your sadistic father's fault. He's the one who decided to kill my family."*

*David shook the knife. "No, if Dillon hadn't testified, I would have still had my family. I need to finish what my father started. Give Dillon the opportunity to experience what losing your entire world can do to you."*

*Jonas started to get up.*

*Kitty's bottom lip trembled. "I love you, Jonas."*

*"Oh, isn't that sweet." David grabbed Kitty by her hair and pulled her head back exposing her neck.*

*The tears now flowed down her cheeks. Kitty felt the sting of the blade for a split second then the rush of warmth as her blood poured from the wound. Her eyes widened as she gasped at Jonas.*

*"No!" Jonas stood as the blood sprayed across his face and the table. He charged the man knocking him off his feet. He hit David two times in the face as they both crashed to the ground. The crunch of the man's nose gave him just a small bit of hope. He could hear Gunner barking wildly and banging against the door. "Gunner! Get in here boy!" Jonas punched the man in the side several times as he tried to get up.*

*David slashed the air with his blade. "You stupid fucker." His blade caught Jonas across his chest. Jonas fell to his side clutching the wound. David took the opportunity to gain the upper hand. The blood from Jonas' wound made the blade handle slippery, it fell from David's hand during the struggle.*

*Jonas tried to get a few more punches in, but he was no match for David. He felt the burn on his chest. He reached up touching the deep wound. From the amount of blood that ran down his shirt, he knew he wouldn't be able to fight for long. "Gunner!" He grunted as David's fist landed on his kidneys. David flipped him over and sat across his body. The punches landed with hate and fury one after the other. Bones in his face crunched. The pain spread like a rippling pool. "I hope you see your father in hell." Jonas spat at David.*

*David stopped punching the man. He looked down at the swollen and bloodied face. He wrapped his hands around his throat and squeezed. Jonas clawed and squirmed under him. David clenched his jaw shut. His nostrils flared as he tightened his fingers around Jonas' neck. "I'll be sure to tell him hello for you." He loosened his grip when Jonas quit squirming, and he reached for his knife. He heard the loud crash and looked up to see Gunner charging him.*

*Gunner's teeth latched onto David's left forearm ripping through his flesh. "AHH!" David struggled against the mad creature. He stretched out reaching for his knife. His right hand just touching the handle. "Let go of me!" David stopped reaching for the knife and punched the dog. The dog released his grasp long enough for David to grab the knife.*

*Gunner latched on to his upper arm this time. David screamed out as the dog's canines tore through his bicep. Getting a hold of the knife, he stabbed the dog twice. Gunner yelped and released his arm. David stuck the dog one last time.*

*He staggered to his feet as the dog lay bleeding on the floor. He hadn't anticipated the old man getting a few punches in nor had he planned to be almost eaten by a dog. David grabbed the camera. He held it up to his face. "This is your fault, Dillon." He panned the destruction. Stopping on the dead bodies of her grandparents before turning the camera back on himself. "This is all your fault."*

*David turned off the camera. He placed it in the pocket of his sweatshirt. The entire left arm of his sweatshirt was in tatters. "Fucking dog. Shit!" He glanced around wanting to get out of there as fast as possible. He looked down at the dying dog. "I fucking hate dogs." He kicked Gunner as he walked by.*

*Once in his truck, he placed the camera on the seat and pulled off his sweatshirt, wrapping it around his arm. Some of the cuts needed to be stitched up. Something he couldn't go to a hospital for. That would bring out all kinds of questions. No, he was going to have to do the best he could himself. He rummaged around in the backseat and found a shirt. He knew there was a twenty-four-hour store on the way out of town. That would have to do until he got to the cabin.*

***

*Jonas heard Gunner's whimpers and felt the nudge of his nose against him. He tried to speak but couldn't get his mouth to work. His face felt puffy, and he couldn't see anything but a sliver of light. He tried to touch Gunner, but his arms felt as heavy as lead filled pipes. He thought of his Kitty and*

*Dillon. The tears stung as they fell from the corners of his eyes. The light dimmed as he heard Kitty calling for him.*

# CHAPTER THIRTY-FIVE

Wednesday 7 p.m.


Joe and Taylor drove in a comfortable silence from the Chinese take-out. He kept glancing at her. He started to say something, then stopped. He pressed his lips together. He knew Damien expected him to keep his secret, but Joe also knew Taylor could help. He pulled the vehicle into his driveway, parking behind his. "Hey babe, you gonna eat that all by yourself or you going to share it with me?"

She tilted her head in his direction. She batted her eyelashes at him. "If I share, what will I get in return? Hmm?"

He leaned into her, lifting her chin. "You should be more concerned with what will happen if you don't share it with me." He placed his lips on hers. Her mouth opened, allowing his tongue entrance. What was intended to be a quick peck, escalated into a passion-filled kiss. He pulled away, the mint of her gum lingering on his tongue.

Joe led the way into his apartment. They shuffled around the kitchen. Muffin, Taylor's hundred-year-old cat, stumbled into the room. He frowned as he watched her head to her kitty bowl. "Seriously, I don't get it. Most of the time she can't find her way around my apartment, but you come in this house with food, and she can all of sudden hear, see, and move with the stealth of a kitten."

Taylor chuckled as she put some soft food into her beloved's bowl. "Since I have been traveling on business for the lab, she has been here more often. It makes sense she is getting used to this place."

"Hmm, no. It all revolves around food. She's been talking to Coach." Joe placed the Chinese food on the table. "You know, she wouldn't have to get used to my apartment if you moved in here."

Taylor stopped spooning shrimp fried rice onto her plate. "Excuse me?"

"You heard me. Don't act like you didn't."

"Yeah, I heard you, and I'm wondering what the hell you did with Joe, and what planet you're from?"

"Why is it hard to believe I want you to move in here?" Joe took a bite of his egg roll. "I asked you a few days ago, you never answered."

"Uhm, when you asked me I thought you were just in the moment. We had some great sex, and I thought you were, you know, caught up in the moment."

Joe snorted. "If that were the case, I would have asked you to move in the first time I did you." He winked at her.

She laughed, almost choking on her rice. She squinted at him. "Are you really serious?"

"Yes Taylor, I am. You spend most of your nights here." He smiled at her. "Look, I know your lease is for six months. I will pay to break it." He reached over and took her hand. "I want you here with me. I want to wake every morning to you and go to bed every night with you. Move in with me, Taylor."

Tears welled up. The tears crested over spilling down her cheek. "Oh, Joe. Yes, I will move in here." She stood and walked to him. Sitting on his lap, she wrapped her arms around his neck. "Are you sure?"

"Yes, baby. I've never been surer of anything." He kissed her, tasting the ginger from her soup. "Now, get off me so I can finish eating."

She smacked him on the head. "I guess that's about as romantic as I'm ever gonna get from you." She grabbed two beers from the fridge before sitting back down. She started to say something when saw the pinched, tension-filled expression on Joe's face. "You can't change your mind."

"Huh? What?"

"You look like you're having second thoughts." She smirked at him.

"No. Never. But I do have a problem." He set his fork down and took a long sip of his beer. "Taylor, I'm telling you something because I need your help. However, I need you to promise me you won't breathe a word of this to anyone. Not even Dillon. Can you promise me?"

She flinched. "Why would you ask me that? You should know the answer to that question. If you tell me something in confidence, I will not tell anyone, not even Muffin. Tell me what it is, Joe?"

Joe ran her through everything that Damien had told him. When he finished telling her, he felt as if a weight had lifted off him. How Damien kept this to himself for as long as he did, Joe had no idea. "Taylor, close your mouth."

"I can't believe this. I can't believe Damien hasn't told Dillon."

"Well, I bet he tells her tonight. He got a call from Camilla."

"Wait, What the heck? Why did he get a call from Camilla?"

"Oh hell, that fucking bitch is after him. She is bound and determined to get him back."

"What about Dillon?"

"Damien has no intention of getting back with her, but she went to see Dillon, called Damien and told him about the flowers. That's when he told me everything."

"I hate Camilla." She sighed as she continued to eat. "What are you going to do? I saw you put the card from the florists in your back pocket. Why?"

Joe swallowed his bite of food. He glanced down at the floor and saw Muffin laying there. He gently nudged her with the tip of his shoe. When she lifted her head, he let out the breath he held.

"Why did you do that?"

"Huh?"

"Kick Muffin?"

"Kick her? I nudged her. Making sure the old bag of bones was still alive. Shit, half the time I can't tell if she is breathing or not."

Taylor giggled. "I know you are worried she is going to die any day now." Taylor reached out with a piece of chicken. Muffin perked up and snagged it with gusto. "See, she's fine."

"Yeah, she's fine. I know when she dies, it will be when you are gone. You cannot hold it against me."

"You're silly. Now finish the story."

"Damien is sure the killer from the Lockhart case is George's son. He is also convinced he hand-delivered those flowers to get close to Dillon. Some kind of mind fuck, knowing this guy. Damien has missed meetings, he almost missed shit in the last case we had. I figured the guy needed some help."

He held up his finger. "Hang on." He pulled the card from his back pocket and called the number on the front. "Hi, this is Detective Joe Hagan, I need to ask you a few questions. Earlier today you had an order for a rather large bouquet." Joe rolled his eyes at Taylor. "I don't know, you're the florist. All I can tell you is this bouquet would have been expensive. No, I don't know what flowers they are. Hang on." He handed the phone to Taylor. "You know flowers, explain what they were."

Taylor took the phone. "Hi, I'm Detective Reese. The bouquet had hydrangeas, tulips, lily of the valley...yes, that was it. Can you tell me anything about the buyer?" She smiled at Joe as he fed the cat a piece of chicken. "Listen, this guy is wanted for questioning in a murder. If I gave you my email would you send me the footage from your security camera? We could get a warrant, but you would save me a lot of time. That's fantastic. Send it to TaylorReese@CrimeLabofChicago.net. I can't thank you enough."

Joe raised his eyebrow. "Detective Reese?"

"Hey, it worked. She has the video. She said he paid cash and wore sunglasses the whole time. But she said we could have what she had. She is going to send everything from the video feed. Some of the cameras pick up out front where people park. It may yield something."

"I knew I found the woman of my dreams. However, I need your help with one more thing."

"Ahh, now the truth comes out. What else do you need my help with?"

"Didn't you go to a conference last year with some of the prison officials from around the country?"

"Yes, I did, it was a blast too. The stories those guys tell are too funny. Why?"

"I need you to get me the names of any visitors before George Henry Parker was put to death in Arkansas, as well as the roster of witnesses to the execution."

"Okay." She glanced at her watch. "Hang on." She went into the living room and grabbed her phone. When she came back to the kitchen, Joe was cleaning up dinner. "I have several of the warden's phone numbers."

Joe stopped putting the leftovers in the fridge. "Why?"

She giggled at his expression. "For moments like this. Dork." She smiled at him when he gave her the evil eye. "Hi, Warden Mitchel? This is Taylor Reese from the Chicago Crime Lab. Yes, sir, I love my job. How is your wife doing? Wonderful. I'm calling for a favor."

She winked at Joe. "I need some information, but it's a case I can't tell you anything about. I'm hoping I can get the visitor log for George Henry Parker. It was about six years ago. Okay. How about the list of witnesses present during the execution? Listen I will take whatever I can get. I need one more favor. I need you to not mention this to anyone. It's imperative. There is a chance this guy will get wind of this. Warden, I can't thank you enough. Yes, send it to my email. Thank you again. I owe you for this."

"Can he get it to you?" Joe asked.

"Yes, he said he wasn't sure about the visitor log. They must keep the witness list, but they don't always keep the visitor logs. He will pull what he can and email me. He thinks he may have it on his home computer." She went to him and wrapped her arms around his waist. "Promise me you won't keep secrets from me? No matter how bad you think they are?"

Joe tilted her head up. "Well, I guess now is as good a time as any. I have been keeping a secret all day, and it's killing me."

She stepped back and squinted at him. "What is it?"

He looked at his feet then back at her. "I have been thinking about fucking you all day." He reached down and picked her up, throwing her over his shoulder.

She squealed and laughed as he carried her down the hall to the bedroom. "Joe put me down. You're going to drop me." She laughed harder as he spanked her.

"Oh, I'm going to drop you. First on your knees, then on all fours."

# CHAPTER THIRTY-SIX

*Late Wednesday night*

*David pulled into the driveway of his cabin. It was close to midnight. He had found a little country doctor just inside the Illinois state line, and he managed to sew up his wounds. He didn't ask any questions, and David gave the man a hefty tip to keep his mouth shut.*

*The doctor had given David some pain meds and told him how to keep the wounds clean. He recommended that he seek an orthopedic surgeon if he found he had trouble gripping anything. The damage to the muscle in both the forearm and the bicep was extensive. But the doctor thought, with time, it should heal.*

*David looked at his face in the cloudy mirror that hung above the pedestal sink. "Fuck, Dillon. I will have so much fun taking this out on you." He was tempted to remove the bandage that covered his nose, but the doc had expressed if he wanted his broken nose to set with a minimal hump he needed to leave it on. His eyes were now black and blue. The swelling on his cheeks, nose, and under his eyes looked as if he had an allergic reaction to a bee sting. He should just cut his losses and get the fuck out of here. He could come back for Dillon another day.*

*He used a warm washcloth to remove some of the dried blood from his face and neck area. As irritated as he was at this situation, there was no way he would let that bitch go now. He figured he had about twelve, maybe twenty-four, hours before the bodies of Jonas and Kitty were found. He wanted more time with Dillon, but he didn't want to run the risk of being caught.*

*The sink water was red. A stark contrast to the white sink. He cleaned the basin rinsing the cloth, he wiped his face one last time. He brushed his teeth, taking care not to push too hard against his sensitive jaw. With one last look at himself in the mirror, he turned and went to his bed.*

*David took a pain pill and washed it down with a beer. He laid down on the bed and waited for the pain to subside. The last thing he saw as he drifted off, was the look in Jonas' eyes when his precious Kitty bled to death in front of him. A thin smile filled David's face as slumber overtook him.*

# CHAPTER THIRTY-SEVEN

Thursday morning

Damien sat at his desk in the VCU. His head pounded out a beat just behind his eyes. He rubbed his temples. The morning routine had been strained, but at least he and Dillon were on speaking terms that morning. He'd begged her not to say anything until next week. He just asked for a few more days to hunt this guy down. He was sure that he would be able to find this guy and he just wanted a little more time. When she left, he had no idea whether she would say anything. He still had not told her who David really was, and it ate at his gut. He popped a few antacids from his desk and said a prayer that it would relieve the discomfort in his belly.

He dialed the number to the Cummins Unit in Grady, Arkansas. He had no warrant or even any information to compel them to give him what he needed, but he had to try. Damien leaned back in his chair. "My gosh, who the hell picks this music?" Damien had to stop himself from poking his pen into his ear as he listened to a symphonic rendition of Air Supply.

"Cummins Unit, how may I help you?"

"Hi, this is Lieutenant Damien Kaine, I need some help with a case. I'm hoping you might be able to give me some assistance."

"Sure, sugar, what can I do for you?"

Damien smiled at the southern accent. He pictured an enormous-breasted woman sitting on the other end of the phone. "I need a witness list of a past execution."

"Hmm, when was the execution?"

Just as Damien was about to answer, Joe knocked on the door and walked in. He nodded at his partner as he watched him take a handful of jelly beans. "Um, the execution took place five years ago. I need...."

"Sugar, before I can even give you any information I need you to fill out some paperwork."

"I don't have time to fill out paperwork. Can't you help me?"

"Oh honeybuns, I wish I could. I can email you the forms. But I can't give you anything without those things."

Damien glanced up to see Joe waving at him. He covered the mouth-piece of the phone. "What is wrong with you? Are you about to shit your pants?"

"Hang up."

"What? Hang up, why?"

"Do it."

Damien watched as his partner was about to have a brain hemor-rhage. He hung up on the southern belle. "Okay, there I hung up." He dragged a hand down his face. "I wasn't getting anywhere anyway."

"I got what you need. Well, Taylor got it." Joe opened the folder he held in his lap. "Alright. Last night Taylor called the prison warden, out there in Arkansas."

"Huh? Wait, you told Taylor?"

Joe winced. He realized he just let Damien know that he told some-one about his secret. "Look, she won't tell anyone. Not even Dillon. But I needed her help. And you do too."

Damien leered at Joe.

"I bet you want to punch me, huh?" Joe asked.

"How do you know?"

"I would if I was you. But hear me out. You can't do this alone. As smart as you are, have you gotten anything yet, anything substantial?"

"No." Damien pouted.

"Well, I have." Joe handed him the folder. "As I was saying, Taylor called the warden. He emailed the roster of the people who attended George's execution."

Damien squinted at his partner. "I may not want to punch you as bad right now."

Joe laughed. "You're so easy. Now the second list has visitors from the month before George's execution." Joe waited for Damien to read through the lists. "You know his aliases. Do you see any of them on the list?"

Damien skimmed the paper. He grabbed his pen and circle the same names that were on the witness list and the visitor's log. "Okay, we know he uses the middle name of Allen for a lot of things. Look, here is the name Allen Drake Pravid. This has to be him."

Joe nodded. "It could be."

Damien stared at the name. "Rossdale said David used an anagram to hide the guy on the platform." He scribbled on a piece of paper. "He's getting kind of sloppy. Allen Drake Pravid is David Allen Parker."

"Is the name on the visitor's log?"

"Yeah, it is. It looks like he visited several times before his father died." Damien looked up to find Joe smiling at him. "Do you need medication?"

"You may have wanted to hit me a few minutes ago, but you're going to want to kiss me when you hear the last bit of information."

Damien placed his arms on his desk. "Okay. What do you know that I don't?"

"Well, the Cummins Unit makes a video recording of the execution. The people who come in as witnesses must sign a consent form, but they don't know they are being recorded. The prison does it for insurance purposes and to combat lawsuits. They had the video file of George's execution." Joe pulled his phone out. He tapped out a few commands. "Check your email. I sent it to you."

Damien's eyes bulged. "I can't believe this," he said as he picked up his cell phone. He accessed his email. He angled his screen so that he and Joe could watch it. When the screen filled with the video, he and Joe searched the witnesses. The camera was positioned so that the gallery was in the entire shot. Each person was seen in full profile. "Look," Damien paused the video. He pointed to a young man. "Him."

"Oh yeah, that's him. His eyes are hard to see, but he has the same intense scowl from the sketch."

Damien attached the file to an email and sent it to Nicky. "Okay. I sent the video to Nicky. He'll isolate him and pull a photo we can use."

Joe took another handful of jelly beans. "Did you tell Nicky who the guy is?"

"No, and I don't plan to unless I am forced to divulge the information."

Joe sighed. "I also called the florist shop. They sent over all their video footage from their store, but there was nothing on the video we could use. I imagine our guy hid from the cameras. The camera inside the store picked him up, but the photo from the prison is way better."

Joe stood and turned towards the door when he stopped and looked at Damien. "After we left last night, did you tell Dillon who the killer is?"

Damien sheepishly looked at his desk.

"Oh, c'mon Damien. Why didn't you tell her? Doesn't she have a right to know who is after her?"

Damien sighed. "No. If you had seen the look on her face when she knew the guy was an associate of George Parker you would understand. I don't want her to worry any more than she needs to." He dragged a hand down his face. "Fuck, Joe. I don't want her to have to relive it all over again."

"Yeah, but she has a right to know," Joe stared at his friend.

"Listen, I told her he was coming after her. She thinks he is just out for revenge for his friend. That's all she needs to know."

Joe started to leave but stopped. "I'm sorry I told your secret. I never repeat anything you tell me. But this time Damien, you were wrong to not ask for help. I love Dillon, and I will do whatever it takes to keep her safe. But you have to trust me."

Damien nodded. "I know I can trust you. I only wanted to protect Dillon. I should have told you, if no one else, I should have at least told you."

"You're damn skippy, you knacker." Joe left the office waving over his shoulder. "Quit staring at my ass."

# CHAPTER THIRTY-EIGHT

*David arrived earlier, before the morning rush of downtown workers, and snagged the spot directly across from where Dillon parked her little red sports car. It wasn't an hour later Dillon had pulled in and parked then entered the building. He sat in his new car ever since. David looked over his shoulder into the back seat of the older model Chrysler 300. A little fancy for his tastes, but it was the best one on the lot, and it had a trunk.*

*He lifted his left arm turning it to check his watch. "Fuck," he hissed out. He breathed in short, shallow pants. Every movement that engaged the muscles in his injured arm sent a searing pain down the length of it. David thought about how he would approach Dillon. Because of his injured arm, he had made sure to soak the rag in his homemade chloroform more heavily than he preferred. He also thumbed the bottle of pepper spray next to him. With his left arm being damn near useless, he couldn't afford to get into a struggling match with this girl.*

*David glanced in the rearview mirror, his face was more swollen, and the bruising around his eyes had darkened to a blue and deep purple color and would continue to do so over the next five or six days. He still wore the bandage on his nose. The pain was relentless, and it pounded between his eyes with the beat of his pulse. "Jonas, you have no idea how much I will make Dillon pay for each of these bruises."*

*He leaned against his seat and went back to scanning the garage. The coffee shop barista said Dillon usually came in during the afternoon on Thursdays. He had decided instead of trying to take her from the street he would wait for her to leave that afternoon. He ran the risk of there being more people in the garage, but he was willing to chance it. Fidgeting with the bandages on his forearm, he looked up when the door from the lobby slammed shut. Within a minute Dillon walked around the corner and headed to her vehicle.*

*David smiled at the pleasant surprise. He popped the trunk open and exited his vehicle leaving his door ajar. He reached into his pocket and pushed the button on the jammer. He walked across the garage and came up behind her.*

# CHAPTER THIRTY-NINE

Thursday afternoon

Dillon spun around in her chair. Several times that day she had ventured into AD Reynolds office. She wanted to tell Reynolds what Damien knew, or thought he knew, but she couldn't bring herself to do it. She should, but he asked for a few more days. The least she could do was give him that. The wall clock across from her desk said two thirty. She pulled her cell phone from her pocket. Still, only two bars and that was pushing it. "Hey, Marks, what's up with our cell phones?"

"AT&T said they were having some problems with their satellite. Something about solar flares or debris. I have no idea, I called IT to see if they could tell me anything. They said it could be down for hours and to expect spotty coverage."

"Ugh, that explains it." Dillon stood and stretched. "Well, I think it's a perfect time for me to go get a coffee. You want anything from the shop from across the street?" she asked SAC Marks.

"Get me one of their Columbian, large with cream and caramel added in." SAC Marks reached into his wallet and handed her a five. "You can keep the change."

Dillon snorted. "You're a jerk. How generous, a ten-cent tip."

"It's the thought that counts."

Dillon headed out to the lobby. "Hey Margaret, I'm heading to the coffee shop, you want anything?"

"Oh Dillon, I would love a café mocha. Large," Margaret said. She started to rummage through her purse for some money.

"Don't worry about it, I got this one," Dillon said as she entered the elevator. She rode the short distance down to the main lobby of the building. She made her way through the dense throngs of people that seem to congregate in the center of the lobby. Dillon stepped out into the frigid air. She had left her coat upstairs and regretted the decision when the icy air whipped around her. She buttoned her sweater and tucked her cell phone into the pocket.

She started to step off the curb when a car horn honked at her. Looking in the direction of the ear-splitting noise she realized she didn't have the right of way. Breathing slowly trying to calm herself, she stared at the crossing indicator waiting for it to tell her when it was safe to proceed. As soon as the green man showed up on the little screen, she crossed the street with several others who seemed to have the same idea in mind as her. Dillon followed three people into the coffee house.

After what seemed like an hour, she carried the three coffees back to her office. "Oh shit," Dillon said. She sighed heavily. "I need that damn file," she said under her breath. She opted to go through the lobby instead of walking around the outside of the building to the pedestrian side entrance of the garage. Her vehicle was parked very near to the entrance to the building. "Oh hell," Dillon said as she fumbled for her keys.

She stared at the tray of coffees and didn't want to risk dropping those, so she placed them on the roof of her car. She opened the driver's side door and leaned in and pulled the file from between the passenger seat and the console. Dillon shut the door. She grabbed the coffee and started to put her keys into her pocket.

"Dillon, Dillon McGrath?"

Dillon turned towards the man's voice that called out her name. "Yes? I'm Dillon."

He stepped up to her. "This won't hurt," he said smiling.

"I'm sorry..." Dillon barely got the words out when the man sprayed a fine mist into her face. She dropped the coffees and file, screaming out as she placed her hands on her face. She recognized the burn of pepper spray. Dillon tried to reach for her weapon, but the man spun her around and placed a rag over her mouth and nose. She struggled to grasp her assailant's arms clawing at his hands. Dillon blinked her eyes trying to hold on to consciousness as long as she could. As the darkness took over, her last thought was of Damien.

# CHAPTER FORTY

*David scooped up Dillon and quickly moved to his vehicle. Her legs began to slip as the pain intensified in his arm. "Crap, crap, crap," David hissed as he quickened his pace. The jammer gave him a few minutes to load her up and exit the garage. He had done a dry run the other day, and barring any crazy event happening, he should clear the exit with seconds to spare.*

*Tossing Dillon into the trunk, he shoved her legs in. He jumped in his running car and pulled out of his spot. He drove up to the exit behind another vehicle. David glanced at his watch, he figured he had less than thirty seconds. He tapped the side of the steering wheel. The driver paid his fee and pulled out. David pulled up and handed the man a ten-dollar bill. "Keep the change," he said without looking at the assistant.*

*"Thanks, man." The kid said as he raised the crossbar blocking the exit.*

*David drove out into traffic and glanced in the rearview mirror. He had no way of knowing if the cameras kicked back in or not. As he drove along Lakeshore Drive, his pulse slowed down and the throbbing in his arm intensified. He glanced at the bandaged area and noticed the blood that began to seep through in various spots. "Damn it!" He gripped the steering wheel. "Fuck, I hate dogs." He continued down Lakeshore Drive, as he hit the expressway leading out of the city, the traffic began to thin.*

*He turned on the radio hoping to catch any news mentioning the FBI agent's disappearance. David scanned the dial until he landed on a local talk radio show. Sixty miles outside Millington, he pulled over at the first rest stop. He parked at the end of the lane, away from the two other vehicles in the lot. He peered through the passenger side window waiting for the old man to get into his car. He pulled out of his space just as the second vehicle's driver got behind the wheel.*

*David got out and walked towards the trunk. He dilly-dallied as the second car drove past. David used the key fob to open the trunk. Dillon lay motionless. His pulse quickened. "Oh shit. You better not die on me." He reached out and checked her pulse. It was faint, but it was still there. He moved her around so that her head rested in a position that didn't cut off her airway. He removed her weapon and tucked it into the waistband of his pants. During the jockeying of her body, her cell phone dropped from her sweater pocket. David picked it up. "Son of a bitch."*

*He stared at the satellite phone. He knew this model. If it was being monitored, it had tracked them to this spot and very well may have them on the satellite feed. He squeezed the phone in his hand. "Fuck, you would carry one of these, you fucking bitch." He threw it onto the ground and stomped on it. He slammed the trunk shut and continued to the cabin.*

# CHAPTER FORTY-ONE

SAC Marks looked around the room. He walked down the hallway and checked in the conference rooms. He walked back down the hall towards the reception area. "Hey Margaret, when did Dillon leave for coffee?"

Margaret frowned pinching her lips together, she glanced at her watch and confirmed it with the clock on the wall. "She left over an hour ago. I got busy doing office work and forgot about her bringing my coffee back." She looked frantically on her desk, she found her cell and dialed Dillon's number. "For crap's sake, the network is still out."

SAC Marks pulled out his phone, "Hey Margaret, you got the menu from the coffee shop?"

Her hand trembled as she handed the menu to him. "Yeah, here it is."

SAC Marks called the coffee shop, but his phone wouldn't connect. He picked up the phone on the desk and dialed the number. "Hey, does anyone remember if Agent McGrath came in and got her afternoon coffee?"

"Oh, she was in about an hour ago. Purchased three coffees and a biscotti."

"Okay, thanks." SAC Marks jogged down the hall to AD Reynold's office. "We have a problem."

AD Reynolds glanced up from his mound of paperwork. "What's the problem?"

"Dillon went for coffee over an hour ago, she isn't back. She left the coffee shop with three coffees."

AD Reynolds picked up his desk phone. "Go to the garage and check and see if her car is still there. I'll call security."

SAC Marks ran down the hall and entered the stairwell. He burst through the door into the parking area and ran to Dillon's parking spot. "Fuck!" He pulled his phone but couldn't get a signal. "Well fuck me." He ran into the lobby and grabbed the phone from the desk next to the security personnel. Dialing the number for reception, he paced the small area as he waited for Margaret to pick up the phone.

"FBI..."

"Margaret, tell the AD Dillon's car is here, and the coffees are spilled all over the ground. Tell him to send one of the agents with a crime scene kit." He hung up the phone without waiting for her response. He stared at the guard. "I need you to pull the video from the last ninety minutes, focusing on Agent Dillon McGrath's parking area."

AD Reynolds and Agent Tanger walked out of the elevator.

SAC Marks looked up. "Agent, get out to Dillon's vehicle and take photos of everything. Bag everything."

AD Reynolds stood next to the desk as the security guard pulled up the feed for the time specified.

"Okay, here it is. I'll skim through it till you say stop," the guard said.

When Dillon came into view of the cameras, AD Reynolds told the guard to slow the tape down. "Alright, there she is."

They all watched as Dillon opened her car door, pulled a file from her car, and next the screen went fuzzy.

"What just happened?" AD Reynolds asked the head security guard.

"I'm not sure. Hang on." He fiddled with the controls, but when the video came back up, Dillon was gone, and the coffee was on the ground.

"You have got to be kidding me." SAC Marks said. "There is no way something went wrong with the feed at the same moment Dillon disappears."

AD Reynolds looked at the guard. "Can you tell what happened? Can you pull up another angle from a different camera?"

"It looks like something jammed our cameras. Long enough to make our feed go down." The guard typed away on his computer. "I can't tell you anything. But here are the views from other angles."

AD Reynolds and SAC Marks peered over the guard's shoulder. "There," AD Reynolds pointed to the screen. "Can you get anything else off the tape? I saw a quick flash of someone walking across the garage."

The guard scrolled through the feed. "I can't get it any clearer than this. Whatever he used to jam our cameras, he did it before he came into view of the camera." The guard looked up at AD Reynolds. "I can also pull up all the exit cameras and see if we can see anything."

"Do it. Send me whatever you get." AD Reynolds followed SAC Marks out to the garage. "Agent Tanger, did you get everything?"

"Yeah. I gathered all the cups and some swabs of the various surfaces.

I used the layout of the cups to surmise how she may have been attacked. I left the file where I found it." He moved around the area.

"We saw the video, she placed her cups on the roof of the car, grabbed that folder from inside, next thing the cameras go blank."

Agent Tanger nodded. "Okay, makes sense." He stood where Dillon was last seen in the video. "I have the tray of coffee, I tuck the file under my arm, I put my keys in my pants pocket, and I start to turn around."

"Her assailant must have come up behind her," SAC Marks stepped up behind the agent and grabbed him, "and subdued her."

"If he planned this, he would have used something to stun her. A stun gun or pepper spray. No way Dillon would have been grabbed and her not fight off her attacker. I've seen her in action."

"Damn it." AD Reynolds paced the garage area. "I need to call Director Sherman, then Damien." He waved his hand around. "Make sure you gather everything, then gather everyone in the conference room." AD Reynolds left the two to find out what the hell happened to his agent.

# CHAPTER FORTY-TWO

Damien sat in the pen with his detectives. He kept trying to call Dillon but hadn't been able to get through. Something with the AT&T network. His phone was spotty at best. He didn't like it. Not being able to get ahold of her.

"Yo, Lieutenant, what do you think?" asked Detective Harris.

Damien furrowed his brow. "Huh? What did I miss?"

"Are you not even paying attention to us? About our case, Detective Cooper thinks our perp will cave in under twenty when we question him. You want in on the bet? Loser has to buy pizza next week."

"I'm in." He stood and stretched about to go to his office when Detective Jenkins desk phone rang. "VCU." He snapped his fingers at Damien. "He's right here." He stretched the phone out to his lieutenant.

Damien took the phone. "Why are they calling me on here? Kaine here."

"Damien, its AD Reynolds."

"Hey AD, what's up?" Damien sat on the corner of Jenkins' desk.

"Listen, Dillon is missing."

Damien stood. "What the fuck do you mean Dillon is missing?"

Everyone in the pen stopped what they were doing.

Damien wiped away the cold sweat that formed on his brow. "Tell me what the hell you mean, Dillon is missing?"

"She went out for coffee, and when she didn't come back, we checked the garage to see if her car was there. It was, along with the coffee she had purchased, it was on the ground. You need to get over here."

"I'm on my way." Damien handed the phone back to Jenkins. He ran to his office for his jacket.

Joe was putting on his jacket when Damien came back into the pen. "I'm going with you."

"Yeah yeah. Davidson, you're in charge. I'll call Captain Mackey on the way, I'll tell him to get in touch with you."

"You got it, boss." Detective Davidson said.

Jenkins stood. "Keep us updated. Whatever we need to do, we will."

Everyone nodded in agreement.

"Okay," Damien answered as he and Joe ran down the hall to the stairs.

# CHAPTER FORTY-THREE

Damien dialed Captain Mackey as he pulled into traffic with his flashing lights and siren.

"What is it, Damien?" Captain Mackey's voice boomed through the speakers of the SUV.

"Captain, Dillon is missing. I'm on my way over to the FBI office, Joe is with me."

"Dillon is missing? What do you mean she is missing?"

"Dillon went out for coffee, and it seems she was abducted in the parking garage. That's all I know. I will call with an update." Damien glanced at Joe who typed a message on his phone.

"Call me the minute you find anything out. Who did you leave in charge of the unit?"

"Davidson."

"Okay, he should do all right for a few days. If you need more time come Monday, I'll bring in another Lieutenant to fill in. Keep me posted Damien. I don't care what time you need to call me." Captain Mackey remained silent for a moment. "Damien, it's going to be okay. Dillon has a good head on her shoulders, and she knows how to handle herself. Call me, you understand?"

"Yes, sir. I will."

The SUV filled with a heavy silence. Joe gave his friend a few minutes before he spoke. "What are you going to tell them? You are telling them everything, aren't you?"

"No. I'm not telling them about the photo from the prison or about her satellite phone. Fuck!" Damien dialed Nicky.

"Yo fratello, what's up?"

"Nicky, Dillon was taken from the garage. I'm not getting any logs on her movement. I need you to pull her up on the satellite."

"Are you serious?

"Yeah, pull her location from the satellite!"

"Damien, I can't."

"What the hell Nicky, do it!"

"No, I can't. All those networks that are offline, the satellite also feeds us. We are working on it now, but we are having problems getting it back online."

"Can't you redirect the feed?"

"Dude there are like two satellites out. It's all fucked up. We got a crew over in Saudi, and we are using a relay just to keep them informed."

Damien pulled on the ends of his hair. "Nicky, *questo è male. Io non so cosa fare.*"

"Damien, I know it's bad. Are you on your way to the FBI?"

"Yeah. We are about to pull up."

"Okay. Get all the information you can and call me as soon as you can. I will keep working on this end and see if I can find some way to track her. I'll call a buddy at the cell phone company too. See if he can do anything for us."

"Alright. Listen, trust me on this. Don't tell anyone anything, only me. You got it?"

"What's going on Damien?"

"You have to trust me. Promise me?"

"*Lo prometto*, Damien. I promise."

Damien caught the look from Joe as he hung up. "I don't need your fucking judgment."

"Damien, you have to tell them everything."

"I am. Except for the satellite phone and the photo from Arkansas."

"Why? Explain it to me."

"This guy is going to kill her. I know we may not find her in time. But if I can get a few hours head start on this fucker, I am going to take it. And I am going to kill him. If I have to chase him across this fucking planet, I will do so. But I will kill him."

Joe sat in silence.

Damien slowed his breathing. As he pulled up in front of the building that housed the FBI offices, Damien looked over at Joe. "I don't expect you to help me or approve. I would never put you or your career in danger."

"I'm not letting you do this alone. But I do think you are making a mistake. You need to tell them everything, and you still go through with your plan."

Damien didn't say anything. He left the lights on and turned off his siren. He placed the on-duty placard on the dash and exited the SUV.

# CHAPTER FORTY-FOUR

Damien and Joe entered the reception area of the FBI offices. Margaret's puffy eyes and red nose made Damien's voice stammer in his throat. "Margaret, have you heard any news?"

Her bottom lip trembled. "No Damien. Go on in, they're expecting you." She pushed the button to release the door lock. As Damien stepped passed her, Margaret reached out for his arm. "She's going to be okay. She knows how to protect herself, and she knows how to get in your head. She will buy enough time for us to find her."

Damien pinched his lips together and patted her hand. "I hope so Margaret." He left her with tear-filled eyes. He pushed open the door and walked into chaos. In offices agents and office staff manned phones and laptops. As he walked down the hallway, Joe on his heels, he heard several voices coming from the main conference room.

He and Joe entered to several agents and office personnel bustling around. Damien searched their faces looking for unspoken reassurance, he found none. The coil in the pit of his stomach ignited and the bile churned. He stepped towards AD Reynolds and SAC Marks. "What do you know?"

AD Reynold turned towards Damien. "Not a lot at the moment. We have been in touch with the phone company. They have a trace set up and ready to go as soon as the network comes back online. I have several agents looking through her case files to see what she was working on."

"You won't find anything there. I know who abducted her."

All movement stopped. All heads turned towards Damien and Joe.

"What do you mean you know who abducted her?" AD Reynolds asked.

"The same guy who did all the killing for James Lockhart."

AD Reynolds furrowed his brow as he drew his lip back into a thin line. "Why would he want to abduct Dillon? If anything, he has been using her to nail James and Robert Lockhart."

Damien exhaled a searing breath. "He knows her from her past. I believe he holds her responsible for things he experienced when he was a child."

SAC Marks crossed his arms. "Damien you aren't making much

sense."

"How do you know he knew Dillon as a kid?" AD Reynolds stared at Damien.

Damien hung his head and sighed as he looked at his feet. "I was given a jump drive by Gage Price. It had some information on it which pertained to Dillon."

"Excuse me?" asked the AD.

"You heard me. Gage Price gave me a jump drive from Glenn Rossdale."

"Damien, why wouldn't you turn the jump drive in? You know you were supposed to turn in all evidence having anything to do with the Lockhart case?" AD Reynolds stared at Damien. His pulse pounded behind his eyes. "What were you thinking?"

"It was separate from the Lockhart case. It was personal and meant for me. Besides the information had to be verified."

"What did the drive have on it?" SAC Marks asked.

"When Rossdale started investigating James Lockhart, he came across some information associated with our case from five years ago." Damien nodded in Joe's direction. "A murder victim in our case had a name linking back to Dillon's past."

"Wait, you mean the dead guy on the train platform Lockhart had murdered?" SAC Marks asked.

Damien nodded. "The hitman used an anagram, a name linking back to Dillon. It was David Allen Parker."

AD Reynolds threw his hands in the air. "And you think this information isn't related to the Lockhart case?"

SAC Marks held up his hand. "Wait, you lost me. What am I missing?"

"Well, Damien, why don't you fill everyone in on who David Allen Parker is." AD Reynolds paced the area in front of the table.

Damien looked at Joe who nodded at him.

"Tell them, Damien," Joe said.

"David Allen Parker is the son of George Henry Parker, the man who killed her family. I wanted..."

"Are you kidding me? You didn't think this was important to us, to this case? Why?" SAC Marks stared with his mouth open wide. "Tell us, Damien."

"I wanted to verify the information. I wanted to make sure. All through the last investigation, this guy seemed to have an ear to the ground and knew our every fucking move during the case. I didn't want him to get a whiff of what I had been given and disappear. I couldn't afford for that to happen." Damien turned to see Agent Johnson had stepped into the office.

AD Reynolds voice raised causing those in the hallway to stop and listen. "Damien, I don't know who the hell you think you are, but you should've turned over all the information. We could've warned Dillon. We could've set up surveillance to keep an eye on her."

"Don't you for one fucking minute blame me. Nothing I did caused this asshole to do this. He had this planned from the start." Damien rocked on his heels. He kept glancing at the doorway. Agent Johnson stood with his arms crossed and a smirk on his face.

Joe followed Damien's stare and saw the reason for his rigid posture. He took a small step to position himself a little better to keep an eye on Johnson.

SAC Marks looked at one of the agents that manned a laptop. "Search for anything on David Allen Parker. Find out where he is now."

"You won't find anything," Damien said.

"And you know this how?" SAC Marks asked.

"I told you I verified the information, I found out David's mother changed their names shortly after the trial. She changed his name to David Arthur Lindquist. Sometime into his junior year, he left college. No one has heard from Lindquist since. Not sure what name he is using now." Damien cut a sideways glance at Joe. He turned back to see AD Reynolds face taut with tension.

"Damien, you may have just fucked yourself this time. You withheld vital information you were instructed to turn over to us. You..."

"I don't work, nor have I ever worked for you. I turned over everything having to do with your fucking case. The information Gage gave me was for me personally. You don't own me or anything I do." Damien said.

"You think you are a wild west lawman." AD Reynolds was about to say something when a noise made him look towards the door.

Agent Johnson snickered and snorted. He glanced around the room then landed his gaze on Damien. "The great Damien Kaine does whatever the hell he wants. This time it caught up with you."

Damien spun around and faced him. "At least I don't have to hit a woman who rejects me, so I can feel more like a man." Damien took half a step towards him. "If you ever lay another hand on Dillon, I will bury your body where they will never find you."

"Aw, you sticking up for your little woman? I wouldn't fuck her anyway, she's a whore who fucked her way to where she is and fucked a Wop."

Damien lowered his shoulders and charged. His body slammed into Agent Johnson, and they both crashed through the glass wall that separated the conference room from the hallway. Glass shattered like a small bomb had exploded. Damien's fist landed on Agent Johnson with crushing force. Blood sprayed as his fist made contact with Johnson's nose.

The conference room erupted into screams. Several agents knocked over their chairs as they ran to the two brawling men. By the time Damien was pulled off the agent, Johnson's face looked like it had been through a meat grinder.

Joe leaned into his friend. "Get ahold of yourself, Damien. I know you're fucking crazy with worry, but this is going to get you kicked off the force. Just stop."

AD Reynold stood between the two men. "Agent Johnson get yourself cleaned up."

"I'm pressing charges. He came at me first. I'll make sure you fucking pay for this." Agent Johnson pinched the tip of his nose, wiping the blood on his jeans.

AD Reynolds turned on Agent Johnson. "Your ass is already in a sling. You may want to think about what you do from this point forward." He turned to Damien. "You need to get the hell out of this office. I don't want you anywhere near this investigation. You're too close to it. I'm calling your captain. I hope you still have a career at the end of this."

Damien glared at AD Reynolds and SAC Marks who now stood next to him. "I don't give a fuck about my career. And you can't tell me what to do. I'll find this asshole, and if Dillon has one hair hurt on her head, you won't have to worry about bringing him in on charges. Because there won't be anything left. Send me the fucking bill for your glass." Damien walked down the destroyed hallway, his shoes crumped down on the broken glass.

Joe turned towards the two men. "He will do what he says. I hope for his sake you find this guy before he does." Joe followed his friend out of the office and into the waiting elevator. "Give me your keys."

"What the fuck for?"

"Cuz I don't want to die anytime soon. And you are in no shape to drive. Now give me the fucking keys. Please." He glanced at his watch as he took the keys from Damien's hand, "I bet you got about ten minutes before the captain calls you."

They stepped out into the frigid air of January. Joe inhaled the crisp air filling his lungs. He had just pulled away from the office building when Van Halen's *Jump* rang out through the speakers of the vehicle. "Well, I was wrong." Joe pointed to the readout on the radio, the Bluetooth indicated a call from Captain Mackey was waiting to be answered.

"Oh hell." Damien paused a moment before he answered. "Hey Captain, what's up?"

"Do you want to get fired? Or thrown in jail for obstruction? First, you withhold the jump drive, and next you try to single handily destroy the FBI offices? Are you trying to get bumped back down to detective?"

"No, but that asshole Johnson deserved what he got. I'll pay for the damage to the office."

"You don't get it, you may not have a position to come back to. Hell Damien, what were you thinking holding back evidence, can you at least explain it?"

Damien went through everything on the jump drive. He explained to the captain what he had found. He also told him what Johnson had said that provoked him.

"Alright, listen to me, when I speak with the Chief I can smooth things over. God, I hope so anyway. You are under a serious stressor, and something like this goes a long way. Having Dillon abducted by the son of the man who killed her family, will go towards establishing your state of mind." The captain paused, "I don't want to see you in this office until Monday or Tuesday of next week. Better yet, I will call you. You have a shit ton of vacation days, you are officially on vacation."

"Captain, I would like to take a few days as well," Joe said. He felt Damien's stare on him and turned and smiled at his partner.

"That's a good idea. Keep him out of trouble Detective. Also, Johnson doesn't have a leg to stand on when it comes to threatening you with charges."

"I don't care about Johnson. My family's lawyers will bury him. If I don't do it first."

"You stay away from Johnson. You better hope nothing happens to him. Or you will be the first one at the top of the list. Go to your parent's house. You should stay there anyway. I will keep you posted on what is happening with the investigation, Damien." The captain disconnected the call.

Damien glanced over at Joe. "Why are you taking time off to babysit me?"

"It's evident someone has to. And there is no way in hell I would let you handle this on your own. Taylor brought me into work. We can go to your house and take care of Coach and let you pack some shit."

Damien flexed his hand. He had gotten a few cuts on them when he went through the glass. It was safety glass, so at least it didn't shatter into shards. He grabbed a bandana from his glove box and wrapped it around one hand to stymie the small flow of blood. He looked up to see Joe smiling at him as he glanced at him and the road. "What are you smiling at?"

"You went flying through the air and smashed into Johnson like you two were part of the WWE," Joe said laughing.

Damien chuckled. "Yeah." He sighed. "I became so enraged, what he said set me off. I couldn't hear anything around me, it sounded like the whirl of a jet engine."

They rode the rest of the way in silence. Joe pulled up in front of the garage. As Damien opened the door, Joe asked, "What are you doing with Coach? Isn't Mrs. C. still out of town?"

"I could give Jenkins the code and let him come in and feed him." Damien exited the vehicle. "Nah, I'll take him with me. He's gone to my parent's house before, he'll be fine. The kids love him, and he gets fed fifty times a day over there."

Entering the condo, Coach bounded off the sofa and rubbed himself on Damien's legs. He stood on his hind legs and pawed at Damien. He reached down and picked up the cat. "Hey, Coach." He scratched his head and then tucked him under his arm. "I'll be right back. I need to go upstairs and get my bag packed." He handed the cat to Joe. "His food is in a bin under the sink. Will you grab it and his bowls? I'll bring his carrier."

Joe took the hefty furball. "Sure. When we leave here, we can stop at my house. I'll get my shit and ride with you." Joe placed Coach on the sofa and pulled out his phone to text Taylor. Coach meowed rubbing his head against Joe's leg. Joe scratched the cat's head. "How about we get your bowls and food, huh?"

Coach meowed and jumped from the sofa, sprinting into the kitchen.

# CHAPTER FORTY-FIVE

Damien pulled up in front of Joe's apartment. They both exited the SUV, leaving Coach asleep in his crate.

"Why is Taylor here?" Damien asked.

Joe shrugged. "I dunno. I texted her about what was going on. I guess she wants to give me a blowjob before we head to your parent's house."

Damien shook his head as he followed Joe up the stairs. "You have a serious problem, you know that right?"

Joe laughed. "Taylor? Where you at?" Joe yelled as they entered the apartment.

Damien looked at all the boxes. "How's the move going?"

Joe shook his head laughing. "I love this woman, but if I had known she had four thousand pairs of shoes, I'm not sure I would have ever started dating her."

Damien laughed. "I'm glad Dillon isn't your typical woman. I have more pairs of shoes than she does."

Joe noticed Damien's stooped posture and his empty stare. He reached out and grabbed his shoulder. "We will find her in time. You need to trust the process."

Damien nodded looking away hoping the tears would recede before they spilled over.

Taylor came into the living room dragging two large suitcases and carrying a third smaller one.

Joe exchanged a glance with Damien. "Uhm, Taylor baby, you going on a trip?"

She placed her hands on her hips. "Not unless you guys found Dillon and we are all going far away for a while."

"Then what's with the two—round the world size—suitcases?" Joe asked pointing to the two large bags.

"I'm going with you. But first I have to find someone to watch Muffin." She smiled in the direction of the cat. "Got any suggestions?" she asked turning back to Joe.

Damien's gaze shifted between the two of them. "Taylor, you don't need to do this. As a matter of fact, Joe, you don't have to go out to my parent's house with me. Stay here with Taylor. I..."

"Whoa, stop right there. Dillon is just as important to me, there is no fucking way I'm going to sit around and not do something to help you." Joe turned to Taylor. "I want you to stay here, and I'll call when we know something..."

She held up her hand. "Nope. Not going to happen. Dillon is the closest thing to a best friend I have. I'm not sitting around waiting for you to call me. I can call the vet even though Muffin doesn't like staying there."

Joe frowned. "Ah hell, Taylor." Joe sighed dragging a hand through his hair. "Jenkins has a key to my place. Besides Damien, I made sure to give a key to one other person. I'll call him. Knowing him, he will stay, eat my food, watch my TV and have sex in my bed." He walked down the hall to his bedroom as he dialed Jenkins' number.

Taylor turned to Damien. "I'm sorry this is happening. I know, if anyone can find her, it's you two." She walked over to him and wrapped her arms around his waist.

Damien clung tight to her. He squeezed his eyes shut hoping to make the tears vanish. They didn't. They rolled down his cheeks, wetting her hair.

"We will find her, Damien. I know it." Taylor said.

Joe carried a bag as he walked back into the living room and stopped. The despair on his friend's face smacked into him, gutting him. "Alright. You two. Break it up. Jenkins said not to worry. He will come by later tonight and stay the night." Joe glanced at them. "You ready?"

Taylor nodded wiping her cheeks. "Did you set out Muffin's food?"

"Yup. I told Jenkins what to do. She'll be fine." He took a step towards the oversized loveseat that had become her favorite spot. He stared at her making sure she was breathing. "She won't even know we're gone."

"Yes, she will," Taylor said grabbing her purse and the smallest of the three bags she had packed.

"Uhm, no she won't. She's like a hundred years old. She wouldn't know if a serial killer was feeding her. She just wants to eat."

Taylor frowned as she walked out the door. "You're an ass."

"At least I know how to pack. Shit Taylor, we're going fifty miles up the road, not to South fucking America."

Loading the bags into the SUV, Damien checked on Coach. He was sound asleep in his crate. Shaking his head, he got in the driver's seat and pulled out and pushed the Bluetooth control on the steering wheel.

"Hey, Damien. Any word on Dillon?" Nicky asked. "Where are you? What's going on?"

"Calm down, brother. Man, give me a minute to answer. No word yet on Dillon. Joe, Taylor, and I are on our way out there. Do you have anything on the satellite yet?"

"No. The sat system is still down. We are working on setting up a relay. As soon as we can download information, it may help us retrieve the location of her phone."

"Wait, if the satellite is down, how can you get info from it?" Damien gripped the steering wheel with white-knuckled hands.

"Parts of the satellite are working. Once we set up the relay, we can retrieve information from it. The satellite won't have the data in real time, but if we can access it, we can transfer all internal files and try to use the relay to pick up its slack. Hopefully, we can get it back online before too much time goes by."

Damien sighed. "Okay. Keep working on it, please. We should be there in under an hour."

"Alright, Damien. See you when you get here."

# CHAPTER FORTY-SIX

*Thursday 6 p.m.*

*David arrived at his cabin and parked with his trunk facing the porch. The early nightfall gave him the cover he needed. The foliage that lined the driveway was bare this time of year, offering no protection from possible prying eyes. He ran up the steps, unlocked, and opened the front door. He came back to the car and popped the trunk and stared down at the leggy woman. He tilted his head to one side. She was a pretty lady. Any other time, she would be his kind of woman to pursue. However, the only thing he wanted from her now was blood.*

*He bent over and scooped her up. "Shit," he hissed out as the pain erupted at the bicep and traveled down his arm. He dropped her back in the trunk. David grabbed his arm squeezing it against his body. He breathed in and out, focusing on the sound of his breathing as he pushed the searing pain from his mind. He reached under the unconscious Dillon and lifted. Grunting and panting, he moved quickly up the stairs and entered the cabin.*

*He placed Dillon in the chair he had set up in front of the TV. Even with the radiating pain in his arm, his lips were pulled into a tight smile at the thought of showing her the video of her beloved grandparents. David would have to wait though. He checked her pulse. Still weaker than he liked, but he didn't think she would die on him. The chair reclined just enough that he didn't have to worry about her head falling to one side.*

*He removed her clothing except for her panties and bra. David secured her legs with hook and loop straps at the ankles to the foot of the chair. Once secured, he moved to her wrists. He used the same kind of hook and loop straps to secure her arms.*

*Once her hands were tied down to his satisfaction, he rechecked her pulse. "Damn." He worried he made the chloroform a little stronger than he should've. He stepped back and ogled her face. The pepper spray had caused the sensitive tissue around her eyes and cheeks to swell. They looked irritated, like a severe sunburn. He imagined when Dillon woke, she would feel significant discomfort, especially when the salty tears ran down her cheeks. The last thing he did was place a dark hood over her head.*

*David set her weapon on the table and turned on his computer and accessed the internet via his portable WIFI connector. With no cable to the cabin, he needed to keep an eye on the news. He navigated to the local channels, checking their listed stories for reports of a missing FBI agent. Nothing. He let out a small breath. He glanced at his watch "Shit, I'm hungry." Going to the small galley kitchen, David made a sandwich with chips and sat back at his computer. He enjoyed his meal while he read the day's news.*

# CHAPTER FORTY-SEVEN

Thursday 6:30 p.m.

Damien parked in front of his parent's house. The weight of the day pushed his shoulder's down. He leaned his head against the steering wheel. The last time he had been here, Dillon had been with him. He uncurled his fingers from the steering wheel. Opening and closing his fists, the sore, achy stiffness dissipated.

They exited the SUV. He and Joe grabbed the heavy bags while Taylor carried a now vocal Coach.

"He's going to be glad to get out of his portable cell," Joe said.

"It's okay Coach. I'll take you out in a few minutes." Taylor crooned to him as they entered the foyer of the house.

Nicky met them at the door. He smiled, hugging his brother. "Hey, glad you guys are here."

"Hey Damien," Catherine, Nicky's wife, wrapped her arms around Damien's neck and kissed his cheek.

"Uncle Joe, Uncle Joe." The three kids yelled as they jumped into Joe's arms.

"Whoa, you guys trying to tackle me?" Joe asked as he scooped all three kids up.

"What the heck?" Damien asked with his mouth turned down. "I'm your actual uncle, and you guys just ignore me?"

"Yeah, but we haven't seen Uncle Joe for like a billion years," Nicholas junior said. Catherine and Nicky's oldest son wrapped his arms around Joe's neck.

"Yeah, Uncle Joe, we missed you." Gia planted a big kiss on his cheek.

"Well, I have missed you guys too. Hey, this is Taylor. Can you guys say hi to her?" Joe said as he kissed little Lorenzo's cheek.

Gia squinted at Taylor as she hugged Joe's neck tighter. "Are you Uncle Joe's girlfriend?"

"Yes, I am." She held out her hand to the little girl. "Nice to meet you."

Gia frowned. She squinted at Taylor. "Is she nice?"

Lorenzo smiled at Taylor, hiding his face in Joe's neck.

Joe nodded. "She's very nice." He placed the kids on their feet.

Gia shrugged as she took Coach's crate from her. "Okay. Hi."

Gia, Nicholas, and Lorenzo took Coach to the large living room screaming and yelling who would get to sleep with the cat first.

"I'm not sure if they like me or not," Taylor said. The corners of her mouth turned down.

Catherine hugged her and led them to the kitchen. "They do. They just love the cat more. Have you guys eaten yet?"

"I don't think I could eat," Damien said.

Nicky placed a hand on Damien's shoulder. "*Fratello, devi mangiare.*"

"I don't know if I can keep from throwing it back up." Damien sat at the sizeable Italian marble island.

Catherine put some pasta and gravy in a bowl. "Mangiare. Eat Damien." She also placed a bowl of warm fresh baked bread between him and Joe. "All of you. Eat."

Taylor took one bite. "OMG. This is the best sauce ever. What kind of meat is in this?"

Catherine smiled. "It's a mix of Italian sausage and pork sausage."

"I need this recipe." Taylor dipped her piece of bread into her bowl and sighed in pure delight as she chewed the warm crusty bread.

Nicky grabbed a piece of bread and sat next to his brother. "What are we going to do while we wait for the satellite? What did you tell the FBI?"

Damien poked at his food. The only thing that tasted good was the bread. "I didn't tell the FBI everything. I withheld some information. Did you ever get the photo isolated?"

"Wait for a second, what do you mean you didn't tell the FBI everything?" Nicky asked.

Damien winced. "I didn't tell them everything. I withheld the fact he was at his dad's execution, and that Dillon still carried the satellite phone."

Nicky rubbed his forehead. "What are you talking about? Who is he?"

Damien's jaw slacked. His head hung as he pushed his plate of food away. "That photo I sent you, that's the guy who took Dillon."

"Okay. I'm confused. If you know who took her, why the hell can't you track him."

Damien rubbed the back of his neck. He glanced at Joe.

Joe placed a hand on Damien's shoulder. "I got this. The guy in the photo is the guy hired by James Lockhart to kill all those people. He is also the son of George Henry Parker."

Nicky, Catherine, and Taylor exchanged glances. Nicky pinched the bridge of his nose. "I don't know who that is."

Damien felt the bile creeping up his throat. He took a long sip of his bottled water. "George is the guy who killed Dillon's entire family." Damien looked at their faces, each with bulging eyes and open mouths.

Joe filled the three in on all the details of David Allen Parker.

When he had finished, Nicky stared at his brother. "What are you going to do Damien?"

Damien closed his eyes but didn't answer.

"Damien?" Nicky asked. When Damien still didn't answer, he glanced at his wife.

Catherine pursed her lips into a thin smile. "Taylor, why don't you grab your bag and I'll show you where you and Joe will be sleeping. Your room has this great jacuzzi tub."

"That sounds heavenly. I'm gonna soak in it before bed." She kissed Joe on the cheek. "You can bring the heavy bags later."

"Gee, thanks, babe." Joe rolled his eyes at her.

"Whatever." She winked at him as she followed Catherine to the foyer.

Once they were out of the room, Nicky addressed his brother. "I know you. You're planning on going after him, aren't you?"

Damien leaned back in his chair. "Yes."

"Have you completely lost your mind?" Nicky turned towards Joe. "Have you tried to convince him not to do this?"

"Yes. You know your brother. He's pig-headed." Joe grinned at Damien when he glared at him. "You are pig-headed."

Nicky grabbed a bottle of whiskey from the cupboard and three glasses. "Alright. I put in a call to my friend at the phone company. Unfortunately, they're suffering from the satellite outage as well. But he put a ping tracer on the number. As soon as the network comes back online, he will tell us her last registered location."

Damien nodded. He downed the whiskey in one gulp. "Okay, thanks. Did you isolate the guy in the photo?"

Nicky nodded as he poured another round in their glasses. "Yes. I have it in the cave." Nicky finished off his whiskey. "What is your plan?"

"I'm not sure."

"How much trouble are you in with your Captain?"

Damien shrugged. "I don't care. If they want to fire me, that's fine. If they want to take the unit from me, that's fine too."

Joe scoffed. "They aren't going to do anything to you. Johnson is an asshole, and he deserved it. Not to mention, you're going to pay for the glass, so the department isn't even out any money."

"I shouldn't have let Johnson get to me. But he gets in my craw." Damien swallowed the last of his whiskey.

"What are you talking about, what glass?" Nicky asked.

"Damien decided to pull a WWE move and take him and Johnson through the glass wall at the FBI offices."

Nicky shot his brother a sideways glance. "You're losing it."

Coach wandered into the kitchen. Meowing and sniffing the air looking for his food.

Damien went into the foyer to get Coach's food. The minute he pulled the bowl out of the bag Coach spun in circles, his meowing escalating in pitch. "Okay, sheesh man. Give me a second." Damien opened a can, dumped it, and placed the bowl on the floor. "Is the kitty litter box still in Nona's bathroom?"

"Yup. We left it there. Figured you would bring him back." Coach rubbed up against Nicky's leg and stared up at him. Nicky bent down and picked him up. "Man, what are you feeding this guy? He must weigh twenty pounds."

Damien chuckled. "Dillon feeds him eight times a day."

Coach snuggled under Nicky's chin. "Hey, buddy." He scratched the cat's head.

The kids came in. "Good night, Daddy. Mommy says we get to sleep here tonight since Grandma and Papa aren't here."

Nicky hugged and kissed them. "Yes, you do. I'll be up to tuck you in bed." His gaze followed them as they ran off to get their baths.

Damien's brow wrinkled. "Where's Mom and Dad?"

"Mom went with Dad out to San Fran. He is working a case out there, and they wanted him to come out and triple check the security system."

"Oh," Damien said without looking up.

Joe finished the last of his whiskey. He glanced at his watch. "Shit.

It's only eight thirty. My body is trying to convince me it's midnight."

Damien nodded. "I'm with you. My head and body are throbbing with pain. It's like I have been hit by a big ass truck." Damien ran his hand through his hair. "Fuck. How the hell am I supposed to sit here doing nothing?"

"You of all people should know sometimes you have to wait. But, how about we go to the cave? We can set up a map of the area and maybe at least come up with a plan." Nicky said as he placed the cat on the floor.

Coach ran from the kitchen and headed up the stairs.

Both Damien and Joe followed Nicky down the long hallway that led off the kitchen. As they reached the end, Nicky punched in a four-digit code into the security keypad. When the door clicked open, they were met by a blast of cool air.

Joe whistled. "Man, this place is like the Batcave." One wall was lined with ten plus TV's that doubled as hi-def monitors. All of which was dark, except for one that had ESPN on it. In front of the TV's sat a curved console. Joe sat down and rubbed his hand along the smooth stone counter. "Man, this looks like a spaceship. I need something like this in my house. Scotty, warp speed."

Nicky pulled over a rolling smartboard. "I can pull up a map of this entire area, and maybe we can get an idea where he might be."

"I don't fucking know where he could be," Damien said throwing his hands in the air and taking a seat next to Joe.

Nicki hurt for his brother. He watched as Damien's posture stiffened and the muscles in his neck twisted into corded braids. The frustration carried in his voice. "That's why little brother, we're going to think about this." Nikki typed out a few commands on the small keyboard. An area map of Illinois popped up on the screen. "Hey, let me go kiss my kids. I'll be right back."

# CHAPTER FORTY-EIGHT

When Nicky walked back into the cave, Joe was messing with the controls on the console, and he had managed to fill all the screens with sports and one with a porn channel. "Seriously, dude?" Nicky pointed to one TV. "Curling? Most boring sport ever."

"I know right? Let's slide a giant donut ball with a hook down an ice shuffleboard and then sweep in front of it with scrub brooms. Not my idea of a sport. But hey, they did win gold in the Olympics, which is kind of cool." Joe said as he tilted his head to the side staring at another of the TVs. "Is that position even possible?"

Both Nicky and Damien glanced at the screen. "Hell if I know, but I might have to try it with my wife later," Nicky said.

Damien went back to studying the map. "Okay, if I was going to abduct someone, and I knocked them out, I wouldn't want them waking up while I was driving. Too much of a risk of them banging on the trunk. Especially an FBI agent."

Nicky stood next to Damien.

Joe rolled his chair over. "That's a good way of looking at it," Joe said.

"Yeah, I think so too," Nicky said. Using his finger, he drew a large circle around a seventy-five-mile radius. "Your guy won't drive farther than that."

Damien studied the area within the circle. "Shit, there are a ton of places he could take her."

"Yeah, but he needs seclusion." Joe went to the board. He crossed out several areas that were large neighborhoods. "Okay, take those out, and you don't have as many places to go through."

"There is still a shit ton." Damien pulled on the ends of his hair. If he kept doing that he wouldn't have any left. He stepped up to the board. "I know this and this area," he crossed out two large sections, "they are protected National Parks and don't allow residences."

Nicky punched in a few commands. The crossed-out areas disappeared. "Alright. If I were him, I would have a place outside the Chicago city limit. He's going to want seclusion, he isn't going to want to be near a large municipality police force within driving distance of him." He tapped a few areas, and they disappeared from the screen.

They all stepped back and stared at the smart board.

Damien nodded. "Okay, okay, this might be doable." The total area now extended sixty-five miles beyond the Chicago city limit. "It's still a ton of small police offices."

"What are you planning?" Nicky asked.

"The photo I asked you for, I'm sending it out to all the police/sheriff's offices. But I'm listing my contact information."

Joe turned from the screen to Damien. "That's a shit ton of offices."

Nicky handed the photo to Damien. "I messed around with the video. It's as good as I can get it."

Damien glared at the picture. "This is good. This will be good. Thanks."

"We can fax this out. I can pull in all the fax numbers for the area law enforcement offices you want to hit," Nicky said.

"That would work. Can you run the program?" Damien asked.

Nicky sat at the console. He pushed a button, and a digital keyboard lit up on the stone counter. After a series of commands, a monitor in front of him lit up. "I'll plug in several parameters. They should pull in all the outlying sheriff and police units. I can check on this from Dad's console. Before I go to sleep, I will check to make sure it is pulling the correct information."

"How long?" Joe asked looking at his watch.

"A few hours. Once the list is populated, I'll set the photo to go out over our fax software. It can send several batches at once." Nicky turned to Damien. He handed him a pad of paper. "Write what you want me to say in the fax."

Damien scribbled what he wanted to go out and handed it back to his brother.

Nicky frowned. "Don't you want to direct all the callbacks to a number the FBI can monitor?"

"Fuck no. If I get a hit off this, I'm going out there." He narrowed in on his brother. "The FBI is not going to know I'm doing this. That's why I listed my contact information."

Nicky shrugged. "This is a bad idea."

Joe nodded. "I agree with you, Nicky. That's why Taylor and I are here. I'm not letting him go at this alone." He glanced again at his watch.

"I'm going to hunt down my woman. I have a feeling come early morning hours we will be stuck in here." He started to head out, turned towards Damien. "Try to rest Damien. I know it's hard. But try to get as much as you can. You won't be any good to anyone without some sleep."

Damien watched his partner leave. "This sucks," he said as he followed his brother out of the cave. He watched him set the lock. "The combo still the same?"

"Yup. You plan on coming down here?"

"I don't see myself sleeping too much." They walked up the stairway Coach came running down the hallway from one of the bedrooms. Damien scooped him up. He frowned as he scratched his head. "His head is wet." He sniffed the tips of his fingers. "Smells like bubbles."

Nicky laughed. "Be glad he isn't soaking wet. The kids probably tried to stick him in the tub." He grabbed his brother, squishing the cat between them. "I know this is going to work out. It has to, Damien. Even though I think you're going about this the wrong way, I'll back you. I'll do whatever you need."

Damien nodded. "Thanks, Nicky." The lump in his throat ached. He squeezed his eyes shut. Before he made an ass of himself, he headed towards Nona's old room. He was the only one who stayed in it. He stared at the bed. Nona died there, and when others were creeped out, he felt an enormous comfort being in there. He placed Coach on the bed and went into the ensuite bathroom. He felt numb. He turned the water making it as hot as he thought he could stand and stepped in.

The water jets pounded against his body. His tears mixed with the steaming hot water. "Oh Dillon, I'm sorry." He leaned his head against the tiled wall. His mind cerebrated on the visions of what this man was doing to Dillon. He pounded the wall with the palm of his hand. "I'm coming for you baby. Just hold on."

# CHAPTER FORTY-NINE

Damien woke to Coach snuggled up next to him. The cat's purring reverberated against his chest. He scratched Coach's head as he thought of Dillon. She slept every night with this furball next to her. Coach rolled over on his back exposing his belly, oblivious to the tears that fell on his fur. His purring increased in speed and intensity as Damien rubbed his fat soft body.

He knew if he got up now, he would be running on fumes by midday. He closed his eyes and pulled the cat into him. He laid there waiting for sleep to overtake him. His brain wouldn't shut off. Visions of Dillon played like a movie reel in his mind. He rolled over onto his back. Coach not happy with the change in position, huffed as he readjusted himself. "Sorry, buddy. I can't sleep. I guess I should let you get your beauty sleep huh?" he scratched the cats head. Damien closed his eyes. Just as his body began to relax, he was jolted back by the sound of his phone ringing. Damien reached over and picked it up making a note of the time, five a.m. "Yeah, Kaine here."

"Damien, it's Sherman."

Damien sat up swinging his legs over the side of the bed. "What? What's happened?" He stood and paced the small room as if it were cavernous and he was a fiddle-footed rambler.

Coached jumped up and scoffed at the sudden movement.

There was a long pause on the phone. "Sherman, talk to me. What has happened?"

"Damn it, this guy killed Dillon's grandparents."

"What? What the fuck are you talking about?"

"I got a phone call from the local authorities. They were found dead in their farmhouse. I'm assuming it's the same guy who took Dillon. AD Reynolds filled me in on everything." Director Sherman paused again. The phone was dead silent. "Hello, Damien? You still there?"

Damien's heart pounded against his chest. Maybe this was a dream, and he imagined what he just heard. "Hell...I'm here."

Sherman heard the quiver in Damien's voice.

"What did this fucker do to them?"

"He cut Catherine's throat. From preliminary reports I have received from the locals, it looks as if a fight occurred between Jonas and David. It looks as if Jonas and Gunner got a few good licks in before David killed them."

"Fuck me," Damien hissed. The tears stung his cheeks. "This is my fault. All of it."

Sherman sat in silence for a moment. He tapped the rage down. "Damien, I get why you did this. I know your plan was to get rid of the threat."

"Yeah, but I fucked up. I should have told you or Joe. If I had told someone...but I never thought he would go after Dillon's grandparents. I never considered that. I was so fucking focused on protecting Dillon. If I had just..."

"Damien, you're right. You should've told someone. But David has had this planned for a long time. He didn't just show up and decide to do this. There is no telling how long he had this whole thing planned," Sherman said.

Damien didn't answer. He sat down on the side of the bed. Damien's head hung as his elbows rested on his knees. He pinched the bridge of his nose. "I made it easy for David to take her. Had I not tried to go after him and protect her, this might not have happened."

"Listen, you can beat yourself up later. Right now, you need to pull your head out of your ass and work with me." Sherman breathed heavily. "Damien, I know you withheld information. Do you have anything? I'm not asking as an FBI Director. I'm asking as someone who loves Dillon like a daughter. I'm not wearing a badge right now. I spoke with SAC Marks, and he told me about Johnson. I understand why you did it."

Damien wiped the moisture from his cheeks. "I know that David attended his father's execution. I was able to get the film from the prison, and I had Nicky isolate his picture. I didn't want to give that to the FBI. Dillon was still using the satellite phone, so I have had Nicky tracing it since I found out about this guy coming after her.

"With this network outage though, Nicky can't give me anything concrete. He has a friend at the phone company who has a trace set up. We are waiting for the network to start working. We narrowed in on a radius we think he will stay in. I was going to send the photo out to the local sheriffs and police, see if anyone recognizes him. I didn't want to use the sketch."

"When are you going to do that?"

Damien glanced at the clock. "The computer program has sent out several faxes by now. We had it set up to run automatically." Damien could hear Sherman's breathing. "What is the FBI doing?"

"They're tracking David Parker's life. They have tracked him to USC using the name you provided. I'm sure you already know, but it dead ends in his junior year. Lindquist, the name he was using, isn't used again when he leaves USC."

"Are you guys releasing anything on him?"

"Oh hell, AD Reynolds wants to. I'm with you on this though, if we broadcast this guy across the airways he will poof. Damien, I want this guy dead. I know my actions may cause me to lose everything, but I don't care."

"I don't know if she will be alive when I get to her or not, but I will stop him."

"I will keep you out of jail. I promise. You need to move on this. If you have something telling you where she is, act on it. I will cover you, no matter what. Let me worry about the FBI. If we get anything I think will help you, I'll funnel it to you."

"As soon as I know something, I will send you a message, as well."

"Save our girl, Damien."

"I will." Damien stared at his phone. If he knew nothing else of David, he knew that the man had no intention of letting Dillon go alive. Damien had already decided there would be no lenity, for this man.

# CHAPTER FIFTY

*The sound echoed in David's head like a wounded animal. "What is that noise?" he rolled over and looked at his phone. Four thirty a.m. He sucked in air through his gritted teeth. His arm had been caught underneath him and when he rolled over the dull ache throbbed even more. The blood seeping through the bandages told him the stitches weren't holding. "This thing is never going to heal if I don't go see a surgeon." He tried flexing his fingers. He had less hand movement and strength than yesterday. He found it hard to hold something as simple as a full beer in that hand, especially if his arm was outstretched.*

*David cocked his head to the side as he sat on the edge of the bed. The noise had subsided. He started to lay back down when the silence was broken again by a screeching wail. He rose and walked into the living room. Dillon screamed at the top of her lungs. He slapped her across the face. The force sending her head to the side and back, smacking the headrest of the chair. "What is wrong with you?"*

*"Who the hell are you?" she twisted her head trying to discern where the man stood.*

*"In due time Dillon. I will tell you who I am when I'm ready." David went into the kitchen. He grabbed a two-liter bottle of water from the fridge then started his coffee pot. He watched Dillon's head twist from side to side trying to figure out his movements. He raised the hood just enough to expose her mouth. "I bet the pepper spray has made your throat feel like a molten asphalt road on a Texas summer day. Would you like a sip of water?"*

*"If you're the asshole who tied my hands, you must know I can't drink it," she said turning towards the sound of his voice.*

*He moved to stand in front of her. "I can help you." He opened the bottle and held it in his good hand, next to her lips. When she had drunk just enough to make her want more, he pulled the bottle away.*

*She turned her head licking her lips. "More. My throat needs more."*

*"You want more? I can give you more." He released a lever which reclined the back of the chair, laying almost flat. David poured the bottle over her uncovered mouth and nose area. The onslaught of that much water had her coughing and gagging. He used his injured hand to hold her head still. David watched as she struggled to catch her breath. He moved the bottle so*

*that the remaining liquid covered her face. "Doesn't that feel good? The nice refreshing cool water on your irritated skin?"*

*Dillon screamed out in pain. She jerked her head breaking free of the man's grip. The skin around her eyes felt as if hot coals had just been placed on her face and pins were being driven into her eyeballs. "Why am I here?" she panted. The words rattled in her head along with the whirling noise that echoed like a train barreling through her skull. A wave of nausea rolled over her. She inhaled through her nose, blowing the breath out slowly as she settled the overwhelming fear that crept into her thoughts. Bits and pieces peppered her mind. She saw her car, the coffee shop, and the parking garage. Her head pounded echoing the beat of her heart.*

*"Well, since we never got to speak to each other when we were younger, and you were the star of the show, I bet you thought I wasn't that important." He grabbed her face again, this time he squeezed hard enough that his fingertips dug into her cheeks. "Think Dillon. I can't imagine you forgot the face of the little boy whose whole world you fucked up." He released her face. "I need a cup of coffee. Since you decided I needed to be up at the butt crack of dawn." He walked into the kitchen whistling.*

*Dillon opened and closed her jaw. Her cheeks radiated with pain. She calmed her breathing trying to figure out what the guy meant by she messed up his life as a kid. Her mind raced. The hood covering her head had tiny mesh holes allowing air to flow through and the faintest amount of light, but she couldn't see anything else. The burning in her eyes felt as if someone had dropped hot wax onto her eyeballs. She pushed her breath in and out. She clamped her eyes shut. She wore only her bra and panties, and yet she felt her body heat rise along with her increasing heart rate. She took long slow breaths, the tightness in her chest making each one labored.*

*"I still don't know what you're talking about," she called out to him. "I'm guessing you're going to kill me. I mean, why go through all this trouble to just hold a conversation with me. But I would hope you would at least explain a few things to me."*

*She listened as the man came back into the room. She was able to discern the building was rather small because it didn't take him but a few steps to reach her. Dillon could smell the dark roast of coffee. One of her favorite smells. For a few moments, she was comforted by the aroma. "You seem to know my name, are you going to tell me yours?"*

*David sat in the chair in front of her and crossed his legs as he put some butter on his muffin. He took a bite savoring the sweet flavor. After a moment he answered her. "Tell me about your mother."*

*Dillon sat up straight. She tilted her head towards the sound of his voice. "Why are you asking me about my mother?"*

*"Humor me. What do you remember about her?"*

*"She was a good mother. She was caring and loving."*

*David laughed. "You're not serious, are you?"*

*"Of course I am. She was my mother. What do you expect me to say about her?"*

*"For starters, how about we discuss what a whore she was?"*

*Dillon bristled. The mention of her mother was the madeleine that sent her mind speeding down memory lane. Only a select few knew that her mother had an affair. "Why do you call her a whore?"*

*David roared back with a hearty laugh. "She had an affair. Broke up a family. Isn't that a whore?"*

*"How do you know what my mother did?" Dillon asked him.*

*"Oh, c'mon now. Think about it. Ask yourself, how would I know about your mother?"*

*"I have no idea. How about you tell me?" She tilted her head from side to side trying to get a better handle on her surroundings.*

*"How about I tell you something about me? Yeah? Okay." He took a long sip of his coffee. "Your mother and I have something in common. My father." He watched her chest rise and fall rapidly. He noticed she flexed her hands, making a fist, clenching then unclenching.*

*"George," she said in a breathy voice.*

*"Hmm. Yes. You do remember. Do you remember my name?"*

*Dillon's heart throbbed in her throat. She felt the coolness from the bead of sweat that formed along her hairline. The bile that had settled in her stomach churned threatening a violent exit.*

*"Dillon, don't you remember my name? I'm a little miffed."*

*Collecting herself, she faced her covered head forward. "Not at all. I do remember a scared little boy." Dillon listened for his reaction. "When did you realize you were a piece of shit like your father?"*

*David stood, looking down at her. "My father was not a piece of shit. If it hadn't been for your mother..."*

*"For my mother? Are you fucking delusional as well as psycho? Your father murdered my entire family. He didn't even want to go back to you and your mother after my mother came to her senses and dumped him."*

*David balled his fist up, pulled back and struck. "Don't you say anything about my mother."*

*The force of the impact snapped Dillon's head back against the chair. Her cheek took the brunt of the hit and luckily, she didn't lose consciousness. She squeezed her eyes shut pushing the pain aside. "I don't need this hood removed to see the resemblance to your father. You're a coward just like he was. Do you have to rape women, like your father raped my mother before he shot her? Tell me, after he slaughtered my family, did he come home and fuck your mother?"*

*David had the coffee mug in his hand. He threw the contents of the steaming liquid onto Dillon. It splashed on her chest and stomach areas. She yelped and sucked in air at the immediate onslaught of pain. He reached down and grabbed her by her hair through the hood. Yanking her head at an awkward angle. "My name is David. And I am nothing like my father. I am so much worse. You keep it up, you smug bitch."*

*"What else can you take from me your father hasn't already? It seems you're a little late to the party." She kept her voice flat.*

*David sneered at her. "If you gave it some thought, you'd figure out what matters most to you. Of course, I am going to kill you, I just need to decide how much I'm going to hurt you first."*

# CHAPTER FIFTY-ONE

Damien walked into the kitchen. He needed a distraction, and the kids would be going off to school soon. If he busied himself with preparing breakfast, he wouldn't fixate on Sherman's phone call. He hadn't been in the kitchen fifteen minutes when Catherine came down the stairs. "Good morning, Cat." He gave her a kiss on the cheek. "Please tell me the kids like pancakes and eggs?"

"They love pancakes and eggs." She went to the fridge and grabbed butter and fruit. She held up a can of whip cream. "We can't forget this." She placed it on the island. She raised an eyebrow at him, "Can't sleep huh?"

A faint smile crested his lips. "No." He opened his mouth to tell her about his early morning call with Director Sherman when the three kids and Nicky entered.

"Pancakes and bacon!" Nicholas Jr. yelled as he sat at the counter.

"Oooh and whipped cream." Gia leaned over and grabbed the can.

The kids ate and laughed, and for a few moments, Damien enjoyed the happiness of his family. Once the kids were loaded into the car for Catherine to cart off to school, Joe and Taylor came down. "You guys hungry?" Damien asked.

"Oh man, I'm starving," Joe said.

He watched as everyone loaded their plates. He listened to their chatter. Coach came in and wanted another helping of food. Damien placed his hands in his lap and stared down at them. "I got an early call from Sherman," Damien said not looking up. All conversations ceased. He looked up to find each pair of eyes boring a hole through him. He took a deep breath.

"Well, what did he say? Spit it out man," Joe said.

"Yeah, Damien. Tell us." Nicky put eggs and bacon on his plate.

"David killed Dillon's grandparents." The words burst out. They smacked into everyone like a bowling ball down a lane.

Joe's fork stopped halfway to his mouth. "Are you fucking serious?"

"No. Oh no." Taylor began to cry. "She is so close to them."

Joe pulled her from her stool and held her tight against him. "Nicky has the network come back online?" he asked.

"As soon as we are finished here we will find out." Nicky went to his brother and hugged him. "*Sono così dispiaciuto fratello. Siamo la sua famiglia ora. Lei ci avrà.* When she comes home, she will have us, we will be her family now."

The worry, frustration, and guilt overtook Damien. The tears flowed and soaked his brother's shirt. Damien clung to Nicky, the weight of emotion cloaking him like a thick wool blanket. "If I had just told her he was coming. We could've warned her grandparents. It never occurred to me he would kill them. If Dillon survives this, she has every right to hate me."

Nicky lifted his brother's face in his hands. "*Cazzate.* Bullshit, pure bullshit. You had no idea this fucker would do this. You must know he had this planned. You wouldn't have been able to stop him."

Taylor sniffled and buried her face in Joe's shoulder.

Joe tightened his grip on her. "You know this, Damien," Joe said. "This asshole had this planned. I may not have agreed with your plan before, but I'm all in. We will take this fucker out. He isn't going to jail. He's going to Hell."


After cleaning the kitchen, Taylor excused herself while the rest went to the cave. Nicky pulled up the network. "Yes! It's back online." He pulled up his email and quickly sent off a message. "Alright, I sent an email to my guy at the phone company. He should get right back to us. Let's pull up the satellite information." He fiddled with a few controls, typing out a series of commands. One of the screens began to fill with line instructions as it told the satellite to dump its memory.

"Because it was offline we won't have any visual. But the phone she carried is programmed to feed its location to the satellite. Even though we couldn't access it, the unit kept recording the data. It's a fail-safe we had put on the system. We often need to track some of our operatives with no visual." Nicky scooted his chair down the long console and turned on another monitor. "It looks like the program I set pulled in all the sheriff and police stations in our area of interest."

Damien glanced over his brother's shoulder. "Has it already sent out faxes?"

Nicky nodded. "It's about one-third of the way through."

"Get me her last location."

Joe frowned at him. "You got to think he got rid of her cell phone. But let's hope he waited till he was in route and out of the city before he did it. We need a smaller radius to concentrate on."

Nicky typed out a series of commands then rolled his chair over to the smart board. He punched a few things into the small control panel and an area lit up. "Okay, this is Dillon's last recorded location. After the last upload of data to the satellite, the record showed the phone system became corrupt."

Damien eyeballed his brother. "You mean he smashed the phone?"

Nicky smiled. "Yes. I believe he smashed the phone. However, before he smashed it, you can see the line he traveled out of the city." Nicky pointed to the map, "he left the city and stayed on a steady course until he hit this place. It's a rest stop about fifty miles outside Millington."

Nicky's email pinged an incoming message. "Okay, my guy at the phone company said Dillon's phone was registered on a tower about fifteen miles away from the satellite location."

Damien dragged his finger in a circle around the town of Millington and a few other outlying townships. "This gives us a much narrower area to concentrate on. We can always expand it. Nicky, can you get me a print out of all the sheriff and police departments in this radius?"

"Sure. Give me a few minutes."

Damien studied the board. He tapped the smart board changing the input to a highlighter. He circled several areas that had cabins or isolated properties. "These four areas are where we should concentrate first. According to this, there are six municipalities in this grouping."

Joe studied the map. "This is a great start. What's your plan?"

Damien took the chair that Nicky vacated. "All right, this guy has to have property, right?"

"Yeah," Joe said.

"I'm going to get this photo faxed to the sheriff offices in each of these areas." Damien counted softly. "There shouldn't be any more than ten to twelve law enforcement facilities to contact."

Nicky walked over with a paper in his hand. "Eleven to be exact." Nicky handed the paper to his brother. "I can program the fax software to send out faxes to each of these now. Are you going to follow it with a call?"

"Yes," Damien said as he nodded at Joe. "He's going to help me."

"Anything I need to do, just tell me," Joe said as he took the drink that Taylor held out.

"I see you guys have made some great progress." Taylor sat on Joe's lap and laid her head on his shoulder.

"You okay babe?" Joe asked as he rubbed the side of her leg.

"I'm okay, my heart aches for Dillon. I wanted a few minutes to collect myself. I'm good now." Taylor ran her hand through Joe's gorgeous red hair. It was thick and soft and just the right length to grab on to. "Damien, what if we send the fax to several of the real estate offices located in this area? Maybe if he bought or rented property, we could get lucky."

"That's a damn good idea, Taylor. Nicky, can you pull that information?" Damien asked.

"Sure can. Give me one second." Nicky sat at the console and typed out a bunch of commands. The printer roared to life. A few minutes later he was rewarded with a prize. "Here you are. It looks like you have about, twenty-five to call. You want me to send out something?"

"Yes, but it needs to say something like, if you recognized this man, please call, and list my information."

"I can follow those up with a phone call," Taylor said. "Maybe if I speak to someone, it will help jog their memory and me being a girl may put them at ease. I can stress he may be in danger and we are trying to find him—instead of scaring them."

"I set the faxes to go out. They are in the queue, but it may take an hour." Nicky handed the paper with the real estate office phone numbers to Taylor.

"Great. Thanks, Nicky. I'll get on this," Taylor said.

# CHAPTER FIFTY-TWO

Friday midday

Stephanie redialed Alicia's number, still no answer. She paced her small apartment. She had been calling her all week but had been automatically forwarded to her voice mail. She had assumed Alicia was up to her old tricks of not answering her phone calls if she was involved in something better. She dialed again. "Alicia pick up the phone." Stephanie bit her fingernails while the phone rolled over to voice mail. "I don't want your voicemail," she screamed into the phone.

When she didn't hear from her on Thursday, Stephanie worried. It wasn't like Alicia to just not call, and even if she were partying every day, if she said she would call, she would call. "Something's not right," Stephanie muttered as she dialed Keith, Alicia's cousin.

"Millington Sheriff's office, how can I help you?"

"Hey Theresa, is Keith there?"

"Oh hey, Stephanie. How was your date the other night?"

Not in the mood to fuel Theresa's love of town gossip, Stephanie steered the conversation. "It was great. Now is Keith in, I have to speak to him?"

"Is there anything wrong?"

Stephanie rolled her eyes. She imagined Theresa drooling over any tidbit of news. "No. can I speak with him? I need to ask him something."

"Hang on."

Silence filled the line. Stephanie tapped her pen on the counter in her kitchen.

"Hey Stephanie, Theresa said something serious was going on, what do you need?"

"Keith, I can't get ahold of Alicia. Have you heard from her at all this week?"

"No. She went to some convention, right?"

"Yes, but I haven't been able to reach her. Can you ping her phone or something? Find out where she is?"

"No. I can't ping her phone, I need a warrant to get the phone company to run a ping trace. What's going on, Stephanie?"

Stephanie squeezed her eyes shut. Her head began to throb. "She said she would call me yesterday and tell me when she was coming into town, but I haven't heard from her."

"Are you serious? You're calling me to ping her phone because you haven't heard from her?"

"Alisha wouldn't ignore me. We talk all the time. I called the realty office, they haven't heard from her either. They have left messages regarding a few clients, and she hasn't responded to them. I spoke with her before she met with her client last Friday.  Something isn't right, Keith. Can't you check on her? You're a sheriff."

Keith sighed into the phone. "Alright. I'll go to the office and see if they'll give me anything. It may not be until tomorrow."

"Can't you do anything today?"

"Listen, I will try and find something out. Quit worrying. You know Alicia can be flakey sometimes. I bet she is on a flight as we speak. If she doesn't come home by tonight, I'll start tracking her. Quit worrying, okay?"

Stephanie sniffled. "Yeah, okay. I'll wait." The line went dead. A wave of nausea stirred around her. This wasn't like her friend. It just didn't feel right, and Stephanie couldn't stop the tears. She decathected from Alicia, preparing herself for the worse.

# CHAPTER FIFTY-THREE

*Early afternoon Friday*


*Dillon's cheek ached. The tissue felt puffy and tight. She opened her jaw and winced. A starburst of pain exploded behind her eyes. It felt as if someone had taken a ball peen hammer and tapped on her cheekbone until it shattered. She had no idea what time it was or how long she had been tied up. At some point, she had figured out that David Allen Parker and David Arthur Lindquist were one and the same, and that Damien had kept a small secret from her. "Hello, David?" no answer. Dillon started screaming.*

*David came out from the back room. "What now?" he stood wrapped in a towel.*

*"I have to pee." Dillon scooted around in the seat.*

*"I don't give a fuck if you have to pee or shit."*

*Dillon heard him walk away. She tried tugging on her wrists. The straps only seem to tighten. "Damien, please hurry," Dillon whispered to herself. She had no idea if she could hold her bladder much longer. The thought of sitting in urine was not a pleasant thought. "Really Dillon, you're tied up, probably going to be killed by a fucking psycho, and you're worried about pissing on yourself." She laid her head back against the seat. The screaming managed to irritate her throat and caused her head to throb again. Another wave of nausea hit her. She breathed in through her nose and out through her mouth hoping to fend off the vomit.*

*David walked back in and grabbed an apple from the kitchen. He sat at his computer and again scanned the local and national news for any word of the missing agent. Nothing yet. "Maybe you aren't the prize possession of your precious FBI anymore. I haven't seen anything on the news regarding your disappearance."*

*"They won't release anything."*

*David turned towards her. "What made you want to be an FBI agent? My father?"*

*"What made you want to be a lame ass hitman, your father?"*

*"I'm not a lame ass hitman. You guys couldn't even figure out who I was. Who is the fucking stupid ass now?"*

*"Evidently you. See Damien researched you back through college, Lind-quist." She giggled. "I don't need to see you to know that your jaw is hanging open. Didn't think anyone would ever figure out one of your aliases, did you? You should have paid better attention. See the sketch from five years ago, Damien still has it."*

*David's eyes widened. Then his eyebrows furrowed. "A sketch given by two dumb teenagers. There is no real likeness to me."*

*"Again, your stupidity is a glowing ember to the other stupid people of the world. But you are once again mistaken. The sketch captures your eyes remarkably well. That's what the FBI will release when they are ready too. I'm sure by now Damien has told them everything he has found out about you, and they are tracking you as we speak."*

*David's hand smacked her hard across the face, twice. He stood and pushed his chair out of the way. He spun her chair towards him and pulled his knife from the sheathing. He moved closer taking the edge of the knife he cut off her bra and panties. He reached out and grabbed one of her breasts, pinching it. "Hmm. You grew into a beautiful woman Dillon. Who would've known a scrawny twelve-year-old would turn into this?" he raised her hood enough exposing her mouth. He grabbed her and kissed her.*

*"Is this the only way you can get women, by raping them? I guess you are more like your dad than you think you are."*

*David squinted at her. He brought the knife up to the largest blister the scalding coffee had caused. He used the tip of the blade and sliced the sensitive skin, allowing the fluid to escape. Using the edge of the blade he scraped off the moist blister, exposing the raw and tender skin underneath. He then proceeded to do that with the half a dozen other blisters that formed across her chest and stomach area.*

*Dillon squirmed with each scrape of the blisters. She bit her bottom lip to keep from crying out. "You can do what you want to me. You're a monster. I wonder if your mother knew you were a monster just like your father."*

*David reached out and grabbed the two middle fingers on her hand. "I told you not to say anything about my mother." He bent back her fingers, breaking them at the knuckle. When she screamed out in pain, he smiled at her. "Ahh, that's better." He pulled his chair back to the table and sat back down to finish his snack.*

*Dillon's breath panted in and out. The hood remained above her mouth, giving her a few breaths of fresh air. Her fingers throbbed making the wave of nausea return. "I'm going to be sick." The heaves began. Dillon fought hard to keep the vomit at bay but was useless in her efforts. Just before the bile made its way out, she made sure to turn her head in the last direction she heard his voice. The vomit spewed out.*

*"You fucking bitch." David stood up covered in Dillon's vomit.*

*"I told you I was about to throw up. If you think for one minute I'm going to sit in my own vomit, you must be more stupid than I thought." She panted. Her throat already raw from the pepper spray reignited in searing pain from the caustic fluid.*

*David grunted as he pummeled her face with his closed fist. After three punches her lifeless body fell back against the seat. David raised the hood enough to look at her injuries. Her previously blackened eye was now swollen shut. Her lip was split in two. The last hit had landed on her nose breaking it, making it crooked and bloodied. He replaced the hood and walked away.*

# CHAPTER FIFTY-FOUR

Damien sat at the console. The others had gone into the kitchen for lunch. He just didn't have much of an appetite.  The computer system had sent out several faxes, but it had over fifty more to go. Damien had Nicky override the system, and he sent out the picture to the eleven offices located in his smaller target area. He wanted to get started on that area first.

He heard the laughter from the kitchen. A slight smile tugged at his mouth. Whenever Joe and Nicky got together the two of them usually had everyone in stitches. Any other time he would've welcomed the distraction. He called the first sheriff's office on the list. He had spoken with two departments when his phone rang. He looked at his screen, his hairline dampened with a thin bead of sweat. "What's happened? Have you found anything?"

"I was about to ask you the same thing. Have you gotten anywhere?" Sherman asked.

"I may have narrowed our area of interest, to within a fifty-mile radius versus a seventy-five mile one."

"How many law enforcement groups do you have now?"

"In my smaller area, eleven. I had two calls in when you called me. What about AD Reynolds, what is he doing?"

Sherman sighed. "He went over my head. He called my boss and told him he wanted to release the sketch. My boss asked me, and I told him I think it may push him underground, but they are going ahead with it. they are using the evening and late evening newscasts to do it."

"Fuck, I better get going on this. I have to stay a few hours ahead of you guys." Damien sat in silence. He heard the drone of a TV in the background. "I'm sorry AD Reynolds went around you. I know you wanted to give me the extra time."

"AD Reynolds is a good man. He is a by the book type of agent. I wouldn't have expected anything less. But I didn't give him any additional information. The phone company pinged her last cell interaction a little farther out than yours."

"Okay. I will keep you posted," Damien said.

"I love Dillon like a daughter Damien. Laura has done nothing but cry. You have to bring her home to us. I don't care what shape she is in. I just want her home."

"Me too, Phillip. Me too." Damien hung up. He was just about to start calling again when Taylor walked in. "I got a call from Sherman. They're going to release the sketch this evening. We need to call as many places as we can. Where's Joe?"

"He went to help Nicky with something in the garage. He will be in here in a bit. I told them I would come in here and help you. I'll start again, calling more of these realtor's offices." She grabbed her paper with the numbers on it. She thought for a moment about what she would say. She decided this time, to call and then send the fax while the person was on the phone with her.

"Kensington Realty. How may I help you?"

Taylor used her best administrator voice. "Hi, I need some information, and I'm hoping you can help me."

"I will if I can. What do you need?"

"I'm with the Crime Lab in Chicago. I'm doing some research into a case we are investigating, and I'm hoping if I fax you a picture of a man, you could tell me if he has been in your office to either purchase or rent some property."

"We don't handle any rentals. Too much work in this area. I can save you a little bit of time if you give me a time frame he may have purchased a place and what kind of place."

"We think he may have bought a remote cabin. Something outside the city limits." Taylor heard shuffling of paper on the other end.

"We haven't sold anything close to a cabin like the one you are describing. Most of our properties are three or four-bedroom homes in gated communities. But let me give you our fax number. We have a few outlying agents who may have dealt with the man you are looking for."

"I would appreciate it. My contact information will be on the fax. Please forward this to your offices."

"I will. You have a good day."

Taylor crossed that office off and repeated the scenario with the next office on the list.

# CHAPTER FIFTY-FIVE

Damien dialed the fifth sheriff's office on his list.

"Sheriff Cantrell."

"Hey, Sheriff I'm Lieutenant Damien Kaine, with Division Central out of Chicago. I'm hoping you can help me locate a person of interest in a missing person's case we have."

"Hell, no problem, Lieutenant. What do you need from me?"

"I've already faxed you a photo of the man. Can you check and see if he looks familiar to you?"

"Yeah? Let me go check."

Damien heard the phone hit the desk and the Sheriff's footsteps leaving the office. A few minutes later, he heard the man re-enter the room.

"Alright, Lieutenant. I got it."

"Could you ask any of your realtors if this man has purchased or rented any properties like a cabin or something similar? Something secluded? Also, could you ask your deputies if they've seen anyone new around the area?"

"I can do that. Maggie is our realtor in this area. She has a small office here in town. I can run over there tonight and ask. If she has anything, I'll call the number on this picture."

"I can't thank you enough Sheriff. I appreciate all your help." Damien disconnected the call. He dragged a hand through his hair. It was almost four pm.

Joe walked into the cave with Nicky. "Where you at in the phone calls, Damien?"

Damien smiled at two of his favorite people. "I have six more in this priority group of eleven. You want to call a couple of them?"

Joe held out his hand. "Sure do."

Damien handed a piece of paper to Joe. "If you could call the ones on this list, I'll call the remaining one on my last paper, then we can get started on the big batch we sent out this morning."

"You got it, boss," Joe said as he started dialing one of the offices.

Nicky placed a sandwich and soda in front of Damien. "You haven't eaten all day. You need to eat, little brother."

Damien didn't think he wanted anything, but looking at the turkey and bacon sandwich, his mouth watered. He took a bite as his brother sat in the chair next to him. "Thanks, man." He guzzled half his soda. "This is really good. Didn't know you even knew how to make a sandwich."

"Haha, asshole." Nicky smiled wickedly at him. "Cat made it. She asked me if you had eaten and then forced me to bring it in here."

"I should've known. Well, it's fantastic." He munched on the sandwich. "You married a great woman, Nicky. You got lucky with Cat."

"You got just as lucky with Dillon." Nicky watched his brother's shoulders sag. He reached out and squeezed one. "Look, you know he would have killed her in the garage if that's all he wanted to do. He took her to hurt her. He won't kill her right away, giving you some time. We will get to her."

Damien pushed his empty plate away. "I'll take anything that buys me some time. It's all I have to hold onto."

"I know sitting here waiting, doing—phone calls—isn't satisfying, but it's what will pay off. Trust the process, Damien."

Damien nodded. "Thanks again for the sandwich. I should've eaten earlier."

Nicky patted him on the back. "Hey, I've been looking out for you all my life. I'm not stopping now. Make your calls. I have to track our guys overseas. They need some recon information." Nicky slid his chair down the long console positioning himself in front of a huge monitor and put on some headphones.

Damien dialed the last number on this sheet. He needed to get through as many of these law enforcement offices as he could before they left for the evening. He had maybe two hours before that happened.

"Millington Sheriff's department."

"This is Lieutenant Damien Kaine with Division Central out of Chicago, could I speak with the Sheriff."

"Sure, Lieutenant. One moment."

The young lady put him on hold. Damien could hear his brother relaying quadrants to their operatives overseas. He figured at the end of this, if it didn't turn out like he hoped, he might just ask his dad to send him on some security jobs.

"Sheriff Martin. What can I do for you, Lieutenant?"

"Listen I want to fax you a picture of a guy who is a person of interest in a missing person case. I was wondering if you could ask your local realtor if they have sold or rented any property to him. I'm also hoping you could keep an eye out for him."

"Sure, my cousin runs the local real estate office. As soon as I can, I will ask her."

"Listen, I need any information I can get. Can you contact her tonight and show her this picture?" Damien's leg began to bounce.

"I would if I could get ahold of her. She went out of town, but it seems no one has heard from her, nor can we reach her."

Damien frowned into the phone. "What do you mean?"

"I got a call from her best friend. She hasn't been able to reach her. I've got the real estate personnel seeing if they can find her. Personally, I think she took the week as a vacation and doesn't want to be bothered."

Damien's sat up straight. "When did she go out of town?"

Sheriff Martin sighed. "Let's see, Stephanie told me she met with her client before she left to go to the airport last Friday."

The hairs on Damien's neck stood on end. "Sheriff, I need you to give me your cousin's phone number. I know it sounds kind of weird, but I have someone who can track her. I'm desperate."

"Okay, Lieutenant, to be honest, I could use the help. My family is now all worked up because Stephanie called all of them too." He rattled off the number. "Will you call me as soon as you know something?"

"Yes. How long will you be at the office? I can call you back pretty quick."

"I'll wait for you to call. Call my cell." He gave Damien the number.

"Give me a few minutes. I'm going to fax you this photo. I'll call you right back." Damien turned towards Nicky. "I need you to call your guy at the phone company."

Nicky raised an eyebrow at him. "You got something?"

Damien dragged a hand through his hair. "I'm not sure if it's related, but this guy's cousin is missing she works at a real estate office. She went missing last Friday, she hasn't contacted anyone. She was supposed to get on a flight. I want to see if she left the state at all."

Nicky took the number. "Hang on."

"Damien," Taylor said. "Give me the city, I will call the real estate office. Let's see if they recognize him."

"Great idea. I don't want to wait for the Sherriff to do it anyway. It's

Millington."

Joe moved to the map. "That's right in the center of our radius." He pointed to the area. This place is perfect too. It has a shit ton of cabins and really nice houses. My family rented a place several years ago. Before we became partners. We had a big family reunion. Fished all damn day." Joe held up his hand. "Sorry. Got carried away. My point is, this is a perfect place for our guy."

Nicky slid his chair over almost knocking Joe off his feet. "Holy shit. My guy says her phone was last online at the airport. It went offline at two last Friday afternoon and never came back on the network."

"Fuck." Damien grabbed his phone and called the Sheriff back.

"Sheriff Martin."

"Sheriff, Lieutenant Kaine. Tell me when Alicia was supposed to get on the plane."

"Ah hell, hang on."

Damien could hear Sheriff Martin speaking to someone, but he couldn't hear what the other person was saying.

"Okay, I have Stephanie on my office line. She said she got off the phone with Alicia around midday Friday. She remembers Alicia said her flight left at five pm. She was heading there right after she met with her client."

"Will you ask her if she remembers Alicia mentioning her client's name?"

"Hang on. Stephanie, do you remember the guy's name? Did Alicia mention it? Well, think about it. You sure? Okay, hang on. Lieutenant, she thinks Alicia mentioned his last name, Bennet. Something along those lines, but no first name. Is there anything else you want me to ask her?"

"Ask her if she knows if the man bought the property, and what property was it?" Damien now paced the cave.

"Stephanie, what property? Yeah, that place is a dump. Hang on again. Lieutenant?"

"I'm here."

"The guy purchased Old Man Winston's place."

"I need the address. Can you give it to me?" Damien waited.

"It's out on Route 3. The address is 4322 Spur Rd."

"Can you tell me anything about the cabin? Anything about its layout?"

Sheriff Martin let out an exasperated groan. "It's pretty much a two-room shack with a kitchen. There is a back door, off the small bedroom. I don't think it was meant as a bedroom. It was originally an oversized mudroom with a shower and bathroom attached. It was never meant to be lived in. It was built as a fishing and hunting cabin." He paused. "Can you tell me what your phone guy said?"

Damien closed his eyes. He slowed his breathing. "My guy at the phone company said her phone was shut off at the airport. It never came back on again."

"Shit. I was hoping this was another one of Stephanie's overreactions. I should've known when Stephanie said she hadn't heard from Alicia something was wrong."

Damien could hear the Sheriff shuffling paper or searching for something. "Sheriff, I need you to not go out there. Do you understand me?"

"Fuck. How can you expect me to just sit here?"

"I understand you want to find out what happened to your cousin, but this guy is responsible for the disappearance of an FBI agent. I am asking you to not do anything. At least give me a few hours. I need to notify a few people, but we can't move on this. If he gets spooked, we may never find out what happened to your cousin or the missing agent."

The Sheriff was silent on the other end.

"Sheriff. Please. Give me a few hours." Damien nodded to Taylor. She smiled back at him.

"Alright, Lieutenant. I'm willing to give you three hours. If I don't hear from you, I'm going out there. I suggest you call me as soon as you have more information."

"I will. Sheriff. I promise. Please don't tell anyone about this call either. I need your help."

"I will do what you asked. But you only get three hours."

"Thank you. I will call you back." Damien hung up the phone and turned towards Taylor. "Please for all that is holy tell me they recognized this guy?"

Taylor's eyes widened. "One of the lady's recognized his photo. She said he came into the office once. But she remembers him because he was scary and when his financials came back, Alicia tried to talk him into buying a bigger property."

"Did you get the financials?"

"Yes. I forwarded it to Nicky's email. I believe he's checking this guy now." She pointed to Nicky at the console.

"Okay. I'm going." Damien turned to leave.

"Woah, there buddy," Joe said rising. "You aren't going anywhere without me, and we need to slow it down a second and gather a few things."

"This is the guy. I know it." Damien screamed at him.

"Dude. I'm sure it is. But you can't go off half-fucking-cocked. Take a breather. Let's gather our shit. We need to do this right." Joe turned towards Nicky. "You got anything?"

"He used Allen Bennet. It's a cover. He has a bank account and his history are all for the show." Nicky looked up. "I think this is your guy."

# CHAPTER FIFTY-SIX

*Early Friday evening*

*David entered the small living room fresh from a shower and dressed in a t-shirt and sweats. He pulled the hood from Dillon's head. He smacked her face several times. "Wake up sleepy head." She twitched. "C'mon. you've had enough beauty sleep." He slapped her again.*

*Dillon blinked her eyes. The bright glare from the lights caused them to water. She squeezed her eyes shut, then blinked them several times in a row. One eye was still swollen; however, she could see out of it. Dillon glanced around the cabin getting her first look at her prison cell. She had been correct. It was small, and it was a shithole. No personal mementos of any kind. This wasn't a place her captor planned to stay.*

*"Ahh, good. I need you to be awake for this." David turned to mess with the camera he connected to the TV. He glanced over his shoulder. "It's movie time." He grinned at her. "I will give you a few minutes for your eyes to adjust." He turned to study her. "I see you couldn't hold your bladder any longer. You kind of stink." He lifted her chin. "It's a shame. Your face is pretty bruised. I bet it hurts huh?"*

*Dillon pulled her head from his hand. She glanced down at herself. She smelt the urine. She looked up and focused on the man before her. She had George's face burned into her memory. She had no trouble seeing the resemblance to the monster. Although he was a younger version, she could see his father. Dillon wondered why she hadn't seen the similarity from the sketch. "I can see your father in you."*

*"My mother used to cry every night my father was with your mother. She knew he was having an affair. She loved him, no matter what he did. She was willing to let it go. Just to keep him and the marriage." David glared at her.*

*"My father traveled. Your father came over to our house a few times. That's how he knew the layout of the second floor. You know, the night he slaughtered my family."*

*David's face flushed with heat. "Your mother brought this on."*

*"How do you figure that? They both made mistakes. When my mother*

*decided to salvage her marriage, your father couldn't deal with it. My mother had nothing to do with him killing my family. Your father decided that all on his own."*

*David stood next to the TV. "My father was seduced by your mother. When she decided she had enough, she dumped him. Maybe he was wrong for having an affair, but your mother caused him to react the way he did." He grabbed a chair and pulled it over. He leaned into her. "I've watched you over the years. I followed you as best I could. When I was in college, I followed your rise in the ranks of the FBI as you became their top profiler."*

*He sat back and crossed his arms. "While your life was going perfect, my mother started getting sick. I lived at home. I took care of her. Watched her wither away. She used to look at me and tell me how much I looked like my father. We never went to see him in jail. I asked a few times, but she said no."*

*Dillon shivered. "Did you ever go see your father, without your mother?"*

*"Yes. My mother died a few months before his execution was scheduled. I decided to go see him. I used an alias and sat with him several times over the next month or two. He told me about your mother. How she told him she was going to leave her husband. Then one day, poof. She said she was going to stay."*

*"She had a right to change her mind. She had kids to consider..."*

*"No!" He stood kicking the chair across the room. "She had no right. When she changed her mind, my father became a different man. He didn't spend any more time with me. He ignored my mother. At least when he was seeing your mother, he was happy. Once your mother broke it off, my mother suffered. I suffered."*

*Dillon shifted around in her chair. The smell of her piss wafted around her. The stale smell made her stomach roll. "Your father had a choice."*

*"What choice did he have?"*

*"He could've checked back into his family. He didn't have to ignore you, that was on him. Not my mother. I didn't have anything to do with your dad going to jail. I testified what I saw and heard. That's it."*

*David paced. "No—no it was your fault. The police would never have found out it was him. You told them, and they arrested him."*

*"You can't be that stupid. The police would've found the evidence leading to him. They would've checked her past and found out she had an affair with your father. That would've put him on their radar. It was not my fault. It was your father's fault. He didn't have to kill my family." She panted. Hot,*

*stinky breath hung in the air. Her wave of nausea intensified. She breathed in and out through her nose, keeping the vomit at bay.*

*David moved towards the TV and turned it on. "No. You are wrong. It was your mother's fault, as well as your fault. You brought all this on." He grinned at her. "As you watch this, remember, this was all your fault. I hope you appreciate this. I went through a lot of trouble to make this for you." He pushed play on the video camera. "Ready?" David stood where he could watch her reaction. He waited a long time to make Dillon hurt. The same hurt he had as he watched his mother die a slow, painful death.*

# CHAPTER FIFTY-SEVEN

*Dillon prepared herself. A knot formed in her stomach. She opened and closed her fists trying to expel the pent-up anxiety that threatened to engulf her. Her breathing came out in short pants. When the video started Dillon gasped. All at once her heart stammered in her chest. David stood behind her grandmother, his hands rested on her shoulder's. Kitty's eyes were wide and pleaded with her grandfather to help her.*

*Her chest tightened. Dillon couldn't control her breathing. Her body trembled as she listened to the conversation between David and Jonas. Dillon watched as her grandmother realized the moment David was going to kill her. She heard Kitty's words as she told Jonas she loved him. It ripped at Dillon's heart. She felt the sting of the tears as they filled her swollen eyes and rolled down her cheeks.*

*Her shaking increased. She wanted to close her eyes, but she couldn't. She couldn't turn away. A soft moan escaped her lips the moment David's blade slid across Kitty's throat. Dillon flinched as her grandmother's blood spurted across the table. "Oh Grandmother, I'm sorry," Dillon said as the wave of emotion overtook her. She dry heaved, gagging at the senseless killing of her grandmother.*

*Dillon continued to watch as the dizziness increased. Her grandfather leaped up and charged at David. "Yes." The word was barely audible over the whirling noise of her pulse as it pounded in her ears. She glanced at David. She took note of his injured arm then turned back to the screen.*

*"Gunner!" She heard her grandfather yell. David's knife sliced Jonas' chest, and Dillon's hands gripped the edge of the chair arms. "Get him, Gunner," her grandfather yelled as the dog barreled at David. She cheered inside as the dog attacked him. Just as quick, her glee was yanked away when David stabbed the dog. The tears flowed down her cheek. She heard the dog yelp and lay on his side, whimpering. Just before the end of the video, David spoke into the camera. "Your fault," she heard him say. She hung her head, and the tears landed on her stomach.*

*David lifted her chin. "Aww, didn't like the movie?"*

*She spat in his face. "Fuck you!"*

*David wiped his cheek. "You need to watch it again." He messed with the controls on the camera, and the video started again. "I'm going to get a snack." He entered the kitchen whistling.*

*Dillon refused to watch the video again. She had seen enough. She laid her head back against the headrest. She hummed to herself to block out the voices on the recordings. She thought of Damien. Dillon had come to accept she would die here. She hoped that Damien would realize how much he saved her. For the last six months, she was happy. Truly happy.*

*The tears burned a trail down her cheeks. Her chest so tight, her shortness of breath and her blurred vision had the room spinning. Dillon gripped the arms of her chair tighter, hoping to slow the spinning room down. She heard David in the kitchen, she didn't have the hood on, and she felt bombarded by the overload to her senses.*

*"Hey David, you got time for a few glasses of whiskey?" Jimmy pulled open the screen door and walked in through the front door with a bottle in his hand.*

*Dillon spun her head around at the sound of another person entering the cabin.*

*"I guess I should've knocked first, but I saw the light on a heard the TV." The screen door slammed behind him. He was about to shut the front door when he glanced up. A young lady sat in an older barber's chair. She was naked and crying. Her arms were strapped to the chair. Jimmy gasped. He moved towards Dillon. "What the hell?"*

*"Help me!" Dillon screamed.*

*"Aww damn Jimmy, why didn't you knock first?" David set his plate on the table and took several steps towards Jimmy drawing his knife from its sheath.*

*Jimmy took a step back. "What's going on?" He glanced at the girl and David. He took several more steps towards the screen door keeping his back to the entryway, as he eyeballed the knife in David's hand. "Listen. I don't care what you do with your women. I will leave you be." Jimmy still held the bottle of whiskey in his right hand. He reached behind him with his other hand pushing the screen door open, about to step over the threshold.*

*"I'm afraid I can't let you leave Jimmy. I wish I didn't have to do this. I kind of liked you." David reached out to grab Jimmy's jacket. He yanked the old man back towards the center of the room.*

*Jimmy didn't wait. He raised the bottle and swung it. He hit David on the side of his head and neck. The bottled shattered.*

*"Fuck!" David yelled out. He stumbled backward but didn't lose consciousness.*

*Jimmy wouldn't be able to outrun the man. The bottle didn't do as much damage as he hoped. He too carried a knife. Not as big as David's, but it would still work. He pulled the knife and charged the unstable man.*

*The stab missed David's chest but sliced a deep wound in his injured arm. "You fucking bastard," David screamed at him.*

*They wrestled and bumped into Dillon's chair.*

*Dillon pulled her arms in at the elbows as best she could. She screamed as the chair fell on its side. Her head hit the floor with a loud crack, and everything went dark.*

*David managed to get out of the tumbling chair's way but not before the headrest smacked the knife out of his hand. David grunted landing on his back with a thud. Jimmy still held his knife and wielded it above his head. David tried to grab Jimmy's wrist, but his hands were slippery.*

*Jimmy's knife sliced through David's cheek. He was attempting to slice him again when David overpowered him and flipped him over. Jimmy felt the crunch of his cheekbone as David's fist rained down. Blow after blow to his face. He couldn't fight anymore. Each strike caused a starburst of light to erupt behind his eyes. Another punch to the face and Jimmy felt no pain and saw no more bursts of light. He simply drifted away.*

# CHAPTER FIFTY-EIGHT

Damien grabbed a few flashbangs. He only took a few small ones. Just enough to cause a distraction if needed.  He checked his weapon and grabbed several fully loaded magazines. He placed his bag next to the blanket, and first aid kit Cat had put together. It had several items that guys on security details used. From pain meds to wound cleaning solutions and a small suture kit. There was enough that would buy them enough time and allow them to get Dillon to a hospital.

Joe loaded his weapon. "What did the sheriff tell you about the place?"

"Says it's a two-room shack. It has a back door. That could prove in our favor. He said it was never meant to be lived in, just a fishing and hunting cabin."

"I hope he doesn't have any boobie traps set. I'm not in the mood to deal with that shit." Joe placed his bag on the console. "If either one of us has a clean shot, take it."

"Yes. I don't care which one of us kills him." Damien looked up as Taylor walked in carrying a small ammunition bag. Damien raised an eyebrow at Joe and nodded in Taylor's direction.

"I've got my two weapons with extra mags. I want one or two of those flash bangs," Taylor said.

"Baby," Joe began to say, "I don't..."

"Don't even think of telling me I'm not going. You two have no idea what you are going into, and you could use an extra person." Taylor crossed her arms over her chest. She poked her lips out daring them to argue.

"Taylor, you aren't law enforcement. You haven't had any law enforcement training." Joe placed his hand on her shoulders. "I don't want anything to happen to you."

"That's the biggest crock of crap you've said in a long time. I've had weapons training just like you two. I did have to qualify to carry this weapon you know." She pointed to the pink Glock on her hip. "I have a Walther CCP in my bag. I am quite capable of handling them both."

Joe pinched the bridge of his nose. "Taylor, you aren't going."

"The hell I'm not. You don't take me, I'm calling AD Reynolds." She glared at both men.

"You can come, Taylor," Damien said. "But whatever we tell you to do, you have to do it. The first thing in any op is trust. I have to trust you will do what I ask."

"You can trust me. I will do what you say." She smiled at Joe, turned on her heels and headed for the SUV.

Joe followed Taylor out. "Taylor, I want to talk to you."

Damien nodded at Nicky. "Give us two hours. It should take us thirty to get there. If you don't hear the code from me, call Director Sherman at the number I gave you. If we get this wrapped up, I'll let you know. Either way, you'll need to call Sherman. He will want to send the FBI out once we take care of David."

Nicky came to his brother. He grabbed the sides of his face. "*Stai attento. Non fare niente di stupido.* You're my only brother. You hear me?"

"Yeah. I hear you." Damien started to leave, turned back to his brother. "I love you, Nicky."

Nicky watched his brother leave. He was coming back with Dillon. He just wasn't sure if Damien would bring her home alive or dead.

# CHAPTER FIFTY-NINE

*David stopped hitting the old man. His arms hung limp next to his body. His breathing came out in short hot bursts. His cheek had bled down the front of his shirt. He lifted his right hand, his knuckles were bloodied and swollen. He touched his cheek and felt the long gash. David had no idea how deep the wound was.*

*He tried to lift his left arm. "Holy shit that hurts." David grabbed his elbow and pulled his arm across his chest to get a glimpse of the damage. The new cut bled at a steady rate. He flexed his left hand, he had a hard time making a fist. "Fuck, Jimmy. Why couldn't you have knocked on the damn door." He stared down at the unrecognizable man.*

*"You put up a hell of a fight Jimmy, I'll give you that." David glanced at the chair. "Oh, fuck me." He crawled off Jimmy and moved to the other side to get a look at Dillon. There was a large pool of blood under her head. "Son of a bitch. I wasn't ready for you to die yet."*

*David staggered to his feet. His head spun. He dropped back down to his knees trying to get his bearings. He moved his head from side to side and regretted it as a sharp pain pierced his temples. The bottle must have done more damage than he thought it had. He gave himself a few more minutes before standing back up. Unsteady on his feet, he used the wall to navigate a pathway to the bathroom.*

*He stared at his face in the mirror. The gash on his cheek was about three inches long. David estimated it was a half inch deep. He was going to need stitches and plastic surgery. The butterfly bandages he had been using on his arm wouldn't do much, but with skin adhesive, he may be able to close the cut on his face enough for travel. He cleaned himself up at the small pedestal sink. The bandage across his nose hung to one side. He pulled it off. David wrapped the arm wound after cleaning it and used the adhesive and butterfly bandages on it as well.*

*David removed his bloody t-shirt and cleaned the blood off as best he could. He heard the ping on his computer indicating a notification. He stumbled his way back into the living room and fell into a chair at the table. "Son of a bitch." Staring back at him was a picture of himself. Dillon had been right. The sketch looked just like him. Just a much younger version. "Well shit, how the hell am I going to get out of this fucking state now." He had to assume this was a nationwide bolo. He had some disguises with him that would allow him to get past the facial recognition at the airport. But he would rather avoid that altogether.*

*He pulled his phone from his pocket. "Hey Havier, I need a favor."*

*"My friend, I was wondering when I would hear from you again. What can I do for you?"*

*"I need a flight out of the states, but first I need to get out of Illinois. You got a plane anywhere I can borrow?" David downed the bottle of water he had left on the table hours ago.*

*"Hmm, I may not have one, but you tell me where you want to leave from, and I will get you one. I can have a private jet pick you up anywhere."*

*David thought for a moment. "Can you have one at the Dane County Regional Airport? I believe they have a small private terminal."*

*"They do, my friend. I can have a plane there within twelve hours."*

*"That'll work. Text me the details when you know them. I'll be at the airport. Thank you, Havier." David disconnected the call and placed the phone on the table. He stood and went into the bedroom. He had to get his shit put together as quickly as he could then set this place on fire.*

# CHAPTER SIXTY

Damien, Joe, and Taylor rode the half hour ride in silence. Damien had his lights and sirens flashing. As he pulled into the township of Millington, he slowed his speed. "I'm sure our element of surprise will be gone the minute we pull into the driveway. But he won't know how many we have with us." Damien glanced at Taylor in the rearview mirror. "Taylor, I understand you have training, but you aren't a cop. However, I need you. I want you to go around the back. I want you to sit on the back door. If he comes out for any reason, I want you to shoot him. Understand?"

"I got that. I won't do anything to put either of you or Dillon in danger. If he comes out the back door, he won't get far."

Damien glanced at Joe. "You need to trust her. She has a good head on her shoulders. I need you present. Can you do that?"

Joe sneered at his partner. "Hell yeah, I can be present. I don't have to like the fact we're bringing my girl on an illegal op that could cost her life, not to mention she may not have a career left after this."

Taylor snorted. "Well, you're going to need someone to run the front of the bar for you. So, you can always hire me.

Damien smiled at him. "She does have a point there."

Damien slowed down about five miles away from the turn that would put them on Route 3. From there they would have about five minutes. He and Joe had tactical bags strapped across their chests. It held the extra ammo and a few flashbangs. He pulled three small ear comms and handed them to Joe. "These have been set already. Turn them on for me. Make sure she knows how to put it in her ear." Damien looked in the rearview again. "Taylor, all you have to do is speak, and this earpiece will pick it up. You don't have to yell, either.

Taylor took the earpiece from Joe. "This is cool." She watched him place it in his ear then mimicked him. "Did I get it in there right?" she turned her head, so he could inspect her handy work.

"You got it in there. Now, there is a tiny button. It will take the unit off standby. Take your forefinger and tap the face of the earpiece. Do you hear the difference?"

Taylor followed his instructions. Her eyes lit up, and a smile pushed her cheeks up high. "Oh my God, yes I do."

Joe chuckled at her reaction. "You're killing me, Smalls."

"Okay, quit laughing at me. I know you guys use these all the time." She stuck her tongue out at him.

"Tap it again to put it in standby. When it is in standby, you can hear everything, but you are muted." Joe winked at her.

Damien pulled onto Route 3. "Alright, while you're getting Taylor into position, I'll hit the front door."

"Uhm, you're going to wait for me before you go through?"

"Of course. I'll go to the front door, I'll let you know what I see." Damien slowed and turned onto Spur Rd. "Check your weapons and ammo. Here we go."

# CHAPTER SIXTY-ONE

*David threw his bag on the bed. He threw his clothes in and gathered any essential belongings he needed to take. He had some dirty clothes in the corner, he just left those. He would buy new when he got to Madison. Anything that wasn't necessary he would leave behind. He didn't need to worry about scrubbing the cabin. He grabbed his gun from the dresser and placed on the bed next to the bag.*

*He stepped out the back door. Just off the steps, he had set two full five-gallon gas cans. He carried them inside. He finished packing. Looking at his chest and arms, he hissed out a breath.  He still had a lot of blood on him. "I can't travel with this blood on me. They would stop me from boarding even a private jet." He stepped back into the bathroom and filled the sink with warm water. Taking care of his newly bandaged wounds, he cleaned off the remaining blood.*

# CHAPTER SIXTY-TWO

Damien pulled down the long drive as slowly as possible. They opted to get out and make the rest of the way on foot. Two cars were in the driveway. "There may be another victim or a helper. Keep alert," Damien said.

Joe and Taylor split off to cover the rear of the house. Just as they came up to the corner, Joe stopped Taylor and motioned to her to stay low and quiet. He peered around the edge and saw an empty back stairwell. He leaned into Taylor. "You stay against this wall. Keep your eye on the back door, I don't want you to be surprised. If you have to, you shoot him. Don't hesitate to do it. Call out for help if you need it." He kissed her forehead. "Taylor, if I tell you to run for cover, run to Damien's truck."

She nodded. "I will. I will run." She watched him leave and took her position on the back door.


Damien inched up the crooked stairs to the small porch. The front door was ajar. He placed his back against the wall and peered around the edge of the door. He saw the bloodied body of an older man on the floor. He noticed Dillon strapped to an overturned chair, blood pooled underneath her head.


David was in the bathroom when he heard the ping of his phone. The hair on his neck stood on end. He had a visitor. He quietly stepped into the bedroom and picked his weapon up off the bed. He inched his way along the wall to the edge of the doorway. He heard someone in the other room.


"Shit," Damien hissed when he saw her naked in the chair. His nostrils flared and collapsed. Her hair stuck to her skin and covered her face.

"Why are you saying shit? Did you go in without me?!" Joe asked as he ran to the front of the house.

"Fuck, Joe, I think she's dead." The words choked out of his throat. He pushed her hair out of her face and inhaled a deep breath at the site of the bruising and swelling.  "What did this fucker do to you?" Damien pulled his knife and cut her legs free of the straps. Her legs fell to the side. She hung at an awkward angle. He scrambled to cut the hook and loop strap that held her hands. He had just released the first strap when he heard a noise behind him. He turned to see the butt of a gun before everything went black.

Joe ran up the front stairs the moment he heard the noise. "Damien? Damien, what's going on?"

"Your partner isn't able to talk at the moment," David yelled across the small living room. He got down on his knees. His left arm was almost useless. He had to use the unconscious man as a shield and a bargaining tool.

Joe placed his back against the wall next to the front door. He glanced in and saw David holding Damien. "Listen, it's just Damien and me. No one else knows we found you. If you kill him or Dillon, I will kill you. I'm willing to make a deal. I'll let you go if you leave them alone. You can walk out of here."

"I can walk out of here anyway. And Dillon is already dead." David tried to position himself so that he could get one good shot and kill Joe. But Damien was heavy. He scooted closer to the chair trying to use that to stabilize the cop. David needed some kind of protection.

"I want my partner to walk out of here. I promise I'm a man of my word. I'll let you go," Joe said.

Taylor heard the conversation through the earpiece. She inched her way towards the back door. Her pulse raced, and her entire body trembled. She blew a shaky breath out and tried to calm herself as she got closer to the door. She remembered the video training on how to enter a room. She pulled the door and found that it opened.

She peeked her head in and quickly pulled back. She didn't see anyone in the small bedroom, but she could hear the man just through the open doorway on the other side of the room. Taylor stepped in and hugged the wall keeping her eyes on the doorframe across from her. She heard Joe trying to bargain with the man.

"C'mon man," Joe said. "You accomplished what you set out to do. You wanted Dillon dead. You did that. Let Damien go. He's nothing to you." Joe leaned around the doorway. He could see David holding Damien as a shield, and he didn't see a clear shot. He could go in guns blazing, but he ran the risk of killing his friend.

Taylor came up to the door separating the small bedroom from the rest of the house. Her heart raced and pounded against her chest. She was sure it echoed and filled the room with the pulsating beat. She closed her eyes and breathed as quietly as she could. She peeked around the edge of the wall. David had Damien in front of him as he crouched down. His head was above Damien's, keeping Joe in his sights.

She pulled back into the room. Her hand holding her weapon shook. She stared at her weapon. *Steady. Calm. Breathe.* She said in her head.

"You know, I could kill him. I'm not going to get out of here alive anyway. If I can at least make your life shitty from here on out, I will die a happy man." David held the gun next to Damien's back. "I've got nothing to lose."

Joe kept poking his head around the corner. He couldn't get a clear shot, and he was running out of time. He steadied himself. The last position of David had his head slightly above the chair. Joe would be uncovered for thirty seconds or more. It was a chance he was willing to take.

Taylor couldn't risk this guy shooting Damien and Joe. She took one last calming breath stepped out from around the edge of the door. Lifted her weapon and shot. Point blank in the back of his head. "Last time I checked, we don't negotiate with assholes."

The impact of the bullet slammed David's head forward into the chair, sending him back onto the floor. Damien fell from his perch and slumped to the side.

At the sound of a gunshot, Joe barreled through the doorway ready to shoot. He saw Taylor standing there. Her gun arm extended. She looked up with wide bulging eyes. "Hey, Annie Oakley. You want to lower the gun?"

"Huh?" she asked. Her brow furrowed.

"Your gun, baby. How about you humor me and lower it? Or better yet holster it." Joe went to her as she realized she was still pointing her weapon.

She looked at the dead man, with half his head blown away and then looked up at Joe. "Ha. I shot him." Her body trembled.

"You did. Taylor, you did well." He grabbed her. She trembled against him. "Help me. Check Dillon. I got Damien."

Taylor took a few deep breaths, trying to shake off what she had just done, and went to Dillon's side. She unhooked the remaining hook and loop strap. She looked at Joe. "Do you think he raped her?"

"No. I think he used it to keep her off balance. He said she was dead. Check her pulse." Joe pulled his phone. "Nicky. We got him. He's dead. Dillon has severe injuries. We are assessing her now. Call Sherman."

"Where's Damien?" Nicky asked.

"She's alive! Joe, she's alive! Dillon, it's me, Taylor." Taylor sucked in a breath at the sight of her face. "Oh, Dillon. You're going to be okay." Tears rolled down Taylor's cheek.

"Nicky, Dillon's alive. Send my phone the closest hospital address. We can get their quicker in Damien's SUV. Let them know we are bringing her in. She looks pretty beat up," Joe said.

"How's Damien? Why didn't he call me?"

Joe let out a nervous laugh. "Your brother is an ass. But he is okay. Almost got himself killed, but it looks like he has a hell of a concussion, and he might need stitches."

"Okay, I sent the address. I'll tell Sherman you are on your way there. I want updates, Joe. Call me when you know something at the hospital."

"I will." Joe disconnected the call and knelt next to Damien. Joe slapped him on the cheek. "Hey, wake up, dumb shit."

Damien blinked and jerked upright. "Dillon?" He turned towards her. He saw Taylor crying. "Oh God no." He crawled towards her. His head pounded with every inch, and a wave of nausea crested over him. "Dillon." He pushed David's lifeless body out of the way. "I didn't get here in time." He knelt next to her. Brushing her hair out of her face. "Baby, I'm so sorry."

"Whoa. Ease up there," Joe said reaching out and stopping Damien from moving her. "Dillon isn't dead. Don't move her, Damien. We need to get her to the SUV." Joe looked at Taylor who had managed to get Dillon flat on the floor. "Taylor, go get the blanket. I need to wrap her up." He turned back to Damien who sat with his eyes open but had a faraway look. "Taylor will help you to the car, I'll carry Dillon. We are going to the hospital."

Damien nodded. "She's okay?" He asked stroking her hair. "Her face. Oh Joe, her face. He hurt her. It's my fault." Damien's head hung.

Joe reached out and helped his friend up onto his feet, steadying him. "Can you stand and walk with Taylor?"

Damien nodded. "I think so. Let's get her to the hospital."

They heard a noise and looked up to see the movie playing on the TV. They stared with wide eyes and their mouths agape, as they watched the video of the murder of Dillon's grandparents.

"The fucker made her watch that. He tortured her physically and psychologically. I'm glad you shot him," Damien said.

"I didn't shoot him," Joe said with a smirk.

"Who blew his fucking head off?"

Taylor stood sheepishly in the doorway holding the blanket.

Joe looked up and pointed. "Annie Oakley."

Damien turned towards her. "You?"

She smiled as tears rolled down her face. "Yeah. It was me."

"Well damn. We need to take her on more ops," Damien said.

"Uhm, no," Joe said as he took the blanket from Taylor. He wrapped the blanket around Dillon and lifted her up. She moaned but didn't wake up. As he laid her in the backseat next to Damien, she muttered something.

"Dillon, it's me, Damien. We're taking you to the hospital." Damien held her in his arms.

"Damien," she coughed out.

"I'm here, baby." Damien pulled her close to him. "I'm here, baby. I'm not going anywhere."

She breathed slowly and tried to say something, but the words were inaudible.

"Dillon?" Damien tried to rouse her. "Dillon? Fuck Joe. She doesn't look good. Her skin is pasty gray. Drive Joe. Hurry. Hurry the fuck up!"

Joe pulled on to Route 3 and flipped on the lights and siren. He listened to the sobs of his best friend as he said a silent prayer and grabbed Taylor's hand.

# CHAPTER SIXTY-THREE

Joe pulled into the hospital ER drive. A team was waiting for them. Before he came to a complete stop, the team had the door open and grabbed Dillon from the back seat and put her on a gurney. One doctor barked out orders as they sped her through the OR doors. Joe pointed to a waiting area. "Let's go sit for a few. Get our bearings."

Damien took stock of his appearance. "Fuck. I'm covered in brain matter." He frowned at Taylor. "Couldn't you shoot him through the back or something?"

"Well, you'd be dead. My bullet would have torn through him and entered you through your back." She scrunched up her face at him.

Damien smiled at her. "Thank you for saving my life, Taylor."

She took his hand. "I wouldn't let anyone hurt you or Dillon. I will pass on any more ops, though. If that's okay with you?"

Damien chuckled. "I bet Joe would like that too." He stood. A little wobbly on his feet. He gripped the back of the chair to steady himself. "I have to get this brain shit off me. I'll be back." He walked to the desk and asked a few questions. Just before the nurse led him away, he turned to Joe. "Hey, call Nicky and tell him to call Sheriff Martin. Let him know he needs to be out there. Also, tell Nicky to inform AD Reynolds the Sheriff's cousin is missing. Tell him they need to search the property. I bet she is there, somewhere."

Joe nodded and pulled out his phone, he watched Damien follow a nurse down the hall. When he finished the call, he reached around pulling Taylor into him. "How are you doing?"

Taylor shrugged. "I know I had to kill him. And I carry a weapon for that purpose. I mean, if I need to protect myself." She smiled up at him. "Or someone I love." She sat up straight and turned to face him. "I still don't like the way it feels. Taking someone's life. Even someone like David who deserved it. I shouldn't feel like that huh?"

Joe's expression softened. "Shit Taylor. I'd be scared if you didn't have those feelings. Those feelings are normal, and they are good feelings to have. You will need to talk about this. If not with me with someone."

"I know that. How do you think Dillon is doing?"

"I don't know. She was beaten pretty bad. The shit he must have done to her. If anyone can get past this over time, it's her. But it's going to be a long fucking road." Joe saw Damien walking towards them in a pair of scrubs carrying a bag. He had his gun and shield clipped to his pants. "Well, hello Doctor Kaine." Joe laughed at the dirty glare he got.

Damien was about to say something when AD Reynolds and SAC Marks walked through the door. "Oh shit," he said as he glanced at Joe.

Joe stood and braced himself. "Hey," he said addressing the two men.

AD Reynolds walked with purpose towards them. "What the fuck? You knew where he was, and you didn't call us? What were you thinking?"

Damien narrowed his stare at the man. "There wasn't time. I did notify Sherman. We had a bead on him and didn't want him getting away."

AD Reynolds paced in front of him. "Damien, we wanted him alive. He could've given us information."

Damien pinched the bridge of his nose. "Are you serious right now? You haven't even asked how Dillon was. What the fuck? I thought you were a better man than that?"

"Wait a second. You know how important he was alive." Ad Reynolds shifted from foot to foot.

"I don't give a fuck about his importance. He was about to kill Dillon. I did what I had to do." Damien stared the man down.

"You may not get out of this. You broke so many fucking laws, I'm not sure you can survive this," AD Reynolds said.

Joe stepped forward. "We were acting as law enforcement officers. We didn't break any laws. We made you guys look bad. You're pissed because we figured out where he held Dillon before you guys did. You know you don't give a rat's ass about his information. You just wanted to look like the heroes."

"That's not true," SAC Marks said. "We wanted nothing but Dillon's safe return. Didn't matter who found her." He glanced at Taylor. "Why is she here?"

"Hello, I'm sitting right here. You could ask me." Taylor stood crossing her arms.

"Did you take her on the OP?" AD Reynolds waved his hands in the air.

"She is fully trained on weapons and tactical. We weren't sure what we were getting into, we needed her," Joe said.

"You have crossed the line. What if she had been killed?" SAC Marcs asked.

"She shouldn't have been there. Which one of you shot him? We will at least need your statements at some point." AD Reynolds paced again.

Damien looked at Joe and was about to say he did it when Taylor spoke up.

"I shot him," Taylor said.

Both men turned towards her. Their jaws hung open.

Damien, Joe, and Taylor couldn't stop the laughter. All three had to take a few deep breaths to settle the giggles. Just as they pulled themselves back under control, their smiles disappeared when the OR doctor made his way towards them.

"Are you with the FBI agent?"

"Yes," Damien said. "What is going on?"

The doctor looked down then met Damien's stare. "She went through a lot. Her nose was broken along with her cheek. Her eardrum was ruptured, and the hit on her head took ten stitches. She has been without food and water for over forty-eight hours. Normally as healthy as she is, she could withstand a lot. But her injuries were severe and made it hard for her body to sustain her. I'm not sure if she will make it through the night."

# CHAPTER SIXTY-FOUR

3 days later

Damien sat next to Dillon's hospital bed. He held her hand in his. His palm was sweaty, but he couldn't let go. He was surrounded by his parents, Nicky and Cat, Joe, Taylor, and Joe's parents. Sniffles echoed throughout the silent room.

"Can you tell us what he said to you? Why he took you?" Agent Richards asked.

Dillon swallowed, her dry throat constricting making the small amount of moisture feel like a rock. She squeezed Damien's hand. "He blamed me for his father being executed. Said if I hadn't testified he never would've been caught. He said I caused the pain his mother went through."

She leaned back against the bed. She hated crying, but she couldn't stop the tears. They poured over the edge streaking her chapped and irritated face with a salty burn. "He made me watch the video of my grandparents over and over again. He kept saying this was all my fault. He killed them all, even Gunner." Dillon covered her face and wept.

Damien had never seen her break like this. "That's enough guys. She's answered everything. We've all given our statements, and it's time you guys give Dillon a break."

The agents stood. "I'm sorry, Dillon. I know this is hard. We're here for you," Agent Richards said. He nodded to everyone in the room as he and his partner left.

Damien stared at the purple bruising spattered across her face. The doctor set her nose taking care to minimize the crookedness. "Dillon, baby, you want me to ask people to leave? I know you must be tired."

She wiped her face with the tissue Angelina handed her. "No. I want them to stay. I couldn't stand to be alone."

"I'm not going anywhere." Damien kissed her hand. "I'm not leaving this hospital without you." He pulled her to him and kissed her forehead as she started to drift off.

She was lightly snoring when a knock on the door woke her. Dillon looked towards it as it opened. Her eyes widened and filled with tears at the same time. "Laura!" Dillon raised her bed to the sitting position and smiled as Laura Sherman came to her side.

"Hi, sweetie." She bent down and gave her cheek a whisper-soft kiss. She stroked her hair as she took the seat that Damien vacated for her. "How are you? Are you okay?"

Dillon couldn't say anything. She nodded as the tears flowed again.

"I'm here for you. I will always be here for you." She kissed Dillon again. "I have someone else who wants to see you. Can he come in?"

Dillon's eyebrow furrowed. "Yeah, it's Phillip, right? I mean Director Sherman? I mean Phillip. Where is he?"

Everyone glanced at each other.

Damien's father came over and kissed Laura on the cheek. "Where is Phillip?"

A smile filled her face. "He wanted me to make sure you were up for one more visitor. Let me get him." She walked to the doorway. She opened it up and peeked out. "Come on in." She moved back towards the bed.

Director Sherman pushed the door open, he started to walk in, then looked over his shoulder out into the hallway. "Well, c'mon we don't have all day."

All at once the door slammed open.

A gasp came from Dillon as well as everyone else in the room.

"Oh my God, Gunner! It's Gunner! Come here, boy!" Dillon yelled.

Gunner ran full force and leaped onto the bed. The huge dog had several bare spots with several dozen stitches on each. He licked Dillon and whimpered as she kissed him, wrapping her arms around his neck. She grabbed his jowls and kissed his nose, barely able to see him through the flood of tears. "I don't understand," Dillon said as the dog laid on her lap. "I watched David kill him."

Gunner snuggled right up next to Dillon. And the look on his face just dared anyone to try to move him.

Damien's mouth was still open. "I can't believe it, either. I've seen the video." He reached out and rubbed the dog's side. He noticed the large piece of plastic in Sherman's hand. "Is that a cone of shame?"

Sherman laughed. "Yeah. The damn dog kept bumping into everything. Almost knocked over a cart in the hallway. I figured I better take it off before he hurt Dillon with it."

Everyone surrounded the Shermans, waiting to hear the explanation about how Gunner survived the attack.

Phillip sat on the end of Dillon's bed. He placed his hand on her leg. "When your grandparents were found, paramedics were called. When they got there, they could tell it was too late. One of the paramedics had reached out to move Gunner, and he whimpered. The paramedics worked on him doing what they could to make sure he was stable. They used the ambulance to transport him to the emergency vet clinic."

Phillip looked at Dillon. "When I got the call about your grandparents, they told me about Gunner. I called the vet and asked when Gunner could travel. Laura and I went there last night to get him." Phillip looked up at Damien. "I have his vet records in my truck. I will make sure you get those for your vet." He reached out and scratched the dog's ears. "The vet said he should have no problems. In about a week, you will want to have him looked at and have your vet check the wounds to make sure they are healing properly."

"That won't be a problem. We'll make sure he gets everything he needs," Damien said.

Dillon's tears splattered on the dog's head as she held on tight to him. "Oh, Gunner. I'm sorry. I'm so sorry he hurt you. You'll come live with us, okay buddy?" The dog licked her face snuggling closer to her. She looked at her boss and his wife. No longer was she confused about her feelings for them. They have treated her like a daughter since she came to the Bureau. The feelings she had stuffed way down came bubbling to the top.

Laura scooted down as Phillip moved to sit right next to Dillon on the bed. He reached out and brushed her hair out of her face. "Dillon, you are more than an agent to me, to Laura. You are way more important to us. You have to know we're here for you and we want you to lean on us. To call us. We want you to know how much we love you. I know I ride you hard as my agent, but these feelings are separate from that. The FBI is business, this between us," he motioned to Laura, "this is family."

Laura kissed her forehead. "We arranged to stay here for a few days. When Phillip has to leave, Damien said I can stay in the spare room. I plan on taking care of you for a while. At least until you are healed or tired of me." She smiled at Angelina. "I've already recruited Damien and Joe's mother to help me. We plan to spoil you rotten."

Angelina stepped up to the other side of the bed. "My sweet *bella donna.* I know this is a hard time, but you will not go through this alone. Darcy, Laura, myself, we'll be here for you."

Joe's mother stepped up pushing Damien to the side. "We can't replace your grandparents. Or your family. But we can be your new family."

Snot ran from Dillon's nose. She tried to wipe her face on the bed sheet, but Gunner's weight kept that from happening. Angelina handed her another tissue. She tried to collect herself, but the words wouldn't come.

The room remained quiet for a few moments before Joe broke the silence. "How the fuck did you get a dog into the hospital?"

Taylor rolled her eyes.

Dillon snorted, then chuckled. Then snorted some more, this time breaking out into laughter. When the giggles had passed, she glanced down at Gunner's big head. She frowned and stared at Phillip. "Umm, how the hell did you get Gunner in here?"

"Well, I'm a Director in the FBI. I may not be in this position for long. But for now, I still have a little pull."

Dillon ogled him. "May not be for long, what do you mean?"

Laura grabbed his hand. "It means he loves you more than this job. And he did what he needed to do, to make sure you came home to us."

Dillon turned towards Damien. "Is there something I should know?"

Damien looked at Joe and Taylor.

Dillon caught the glance. "Okay, what the hell is going on with all of you?" her head swiveled between Phillip, Joe, Damien, and Taylor. "What happened at the house?"

"Well," Damien started. "We got the information about where you were, and with the help of Sherman and Taylor we were able to rescue you."

"Taylor?" Dillon's eyes bulged. "I remember now, you were there. Taylor, why would you be at the cabin?"

Taylor looked at Damien then Joe. "Umm, they needed help. An extra set of eyes."

"Oh hell." Joe stood and walked next to the bed. "Okay, we all broke a hell of a lot of rules. No real laws. But assmunch here," he smacked Damien on the back of the head. "He decided to go in without any backup and almost got himself killed. Had it not been for Taylor, he and you would be dead."

Dillon's jaw dropped. She stared at the motley crew. "How could you sanction this OP?" she asked Phillip.

"My goal was to get my agent back at all costs. That's what I did," Phillip said.

The pain meds fogged Dillon's brain. "Wait, wait a second. You said if it weren't for Taylor, we'd be dead. What did Taylor do?"

Joe smiled. "Taylor was covering the back door. She heard the exchange between David and me. He had taken cover behind the chair and was using Damien as a shield. I was unable to get a clean shot without either getting shot or shooting my illustrious partner." He nodded towards Taylor. "She kind of went all Bronson on us."

Dillon stared at Taylor. Her jaw slacked hanging open. "You killed David?"

Taylor made jazz hands. "Surprise."

"I get kidnapped, and you all lose your minds," Dillon said.

Damien smiled at her. "Yes, but between Phillip, Joe, myself, and Taylor, we should be able to open one hell of a bar."


The End.

**Other books by Victoria M. Patton**

**Damien Kaine Series**
Innocence Taken
Confession of Sin
Fatal Dominion
Web of Malice
Blind Vengeance
Series Bundle Books 1-3
Series Bundle Books 1-5

**Derek Reed Thrillers**
The Box
Buried Secrets

**Novellas**
Fleeting Glimpse

**Short Stories**
Deadfall

## ABOUT THE AUTHOR

Victoria M. Patton lives with her husband of twenty-five years, two dogs—Bogart and Georgie, and two cats—Squeakers and Pumpkin.

Her years in the Coast Guard doing Search and Rescue/Law Enforcement and her BS in Forensic Chemistry helps her figure out the best way to hide all the bodies, and then write thrilling stories to keep you up at night. If she has any free time, she drinks copious amounts of whiskey and binge watches Hulu and Acorn TV.

Check out her blog Whiskey and Writing where she tries to help new authors navigate the indie publishing world. If all else fails, she provides great whiskey recipes.

Email her at: victoria@victoriampatton.com.
Check out her author website at www.victoriampatton.com. Be sure to join her Email List for updates on her latest book.
Follow her at Facebook @WhsikeyandWriting
Twitter @victoriampatton and on Pinterest.